Andersen's Fairy Tales

HANS CHRISTIAN ANDERSEN

Published by Paperview Ltd. (2005)
ISBN: 2-87427-103-9
www.paperviewgroup.com

Contents

The Emperor's New Clothes

Many years ago, there was an Emperor, who was so excessively fond of new clothes, that he spent all his money in dress. He did not trouble himself in the least about his soldiers; nor did he care to go either to the theatre or the chase, except for the opportunities then afforded him for displaying his new clothes. He had a different suit for each hour of the day; and as of any other king or emperor, one is accustomed to say, "he is sitting in council," it was always said of him, "The Emperor is sitting in his wardrobe."

Time passed merrily in the large town which was his capital; strangers arrived every day at the court. One day, two rogues, calling themselves weavers, made their appearance. They gave out that they knew how to weave stuffs of the most beautiful colours and elabourate patterns, the clothes manufactured from which should have the wonderful property of remaining invisible to everyone who was unfit for the office he held, or who was extraordinarily simple in character.

"These must, indeed, be splendid clothes!" thought the Emperor. "Had I such a suit, I might at once find out what men in my realms are unfit for their office, and also be able to distinguish the wise from the foolish! This stuff must be woven for me immediately." And he caused large sums of money to be given to both the weavers in order that they might begin their work directly.

So the two pretended weavers set up two looms, and affected to work very busily, though in reality they did nothing at all. They asked for the most delicate silk and the purest gold thread; put both into their own knapsacks; and then continued their pretended work at the empty looms until late at night.

"I should like to know how the weavers are getting on with my cloth," said the Emperor to himself, after some little time had elapsed; he was, however, rather embarrassed, when he remembered that a simpleton, or one unfit for his office, would be unable to see the manufacture. To be sure, he thought he had nothing to risk in his own person; but yet, he would prefer sending somebody else, to bring him intelligence about the weavers, and their work, before he troubled himself in the affair. All the people throughout the city had heard of the wonderful property the cloth was to possess; and all were anxious to learn how wise, or how ignorant, their neighbours might prove to be.

"I will send my faithful old minister to the weavers," said the Emperor at last, after some deliberation, "he will be best able to see how the cloth looks; for he is a man of sense, and no one can be more suitable for his office than he is."

So the faithful old minister went into the hall, where the knaves were working with all their might, at their empty looms. "What can be the meaning of this?" thought the old man, opening his eyes very wide. "I cannot discover the least bit of thread on the looms." However, he did not express his thoughts aloud.

The impostors requested him very courteously to be so good as to come nearer their looms; and then asked him whether the design pleased him, and whether the colours were not very beautiful; at the same time pointing to the empty frames. The poor old minister looked and looked, he could not discover anything on the looms, for a very good reason, viz: there was nothing there. "What!" thought he again. "Is it possible that I am a simpleton? I have never thought so myself; and no one must know it now if I am so. Can it be, that I am unfit for my office? No, that must not be said either. I will never confess that I could not see the stuff."

"Well, Sir Minister!" said one of the knaves, still pretending to work. "You do not say whether the stuff pleases you."

"Oh, it is excellent!" replied the old minister, looking at the loom through his spectacles. "This pattern, and the colours, yes, I will tell the Emperor without delay, how very beautiful I think them."

"We shall be much obliged to you," said the impostors, and then they named the different colours and described the pattern of the pretended stuff. The old minister listened attentively to their words, in order that he might repeat them to the Emperor; and then the knaves asked for more silk and gold, saying that it was necessary to complete what they had begun. However, they put all that was given them into their knapsacks; and continued to work with as much apparent diligence as before at their empty looms.

The Emperor now sent another officer of his court to see how the men were getting on, and to ascertain whether the cloth would soon be ready. It was just the same with this gentleman as with the minister; he surveyed the looms on all sides, but could see nothing at all but the empty frames.

"Does not the stuff appear as beautiful to you, as it did to my lord the minister?" asked the impostors of the Emperor's second ambassador; at the same time making the same gestures as before, and talking of the design and colours which were not there.

"I certainly am not stupid!" thought the messenger. "It must be that I am not fit for my good, profitable office! That is very odd; however, no one shall know anything about it." And accordingly he praised the stuff he could not see, and declared that he was delighted with both colours and patterns. "Indeed, please your Imperial Majesty," said he to his sovereign when he returned, "the cloth which the weavers are preparing is extraordinarily magnificent."

The whole city was talking of the splendid cloth which the Emperor had ordered to be woven at his own expense.

And now the Emperor himself wished to see the costly manufacture, while it was still in the loom. Accompanied by a select number of officers of the court, among whom were the two honest men who had already admired the cloth, he went to the crafty impostors, who, as soon as they were aware of the Emperor's approach, went on working more diligently than ever; although they still did not pass a single thread through the looms.

"Is not the work absolutely magnificent?" said the two officers of the crown, already mentioned. "If your Majesty will only be pleased to look at it! What a splendid design! What glorious colours!" and at the same time they pointed to the empty frames; for they imagined that everyone else could see this exquisite piece of workmanship.

"How is this?" said the Emperor to himself. "I can see nothing! This is indeed a terrible affair! Am I a simpleton, or am I unfit to be an Emperor? That would be the worst thing that could happen"—"Oh! the cloth is charming," said he, aloud. "It has my complete approbation." And he smiled most graciously, and looked closely at the empty looms; for on no account would he say that he could not see what two of the officers of his court had praised so much. All his retinue now strained their eyes, hoping to discover something on the looms, but they could see no more than the others; nevertheless, they all exclaimed, "Oh, how beautiful!" and advised his majesty to have some new clothes made from this splendid material, for the approaching procession. "Magnificent! Charming! Excellent!" resounded on all sides; and everyone was uncommonly gay. The Emperor shared in the general satisfaction; and presented the impostors with the riband of an order of knighthood, to be worn in their button-holes, and the title of "Gentlemen Weavers."

The rogues sat up the whole of the night before the day on which the procession was to take place, and had sixteen lights burning, so that everyone might see how anxious they were to finish the Emperor's new suit. They pretended to roll the cloth off the looms; cut the air with their scissors; and sewed with needles without any thread in them. "See!" cried they, at last.

"The Emperor's new clothes are ready!"

And now the Emperor, with all the grandees of his court, came to the weavers; and the rogues raised their arms, as if in the act of holding something up, saying, "Here are your Majesty's trousers! Here is the scarf! Here is the mantle! The whole suit is as light as a cobweb; one might fancy one has nothing at all on, when dressed in it; that, however, is the great virtue of this delicate cloth."

"Yes indeed!" said all the courtiers, although not one of them could see anything of this exquisite manufacture.

"If your Imperial Majesty will be graciously pleased to take off your clothes, we will fit on the new suit, in front of the looking glass."

The Emperor was accordingly undressed, and the rogues pretended to array him in his new suit; the Emperor turning round, from side to side, before the looking glass.

"How splendid his Majesty looks in his new clothes, and how well they fit!" everyone cried out. "What a design! What colours! These are indeed royal robes!"

"The canopy which is to be borne over your Majesty, in the procession, is waiting," announced the chief master of the ceremonies.

"I am quite ready," answered the Emperor. "Do my new clothes fit well?" asked he, turning himself round again before the looking glass, in order that he might appear to be examining his handsome suit.

The lords of the bedchamber, who were to carry his Majesty's train felt about on the ground, as if they were lifting up the ends of the mantle; and pretended to be carrying something; for they would by no means betray anything like simplicity, or unfitness for their office.

So now the Emperor walked under his high canopy in the midst of the procession, through the streets of his capital; and all the people standing by, and those at the windows, cried out,

"Oh! How beautiful are our Emperor's new clothes! What a magnificent train there is to the mantle; and how gracefully the scarf hangs!" In short, no one would allow that he could not see these much-admired clothes; because, in doing so, he would have declared himself either a simpleton or unfit for his office. Certainly, none of the Emperor's various suits, had ever made so great an impression, as these invisible ones.

"But the Emperor has nothing at all on!" said a little child.

"Listen to the voice of innocence!" exclaimed his father; and what the child had said was whispered from one to another.

"But he has nothing at all on!" at last cried out all the people. The Emperor was vexed, for he knew that the people were right; but he thought the procession must go on now! And the lords of the bedchamber took greater pains than ever, to appear holding up a train, although, in reality, there was no train to hold.

The Swineherd

There was once a poor Prince, who had a kingdom. His kingdom was very small, but still quite large enough to marry upon; and he wished to marry.

It was certainly rather cool of him to say to the Emperor's daughter, "Will you have me?" But so he did; for his name was renowned far and wide; and there were a hundred princesses who would have answered, "Yes!" and "Thank you kindly." We shall see what this princess said.

Listen!

It happened that where the Prince's father lay buried, there grew a rose tree—a most beautiful rose tree, which blossomed only once in every five years, and even then bore only one flower, but that was a rose! It smelt so sweet that all cares and sorrows were forgotten by he who inhaled its fragrance.

And furthermore, the Prince had a nightingale, who could sing in such a manner that it seemed as though all sweet melodies dwelt in her little throat. So the Princess was to have the rose, and the nightingale; and they were accordingly put into large silver caskets, and sent to her.

The Emperor had them brought into a large hall, where the Princess was playing at "Visiting" with the ladies of the court; and when she saw the caskets with the presents, she clapped her hands for joy.

"Ah, if it were but a little pussy-cat!" said she; but the rose tree, with its beautiful rose came to view.

"Oh, how prettily it is made!" said all the court ladies.

"It is more than pretty," said the Emperor, "it is charming!"

But the Princess touched it, and was almost ready to cry.

"Fie, papa!" said she. "It is not made at all, it is natural!"

"Let us see what is in the other casket, before we get into a bad humour," said the Emperor. So the nightingale came forth and sang so delightfully that at first no one could say anything ill-humoured of her.

"*Superbe! Charmant!* exclaimed the ladies; for they all used to chatter French, each one worse than her neighbour.

"How much the bird reminds me of the musical box that belonged to our blessed Empress," said an old knight. "Oh yes! These are the same tones, the same execution."

"Yes! yes!" said the Emperor, and he wept like a child at the remembrance.

"I will still hope that it is not a real bird," said the Princess.

"Yes, it is a real bird," said those who had brought it. "Well then let the bird fly," said the Princess; and she positively refused to see the Prince.

However, he was not to be discouraged; he daubed his face over brown and black; pulled his cap over his ears, and knocked at the door.

"Good day to my lord, the Emperor!" said he. "Can I have employment at the palace?"

"Why, yes," said the Emperor. "I want some one to take care of the pigs, for we have a great many of them."

So the Prince was appointed "Imperial Swineherd." He had a dirty little room close by the pigsty; and there he sat the whole day, and worked. By the evening he had made a pretty little kitchen-pot. Little bells were hung all round it; and when the pot was boiling, these bells tinkled in the most charming manner, and played the old melody,

"Ach! du lieber Augustin,
Alles ist weg, weg, weg!"*

But what was still more curious, whoever held his finger in

* "Ah! dear Augustine! All is gone, gone, gone!"

the smoke of the kitchen-pot, immediately smelt all the dishes that were cooking on every hearth in the city—this, you see, was something quite different from the rose.

Now the Princess happened to walk that way; and when she heard the tune, she stood quite still, and seemed pleased; for she could play "Lieber Augustine"; it was the only piece she knew; and she played it with one finger.

"Why there is my piece," said the Princess. "That swineherd must certainly have been well educated! Go in and ask him the price of the instrument."

So one of the court-ladies must run in; however, she drew on wooden slippers first.

"What will you take for the kitchen-pot?" said the lady.

"I will have ten kisses from the Princess," said the swineherd.

"Yes, indeed!" said the lady.

"I cannot sell it for less," rejoined the swineherd.

"He is an impudent fellow!" said the Princess, and she walked on; but when she had gone a little way, the bells tinkled so prettily:

"Ach! du lieber Augustin,
Alles ist weg, weg, weg!"

"Stay," said the Princess. "Ask him if he will have ten kisses from the ladies of my court."

"No, thank you!" said the swineherd. "Ten kisses from the Princess, or I keep the kitchen-pot myself."

"That must not be, either!" said the Princess. "But do you all stand before me that no one may see us."

And the court-ladies placed themselves in front of her, and spread out their dresses—the swineherd got ten kisses, and the Princess—the kitchen-pot.

That was delightful! The pot was boiling the whole evening, and the whole of the following day. They knew perfectly well what was cooking at every fire throughout the city, from the chamberlain's to the cobbler's; the court-ladies danced and clapped their hands.

"We know who has soup, and who has pancakes for dinner today, who has cutlets, and who has eggs. How interesting!"

"Yes, but keep my secret, for I am an Emperor's daughter."

The swineherd—that is to say—the Prince, for no one knew that he was other than an ill-favoured swineherd, let not a day pass without working at something; he at last constructed a rattle, which, when it was swung round, played all the waltzes and jig tunes, which have ever been heard since the creation of the world.

"Ah, that is *superbe!*" said the Princess when she passed by. "I have never heard prettier compositions! Go in and ask him the price of the instrument; but mind, he shall have no more kisses!"

"He will have a hundred kisses from the Princess!" said the lady who had been to ask.

"I think he is not in his right senses!" said the Princess, and walked on, but when she had gone a little way, she stopped again. "One must encourage art," said she, "I am the Emperor's daughter. Tell him he shall, as on yesterday, have ten kisses from me, and may take the rest from the ladies of the court."

"Oh—but we should not like that at all!" said they. "What are you muttering?" asked the Princess. "If I can kiss him, surely you can. Remember that you owe everything to me." So the ladies were obliged to go to him again.

"A hundred kisses from the Princess," said he, "or else let everyone keep his own!"

"Stand round!" said she; and all the ladies stood round her whilst the kissing was going on.

"What can be the reason for such a crowd close by the pigsty?" said the Emperor, who happened just then to step out on the balcony; he rubbed his eyes, and put on his spectacles.

"They are the ladies of the court; I must go down and see what they are about!" So he pulled up his slippers at the heel, for he had trodden them down.

As soon as he had got into the court-yard, he moved very softly, and the ladies were so much engrossed with counting the kisses, that all might go on fairly, that they did not perceive the Emperor. He rose on his tiptoes.

"What is all this?" said he, when he saw what was going on, and he boxed the Princess's ears with his slipper, just as the swineherd was taking the eighty-sixth kiss.

"March out!" said the Emperor, for he was very angry; and both Princess and swineherd were thrust out of the city.

The Princess now stood and wept, the swineherd scolded, and the rain poured down.

"Alas! Unhappy creature that I am!" said the Princess. "If I had but married the handsome young Prince! Ah! how unfortunate I am!"

And the swineherd went behind a tree, washed the black and brown colour from his face, threw off his dirty clothes, and stepped forth in his princely robes; he looked so noble that the Princess could not help bowing before him.

"I am come to despise thee," said he. "Thou would'st not have an honourable Prince! Thou could'st not prize the rose and the nightingale, but thou wast ready to kiss the swineherd for the sake of a trumpery plaything. Thou art rightly served."

He then went back to his own little kingdom, and shut the door of his palace in her face. Now she might well sing,

"Ach! du lieber Augustin,
Alles ist weg, weg, weg!"

THE PRINCESS AND THE PEA

There was once a Prince who wished to marry a Princess; but then she must be a real Princess. He travelled all over the world in hopes of finding such a lady; but there was always something wrong. Princesses he found in plenty; but whether they were real Princesses it was impossible for him to decide, for now one thing, now another, seemed to him not quite right about the ladies. At last he returned to his palace quite cast down, because he wished so much to have a real Princess for his wife.

One evening a fearful tempest arose, it thundered and lightened, and the rain poured down from the sky in torrents: besides, it was as dark as pitch. All at once there was heard a violent knocking at the door, and the old King, the Prince's father, went out himself to open it.

It was a Princess who was standing outside the door. What with the rain and the wind, she was in a sad condition; the water trickled down from her hair, and her clothes clung to her body. She said she was a real Princess.

"Ah! we shall soon see that!" thought the old Queen-mother; however, she said not a word of what she was going to do; but went quietly into the bedroom, took all the bed-clothes off the bed, and put three little peas on the bedstead. She then laid twenty mattresses one upon another over the three peas, and put twenty feather beds over the mattresses.

Upon this bed the Princess was to pass the night.

The next morning she was asked how she had slept. "Oh, very badly indeed!" she replied. "I have scarcely closed my eyes the whole night through. I do not know what was in my bed, but I had something hard under me, and am all over black and blue. It has hurt me so much!"

Now it was plain that the lady must be a real Princess, since she had been able to feel the three little peas through the twenty mattresses and twenty feather beds. None but a real Princess could have had such a delicate sense of feeling.

The Prince accordingly made her his wife; being now convinced that he had found a real Princess. The three peas were however put into the cabinet of curiosities, where they are still to be seen, provided they are not lost.

Wasn't this a lady of real delicacy?

THE SHOES OF FORTUNE

I.
A BEGINNING

Every author has some peculiarity in his descriptions or in his style of writing. Those who do not like him, magnify it, shrug up their shoulders, and exclaim—there he is again! I, for my part, know very well how I can bring about this movement and this exclamation. It would happen immediately if I were to begin here, as I intended to do, with: "Rome has its Corso, Naples its Toledo"—"Ah! that Andersen; there he is again!" they would cry; yet I must, to please my fancy, continue quite quietly, and add: "But Copenhagen has its East Street."

Here, then, we will stay for the present. In one of the houses not far from the new market, a party was invited—a very large party, in order, as is often the case, to get a return invitation from the others. One half of the company was already seated at the card-table, the other half awaited the result of the stereotype preliminary observation of the lady of the house:

"Now let us see what we can do to amuse ourselves."

They had got just so far, and the conversation began to crystallise, as it could but do with the scanty stream which the commonplace world supplied. Amongst other things they spoke of the middle ages: some praised that period as far more interesting, far more poetical than our own too sober present; indeed Councillor Knap defended this opinion so warmly, that the hostess declared immediately on his side, and both exerted themselves with unwearied eloquence. The Councillor boldly declared the time of King Hans to be the noblest and the most happy period.*

* A.D. 1482-1513

While the conversation turned on this subject, and was only for a moment interrupted by the arrival of a journal that contained nothing worth reading, we will just step out into the antechamber, where cloaks, mackintoshes, sticks, umbrellas, and shoes, were deposited. Here sat two female figures, a young and an old one. One might have thought at first they were servants come to accompany their mistresses home; but on looking nearer, one soon saw they could scarcely be mere servants; their forms were too noble for that, their skin too fine, the cut of their dress too striking. Two fairies were they; the younger, it is true, was not Dame Fortune herself, but one of the waiting-maids of her handmaidens who carry about the lesser good things that she distributes; the other looked extremely gloomy—it was Care. She always attends to her own serious business herself, as then she is sure of having it done properly.

They were telling each other, with a confidential interchange of ideas, where they had been during the day. The messenger of Fortune had only executed a few unimportant commissions, such as saving a new bonnet from a shower of rain, etc.; but what she had yet to perform was something quite unusual.

"I must tell you," said she, "that today is my birthday; and in honour of it, a pair of walking-shoes or galoshes has been entrusted to me, which I am to carry to mankind. These shoes possess the property of instantly transporting he who has them on to the place or the period in which he most wishes to be; every wish, as regards time or place, or state of being, will be immediately fulfilled, and so at last man will be happy, here below."

"Do you seriously believe it?" replied Care, in a severe tone of reproach. "No; he will be very unhappy, and will assuredly bless the moment when he feels that he has freed himself from the fatal shoes."

"Stupid nonsense!" said the other angrily. "I will put them

here by the door. Some one will make a mistake for certain and take the wrong ones—he will be a happy man."

Such was their conversation.

II.
What Happened to the Councillor

It was late; Councillor Knap, deeply occupied with the times of King Hans, intended to go home, and malicious Fate managed matters so that his feet, instead of finding their way to his own galoshes, slipped into those of Fortune. Thus caparisoned the good man walked out of the well-lighted rooms into East Street. By the magic power of the shoes he was carried back to the times of King Hans; on which account his foot very naturally sank in the mud and puddles of the street, there having been in those days no pavement in Copenhagen.

"Well! This is too bad! How dirty it is here!" sighed the Councillor. "As to a pavement, I can find no traces of one, and all the lamps, it seems, have gone to sleep."

The moon was not yet very high; it was besides rather foggy, so that in the darkness all objects seemed mingled in chaotic confusion. At the next corner hung a votive lamp before a Madonna, but the light it gave was little better than none at all; indeed, he did not observe it before he was exactly under it, and his eyes fell upon the bright colours of the pictures which represented the well-known group of the Virgin and the infant Jesus.

"That is probably a wax-work show," thought he; "and the people delay taking down their sign in hopes of a late visitor or two."

A few persons in the costume of the time of King Hans passed quickly by him.

"How strange they look! The good folks come probably from a masquerade!"

Suddenly was heard the sound of drums and fifes; the bright

blaze of a fire shot up from time to time, and its ruddy gleams seemed to contend with the bluish light of the torches. The Councillor stood still, and watched a most strange procession pass by. First came a dozen drummers, who understood pretty well how to handle their instruments; then came halberdiers, and some armed with cross-bows. The principal person in the procession was a priest. Astonished at what he saw, the Councillor asked what was the meaning of all this mummery, and who that man was.

"That's the Bishop of Zealand," was the answer.

"Good Heavens! What has taken possession of the Bishop?" sighed the Councillor, shaking his bead. It certainly could not be the Bishop; even though he was considered the most absent man in the whole kingdom, and people told the drollest anecdotes about him. Reflecting on the matter, and without looking right or left, the Councillor went through East Street and across the Habro-Platz. The bridge leading to Palace Square was not to be found; scarcely trusting his senses, the nocturnal wanderer discovered a shallow piece of water, and here fell in with two men who very comfortably were rocking to and fro in a boat.

"Does your honour want to cross the ferry to the Holme?" asked they.

"Across to the Holme!" said the Councillor, who knew nothing of the age in which he at that moment was. "No, I am going to Christianshafen, to Little Market Street."

Both men stared at him in astonishment.

"Only just tell me where the bridge is," said he. "It is really unpardonable that there are no lamps here; and it is as dirty as if one had to wade through a morass."

The longer he spoke with the boatmen, the more unintelligible did their language become to him.

"I don't understand your Bornholmish dialect," said he at last, angrily, and turning his back upon them. He was unable to find the bridge: there was no railway either. "It is really disgraceful what a state this place is in," muttered he to himself. Never had his age, with which, however, he was always grumbling, seemed so miserable as on this evening. "I'll take a hackney-coach!" thought he. But where were the hackney-coaches? Not one was to be seen.

"I must go back to the New Market; there, it is to be hoped, I shall find some coaches; for if I don't, I shall never get safe to Christianshafen."

So off he went in the direction of East Street, and had nearly got to the end of it when the moon shone forth.

"God bless me! What wooden scaffolding is that which they have set up there?" cried he involuntarily, as he looked at East Gate, which, in those days, was at the end of East Street.

He found, however, a little side-door open, and through this he went, and stepped into our New Market of the present time. It was a huge desolate plain; some wild bushes stood up here and there, while across the field flowed a broad canal or river. Some wretched hovels for the Dutch sailors, resembling great boxes, and after which the place was named, lay about in confused disorder on the opposite bank.

"I either behold a fata morgana, or I am regularly tipsy," whimpered out the Councillor. "But what's this?"

He turned round anew, firmly convinced that he was seriously ill. He gazed at the street formerly so well known to him, and now so strange in appearance, and looked at the houses more attentively: most of them were of wood, slightly put together; and many had a thatched roof.

"No—I am far from well," sighed he; "and yet I drank only one glass of punch; but I cannot suppose it—it was, too, really very wrong to give us punch and hot salmon for supper. I shall speak about it at the first opportunity. I have half a mind to go back again, and say what I suffer. But no, that would be too silly; and Heaven only knows if they are up still."

He looked for the house, but it had vanished.

"It is really dreadful," groaned he with increasing anxiety; "I cannot recognise East Street again; there is not a single decent shop from one end to the other! Nothing but wretched huts can I see anywhere; just as if I were at Ringstead. Oh! I am ill! I can scarcely bear myself any longer. Where the deuce can the house be? It must be here on this very spot; yet there is not the slightest idea of resemblance, to such a degree has everything changed this night! At all events here are some people up and stirring. Oh! oh! I am certainly very ill."

He now hit upon a half-open door, through a chink of which a faint light shone. It was a sort of hostelry of those times; a kind of public-house. The room had some resemblance to the clay-floored halls in Holstein; a pretty numerous company, consisting of seamen, Copenhagen burghers, and a few scholars, sat here in deep converse over their pewter cans, and gave little heed to the person who entered.

"By your leave!" said the Councillor to the Hostess, who came bustling towards him. "I've felt so queer all of a sudden; would you have the goodness to send for a hackney-coach to take me to Christianshafen?"

The woman examined him with eyes of astonishment, and shook her head; she then addressed him in German. The Councillor thought she did not understand Danish, and therefore repeated his wish in German. This, in connection with his costume, strengthened the good woman in the belief that he was a foreigner. That he was ill, she comprehended directly; so she brought him a pitcher of water, which tasted certainly pretty strong of the sea, although it had been fetched from the well.

The Councillor supported his head on his hand, drew a long breath, and thought over all the wondrous things he saw around him.

"Is this the Daily News of this evening?" he asked mechanically, as he saw the Hostess push aside a large sheet of paper.

The meaning of this councillorship query remained, of

course, a riddle to her, yet she handed him the paper without replying. It was a coarse wood-cut, representing a splendid meteor "as seen in the town of Cologne," which was to be read below in bright letters.

"That is very old!" said the Councillor, whom this piece of antiquity began to make considerably more cheerful. "Pray how did you come into possession of this rare print? It is extremely interesting, although the whole is a mere fable. Such meteorous appearances are to be explained in this way—that they are the reflections of the Aurora Borealis, and it is highly probable they are caused principally by electricity."

Those persons who were sitting nearest him and heard his speech, stared at him in wonderment; and one of them rose, took off his hat respectfully, and said with a serious countenance, "You are no doubt a very learned man, Monsieur."

"Oh no," answered the Councillor, "I can only join in conversation on this topic and on that, as indeed one must do according to the demands of the world at present."

"*Modestia* is a fine virtue," continued the gentleman; "however, as to your speech, I must say *mihi secus videtur*: yet I am willing to suspend my *judicium*."

"May I ask with whom I have the pleasure of speaking?" asked the Councillor.

"I am a Bachelor in *Theologia*," answered the gentleman with a stiff reverence.

This reply fully satisfied the Councillor; the title suited the dress. "He is certainly," thought he, "some village schoolmaster—some queer old fellow, such as one still often meets with in Jutland."

"This is no *locus docendi*, it is true," began the clerical gentleman; "yet I beg you earnestly to let us profit by your learning. Your reading in the ancients is, *sine dubio*, of vast extent?"

"Oh yes, I've read a something, to be sure," replied the Councillor. "I like reading all useful works; but I do not on that account despise the modern ones; 'tis only the unfortunate 'Tales of Every-day Life' that I cannot bear—we have enough and more than enough such in reality."

"'Tales of Every-day Life?'" said our Bachelor inquiringly.

"I mean those new fangled novels, twisting and writhing themselves in the dust of commonplace, which also expect to find a reading public."

"Oh," exclaimed the clerical gentleman smiling, "there is much wit in them; besides they are read at court. The King likes the history of Sir Iffven and Sir Gaudian particularly, which treats of King Arthur, and his Knights of the Round Table; he has more than once joked about it with his high vassals."

"I have not read that novel," said the Councillor; "it must be quite a new one, that Heiberg has published lately."

"No," answered the theologian of the time of King Hans: "that book is not written by a Heiberg, but was imprinted by Godfrey von Gehmen."

"Oh, is that the author's name?" said the Councillor. "It is a very old name, and, as well as I recollect, he was the first printer that appeared in Denmark."

"Yes, he is our first printer," replied the clerical gentleman hastily.

So far all went on well. Some one of the worthy burghers now spoke of the dreadful pestilence that had raged in the country a few years back, meaning that of 1484. The Councillor imagined it was the cholera that was meant, which people made so much fuss about; and the discourse passed off satisfactorily enough. The war of the buccaneers of 1490 was so recent that it could not fail being alluded to; the English pirates had, they said, most shamefully taken their ships while in the roadstead; and the Councillor, before whose eyes the Herostratic* event of

* Herostratus, or Eratostratus—an Ephesian, who wantonly set fire to the famous temple of Diana, in order to commemorate his name by so uncommon an action.

1801 still floated vividly, agreed entirely with the others in abusing the rascally English. With other topics he was not so fortunate; every moment brought about some new confusion, and threatened to become a perfect Babel; for the worthy Bachelor was really too ignorant, and the simplest observations of the Councillor sounded to him too daring and phantastical. They looked at one another from the crown of the head to the soles of the feet; and when matters grew to too high a pitch, then the Bachelor talked Latin, in the hope of being better understood—but it was of no use after all.

"What's the matter?" asked the Hostess, plucking the Councillor by the sleeve; and now his recollection returned, for in the course of the conversation he had entirely forgotten all that had preceded it.

"Merciful God, where am I!" exclaimed he in agony; and while he so thought, all his ideas and feelings of overpowering dizziness, against which he struggled with the utmost power of desperation, encompassed him with renewed force. "Let us drink claret and mead, and Bremen beer," shouted one of the guests—"and you shall drink with us!"

Two maidens approached. One wore a cap of two staring colours, denoting the class of persons to which she belonged. They poured out the liquor, and made the most friendly gesticulations; while a cold perspiration trickled down the back of the poor Councillor.

"What's to be the end of this! What's to become of me!" groaned he; but he was forced, in spite of his opposition, to drink with the rest. They took hold of the worthy man; who, hearing on every side that he was intoxicated, did not in the least doubt the truth of this certainly not very polite assertion; but on the contrary, implored the ladies and gentlemen present to procure him a hackney-coach: they, however, imagined he was talking Russian.

Never before, he thought, had he been in such a coarse and ignorant company; one might almost fancy the people had turned heathens again. "It is the most dreadful moment of my life: the whole world is leagued against me!" But suddenly it occurred to him that he might stoop down under the table, and then creep unobserved out of the door. He did so; but just as he was going, the others remarked what he was about; they laid hold of him by the legs; and now, happily for him, off fell his fatal shoes—and with them the charm was at an end.

The Councillor saw quite distinctly before him a lantern burning, and behind this a large handsome house. All seemed to him in proper order as usual; it was East Street, splendid and elegant as we now see it. He lay with his feet towards a doorway, and exactly opposite sat the watchman asleep.

"Gracious Heaven!" said he. "Have I lain here in the street and dreamed? Yes; 'tis East Street! How splendid and light it is! But really it is terrible what an effect that one glass of punch must have had on me!"

Two minutes later, he was sitting in a hackney-coach and driving to Frederickshafen. He thought of the distress and agony he had endured, and praised from the very bottom of his heart the happy reality—our own time—which, with all its deficiencies, is yet much better than that in which, so much against his inclination, he had lately been.

III.
The Watchman's Adventure

"Why, there is a pair of galoshes, as sure as I'm alive!" said the watchman, awaking from a gentle slumber. "They belong no doubt to the lieutenant who lives over the way. They lie close to the door."

The worthy man was inclined to ring and deliver them at the house, for there was still a light in the window; but he did not like disturbing the other people in their beds, and so very considerately he left the matter alone.

"Such a pair of shoes must be very warm and comfortable," said he; "the leather is so soft and supple." They fitted his feet as though they had been made for him. "'Tis a curious world we live in," continued he, soliloquising. "There is the lieutenant, now, who might go quietly to bed if he chose, where no doubt he could stretch himself at his ease; but does he do it? No; he saunters up and down his room, because, probably, he has enjoyed too many of the good things of this world at his dinner. That's a happy fellow! He has neither an infirm mother, nor a whole troop of everlastingly hungry children to torment him. Every evening he goes to a party, where his nice supper costs him nothing: would to Heaven I could but change with him! How happy should I be!"

While expressing his wish, the charm of the shoes, which he had put on, began to work; the watchman entered into the being and nature of the lieutenant. He stood in the handsomely furnished apartment, and held between his fingers a small sheet of rose-coloured paper, on which some verses were written—written indeed by the officer himself; for who has not, at least once in his life, had a lyrical moment? And if one then marks down one's thoughts, poetry is produced. But here was written:

Oh, were I rich

"Oh, were I rich! Such was my wish, yea such
When hardly three feet high, I longed for much.
Oh, were I rich! an officer were I,
With sword, and uniform, and plume so high.
And the time came, and officer was I!
But yet I grew not rich. Alas, poor me!
Have pity, Thou, who all man's wants dost see.

"I sat one evening sunk in dreams of bliss,
A maid of seven years old gave me a kiss,
I at that time was rich in poesy
And tales of old, though poor as poor could be;

But all she asked for was this poesy.
Then was I rich, but not in gold, poor me!
As Thou dost know, who all men's hearts canst see.

"Oh, were I rich! Oft asked I for this boon.
The child grew up to womanhood full soon.
She is so pretty, clever, and so kind
Oh, did she know what's hidden in my mind—
A tale of old. Would she to me were kind!.
But I'm condemned to silence! oh, poor me!
As Thou dost know, who all men's hearts canst see.

"Oh, were I rich in calm and peace of mind,
My grief you then would not here written find!
O thou, to whom I do my heart devote,
Oh read this page of glad days now remote,
A dark, dark tale, which I tonight devote!
Dark is the future now. Alas, poor me!
Have pity Thou, who all men's pains dost see."

Such verses as these people write when they are in love! But no man in his senses ever thinks of printing them. Here one of the sorrows of life, in which there is real poetry, gave itself vent; not that barren grief which the poet may only hint at, but never depict in its detail—misery and want: that animal necessity, in short, to snatch at least at a fallen leaf of the bread-fruit tree, if not at the fruit itself. The higher the position in which one finds oneself transplanted, the greater is the suffering. Everyday necessity is the stagnant pool of life—no lovely picture reflects itself therein. Lieutenant, love, and lack of money—that is a symbolic triangle, or much the same as the half of the shattered die of Fortune. This the lieutenant felt most poignantly, and this was the reason he leant his head against the window, and sighed so deeply.

"The poor watchman out there in the street is far happier than I. He knows not what I term privation. He has a home, a wife, and children, who weep with him over his sorrows, who rejoice with him when he is glad. Oh, far happier were I, could I exchange with him my being—with his desires and with his hopes perform the weary pilgrimage of life! Oh, he is a hundred times happier than I!"

In the same moment the watchman was again watchman. It was the shoes that caused the metamorphosis by means of which, unknown to himself, he took upon him the thoughts and feelings of the officer; but, as we have just seen, he felt himself in his new situation much less contented, and now preferred the very thing which but some minutes before he had rejected. So then the watchman was again watchman.

"That was an unpleasant dream," said he; "but 'twas droll enough altogether. I fancied that I was the lieutenant over there: and yet the thing was not very much to my taste after all. I missed my good old mother and the dear little ones; who almost tear me to pieces for sheer love."

He seated himself once more and nodded: the dream continued to haunt him, for he still had the shoes on his feet. A falling star shone in the dark firmament.

"There falls another star," said he: "but what does it matter; there are always enough left. I should not much mind examining the little glimmering things somewhat nearer, especially the moon; for that would not slip so easily through a man's fingers. When we die—so at least says the student, for whom my wife does the washing—we shall fly about as light as a feather from one such a star to the other. That's, of course, not true: but 'twould be pretty enough if it were so. If I could but once take a leap up there, my body might stay here on the steps for what I care."

Behold—there are certain things in the world to which one ought never to give utterance except with the greatest caution; but doubly careful must one be when we have the Shoes of Fortune on our feet. Now just listen to what happened to the watchman.

As to ourselves, we all know the speed produced by the employment of steam; we have experienced it either on railroads, or in boats when crossing the sea; but such a flight is like the travelling of a sloth in comparison with the velocity with which light moves. It flies nineteen million times faster than the best race-horse; and yet electricity is quicker still. Death is an electric shock which our heart receives; the freed soul soars upwards on the wings of electricity. The sun's light wants eight minutes and some seconds to perform a journey of more than twenty million of our Danish* miles; borne by electricity, the soul wants even some minutes less to accomplish the same flight. To it the space between the heavenly bodies is not greater than the distance between the homes of our friends in town is for us, even if they live a short way from each other; such an electric shock in the heart, however, costs us the use of the body here below; unless, like the watchman of East Street, we happen to have on the Shoes of Fortune.

In a few seconds the watchman had done the fifty-two thousand of our miles up to the moon, which, as everyone knows, was formed out of matter much lighter than our earth; and is, so we should say, as soft as newly-fallen snow. He found himself on one of the many circumjacent mountain-ridges with which we are acquainted by means of Dr. Madler's "Map of the Moon." Within, down it sunk perpendicularly into a caldron, about a Danish mile in depth; while below lay a town, whose appearance we can, in some measure, realise to ourselves by beating the white of an egg in a glass of water. The matter of which it was built was just as soft, and formed similar towers, and domes, and pillars, transparent and rocking in the thin air; while above his head our earth was rolling like a large fiery ball.

He perceived immediately a quantity of beings who were certainly what we call "men"; yet they looked different to us. A far

* A Danish mile is nearly 4 3/4 English.

more correct imagination than that of the pseudo-Herschel* had created them; and if they had been placed in rank and file, and copied by some skilful painter's hand, one would, without doubt, have exclaimed involuntarily, "What a beautiful arabesque!"

They had a language too; but surely nobody can expect that the soul of the watchman should understand it. Be that as it may, it did comprehend it; for in our souls there germinate far greater powers than we poor mortals, despite all our cleverness, have any notion of. Does she not show us—she the queen in the land of enchantment—her astounding dramatic talent in all our dreams? There every acquaintance appears and speaks upon the stage, so entirely in character, and with the same tone of voice, that none of us, when awake, were able to imitate it. How well can she recall persons to our mind, of whom we have not thought for years; when suddenly they step forth "every inch a man," resembling the real personages, even to the finest features, and become the heroes or heroines of our world of dreams. In reality, such remembrances are rather unpleasant: every sin, every evil thought, may, like a clock with alarm or chimes, be repeated at pleasure; then the question is if we can trust ourselves to give an account of every unbecoming word in our heart and on our lips.

The watchman's spirit understood the language of the inhabitants of the moon pretty well. The Selenites** disputed variously about our earth, and expressed their doubts if it could be inhabited: the air, they said, must certainly be too dense to allow any rational dweller in the moon the necessary free respiration. They considered the moon alone to be inhabited: they imagined it was the real heart of the universe or planetary system, on which the

*This relates to a book published some years ago in Germany, and said to be by Herschel, which contained a description of the moon and its inhabitants, written with such a semblance of truth that many were deceived by the imposture. Probably a translation of the celebrated Moon hoax, written by Richard A. Locke, and originally published in New York.

** Selenites: Dwellers in the moon.

genuine Cosmopolites, or citizens of the world, dwelt. What strange things men—no, what strange things Selenites sometimes take into their heads!

About politics they had a good deal to say. But little Denmark must take care what it is about, and not run counter to the moon; that great realm, that might in an ill-humour bestir itself, and dash down a hail-storm in our faces, or force the Baltic to overflow the sides of its gigantic basin.

We will, therefore, not listen to what was spoken, and on no condition run in the possibility of telling tales out of school; but we will rather proceed, like good quiet citizens, to East Street, and observe what happened meanwhile to the body of the watchman.

He sat lifeless on the steps: the morning-star,* that is to say, the heavy wooden staff, headed with iron spikes, and which had nothing else in common with its sparkling brother in the sky, had glided from his hand; while his eyes were fixed with glassy stare on the moon, looking for the good old fellow of a spirit which still haunted it.

"What's the hour, watchman?" asked a passer-by. But when the watchman gave no reply, the merry roysterer, who was now returning home from a noisy drinking bout, took it into his head to try what a tweak of the nose would do, on which the supposed sleeper lost his balance, the body lay motionless, stretched out on the pavement: the man was dead. When the patrol came up, all his comrades, who comprehended nothing of the whole affair, were seized with a dreadful fright, for dead be was, and he remained so. The proper authorities were informed of the circumstance, people talked a good deal about it, and in the morning the body was carried to the hospital.

Now that would be a very pretty joke, if the spirit when it came back and looked for the body in East Street, were not to

* The watchmen in Germany, had formerly, and in some places they still carry with them, on their rounds at night, a sort of mace or club, known in ancient times by the above denomination.

find one. No doubt it would, in its anxiety, run off to the police, and then to the "Hue and Cry" office, to announce that "the finder will be handsomely rewarded," and at last away to the hospital; yet we may boldly assert that the soul is shrewdest when it shakes off every fetter, and every sort of leading-string—the body only makes it stupid.

The seemingly dead body of the watchman wandered, as we have said, to the hospital, where it was brought into the general viewing-room: and the first thing that was done here was naturally to pull off the galoshes—when the spirit, that was merely gone out on adventures, must have returned with the quickness of lightning to its earthly tenement. It took its direction towards the body in a straight line; and a few seconds after, life began to show itself in the man. He asserted that the preceding night had been the worst that ever the malice of fate had allotted him; he would not for two silver marks again go through what he had endured while moon-stricken; but now, however, it was over.

The same day he was discharged from the hospital as perfectly cured; but the Shoes meanwhile remained behind.

IV.
A Moment of Head Importance—An Evening's "Dramatic Readings"—A Most Strange Journey

Every inhabitant of Copenhagen knows, from personal inspection, how the entrance to Frederick's Hospital looks; but as it is possible that others, who are not Copenhagen people, may also read this little work, we will beforehand give a short description of it.

The extensive building is separated from the street by a pretty high railing, the thick iron bars of which are so far apart, that in all seriousness, it is said, some very thin fellow had of a night occasionally squeezed himself through to go and pay his little visits in the town. The part of the body most difficult to manage on such occasions was, no doubt, the head; here, as is so often the case in the world, long-headed people get through best. So much, then, for the introduction.

One of the young men, whose head, in a physical sense only, might be said to be of the thickest, had the watch that evening. The rain poured down in torrents; yet despite these two obstacles, the young man was obliged to go out, if it were but for a quarter of an hour; and as to telling the door-keeper about it, that, he thought, was quite unnecessary, if, with a whole skin, he were able to slip through the railings. There, on the floor lay the galoshes, which the watchman had forgotten; he never dreamed for a moment that they were those of Fortune; and they promised to do him good service in the wet; so he put them on. The question now was, if he could squeeze himself through the grating, for he had never tried before. Well, there he stood.

"Would to Heaven I had got my head through!" said he, involuntarily; and instantly through it slipped, easily and without pain, notwithstanding it was pretty large and thick. But now the rest of the body was to be got through!

"Ah! I am much too stout," groaned he aloud, while fixed as in a vice. "I had thought the head was the most difficult part of the matter—oh! oh! I really cannot squeeze myself through!"

He now wanted to pull his over-hasty head back again, but he could not. For his neck there was room enough, but for nothing more. His first feeling was of anger; his next that his temper fell to zero. The Shoes of Fortune had placed him in the most dreadful situation; and, unfortunately, it never occurred to him to wish himself free. The pitch-black clouds poured down their contents in still heavier torrents; not a creature was to be seen in the streets. To reach up to the bell was what he did not like; to cry aloud for help would have availed him little; besides, how ashamed would he have been to be found caught in a trap, like an outwitted fox! How was he to twist himself through! He saw clearly that it was his irrevocable destiny to remain a prisoner till dawn, or, perhaps, even late in the morning; then the smith must be fetched to file away the bars; but all that would not be done so quickly as he could think about it. The whole Charity School, just opposite, would be in motion; all the new booths, with their not very courtier-like swarm of seamen, would join them out of curiosity, and would greet him with a wild "hurrah!" while he was standing in his pillory: there would be a mob, a hissing, and rejoicing, and jeering, ten times worse than in the rows about the Jews some years ago—"Oh, my blood is mounting to my brain; 'tis enough to drive one mad! I shall go wild! I know not what to do. Oh! were I but loose; my dizziness would then cease; oh, were my head but loose!"

You see he ought to have said that sooner; for the moment he expressed the wish his head was free; and cured of all his paroxysms of love, he hastened off to his room, where the pains consequent on the fright the Shoes had prepared for him, did not so soon take their leave.

But you must not think that the affair is over now; it grows much worse.

The night passed, the next day also; but nobody came to fetch the Shoes.

In the evening "Dramatic Readings" were to be given at the little theatre in King Street. The house was filled to suffocation; and among other pieces to be recited was a new poem by H. C. Andersen, called, My Aunt's Spectacles; the contents of which were pretty nearly as follows:

"A certain person had an aunt, who boasted of particular skill in fortune-telling with cards, and who was constantly being stormed by persons that wanted to have a peep into futurity. But she was full of mystery about her art, in which a certain pair of magic spectacles did her essential service. Her nephew, a merry boy, who was his aunt's darling, begged so long for these spectacles, that, at last, she lent him the treasure, after having informed him, with many exhortations, that in order to execute the interesting trick, he need only repair to some place where a great many persons were assembled; and then, from a higher position, whence he could overlook the crowd, pass the company in review before him through his spectacles. Immediately 'the inner man' of each individual would be displayed before him, like a game of cards, in which he unerringly might read what the future of every person presented was to be. Well pleased, the little magician hastened away to prove the powers of the spectacles in the theatre; no place seeming to him more fitted for such a trial. He begged permission of the worthy audience, and set his spectacles on his nose. A motley phantasmagoria presents itself before him, which he describes in a few satirical touches, yet without expressing his opinion openly: he tells the people enough to set them all thinking and guessing; but in order to hurt nobody, he wraps his witty oracular judgments in a transparent veil, or rather in a lurid thundercloud, shooting forth bright sparks of wit, that they may fall in the powder-magazine of the expectant audience."

The humourous poem was admirably recited, and the speaker much applauded. Among the audience was the young man of the hospital, who seemed to have forgotten his adventure of the preceding night. He had on the Shoes; for as yet no lawful owner had appeared to claim them; and besides it was so very dirty out-of-doors, they were just the thing for him, he thought.

The beginning of the poem he praised with great generosity: he even found the idea original and effective. But that the end of it, like the Rhine, was very insignificant, proved, in his opinion, the author's want of invention; he was without genius, etc. This was an excellent opportunity to have said something clever.

Meanwhile he was haunted by the idea—he should like to possess such a pair of spectacles himself; then, perhaps, by using them circumspectly, one would be able to look into people's hearts, which, he thought, would be far more interesting than merely to see what was to happen next year; for that we should all know in proper time, but the other never.

"I can now," said he to himself, "fancy the whole row of ladies and gentlemen sitting there in the front row; if one could but see into their hearts—yes, that would be a revelation—a sort of bazaar. In that lady yonder, so strangely dressed, I should find for certain a large milliner's shop; in that one the shop is empty, but it wants cleaning plain enough. But there would also be some good stately shops among them. Alas!" sighed he, "I know one in which all is stately; but there sits already a spruce young shopman, which is the only thing that's amiss in the whole shop. All would be splendidly decked out, and we should hear, 'Walk in, gentlemen, pray walk in; here you will find all you please to want.' Ah! I wish to Heaven I could walk in and take a trip right through the hearts of those present!"

And behold! to the Shoes of Fortune this was the cue; the whole man shrunk together and a most uncommon journey through the hearts of the front row of spectators, now began. The first heart through which he came, was that of a middle-aged lady, but he instantly fancied himself in the room of the "Institution for the cure of the crooked and deformed," where casts of mis-shapen limbs are displayed in naked reality on the wall. Yet there was this difference, in the institution the casts were taken at the entry of the patient; but here they were retained and guarded in the heart while the sound persons went away. They were, namely, casts of female friends, whose bodily or mental deformities were here most faithfully preserved.

With the snake-like writhings of an idea he glided into another female heart; but this seemed to him like a large holy fane.* The white dove of innocence fluttered over the altar. How gladly would he have sunk upon his knees; but he must away to the next heart; yet he still heard the pealing tones of the organ,

* temple

and he himself seemed to have become a newer and a better man; he felt unworthy to tread the neighbouring sanctuary which a poor garret, with a sick bed-rid mother, revealed. But God's warm sun streamed through the open window; lovely roses nodded from the wooden flower-boxes on the roof, and two sky-blue birds sang rejoicingly, while the sick mother implored God's richest blessings on her pious daughter.

He now crept on hands and feet through a butcher's shop; at least on every side, and above and below, there was nought but flesh. It was the heart of a most respectable rich man, whose name is certain to be found in the Directory.

He was now in the heart of the wife of this worthy gentleman. It was an old, dilapidated, mouldering dovecot. The husband's portrait was used as a weather-cock, which was connected in some way or other with the doors, and so they opened and shut of their own accord, whenever the stern old husband turned round.

Hereupon he wandered into a boudoir formed entirely of mirrors, like the one in Castle Rosenburg; but here the glasses magnified to an astonishing degree. On the floor, in the middle of the room, sat, like a Dalai-Lama, the insignificant "Self" of the person, quite confounded at his own greatness. He then imagined he had got into a needle-case full of pointed needles of every size.

"This is certainly the heart of an old maid," thought he. But he was mistaken. It was the heart of a young military man; a man, as people said, of talent and feeling.

In the greatest perplexity, he now came out of the last heart in the row; he was unable to put his thoughts in order, and fancied that his too lively imagination had run away with him.

"Good Heavens!" sighed he. "I have surely a disposition to madness—'tis dreadfully hot here; my blood boils in my veins and my head is burning like a coal." And he now remembered the important event of the evening before, how his head had got jammed in between the iron railings of the hospital. "That's what it is, no doubt," said he. "I must do something in time: under such circumstances a Russian bath might do me good. I only wish I were already on the upper bank."*

And so there he lay on the uppermost bank in the vapour-bath; but with all his clothes on, in his boots and galoshes, while the hot drops fell scalding from the ceiling on his face.

"Holloa!" cried he, leaping down. The bathing attendant, on his side, uttered a loud cry of astonishment when he beheld in the bath, a man completely dressed.

The other, however, retained sufficient presence of mind to whisper to him, "'Tis a bet, and I have won it!" But the first thing he did as soon as he got home, was to have a large blister put on his chest and back to draw out his madness.

The next morning he had a sore chest and a bleeding back; and, excepting the fright, that was all that he had gained by the Shoes of Fortune.

V.
Metamorphosis of the Copying-Clerk

The watchman, whom we have certainly not forgotten, thought meanwhile of the galoshes he had found and taken with him to the hospital; he now went to fetch them; and as neither the lieutenant, nor anybody else in the street, claimed them as his property, they were delivered over to the police-office.**

* In these Russian (vapour) baths the person extends himself on a bank or form, and as he gets accustomed to the heat, moves to another higher up towards the ceiling, where, of course, the vapour is warmest. In this manner he ascends gradually to the highest.

** As on the continent, in all law and police practices nothing is verbal, but any circumstance, however trifling, is reduced to writing, the labour, as well as the number of papers that thus accumulate, is enormous. In a police-office, consequently, we find copying-clerks among many other scribes of various denominations, of which, it seems, our hero was one.

"Why, I declare the Shoes look just like my own," said one of the clerks, eying the newly-found treasure, whose hidden powers, even he, sharp as he was, was not able to discover. "One must have more than the eye of a shoemaker to know one pair from the other," said he, soliloquising; and putting, at the same time, the galoshes in search of an owner, beside his own in the corner.

"Here, sir!" said one of the men, who panting brought him a tremendous pile of papers.

The copying-clerk turned round and spoke awhile with the man about the reports and legal documents in question; but when he had finished, and his eye fell again on the Shoes, he was unable to say whether those to the left or those to the right belonged to him. "At all events it must be those which are wet, thought he; but this time, in spite of his cleverness, he guessed quite wrong, for it was just those of Fortune which played as it were into his hands, or rather on his feet. And why, I should like to know, are the police never to be wrong? So he put them on quickly, stuck his papers in his pocket, and took besides a few under his arm, intending to look them through at home to make the necessary notes. It was noon; and the weather, that had threatened rain, began to clear up, while gaily dressed holiday folks filled the streets. "A little trip to Fredericksburg would do me no great harm," thought he; "for I, poor beast of burden that I am, have so much to annoy me, that I don't know what a good appetite is. 'Tis a bitter crust, alas! at which I am condemned to gnaw!"

Nobody could be more steady or quiet than this young man; we therefore wish him joy of the excursion with all our heart; and it will certainly be beneficial for a person who leads so sedentary a life. In the park he met a friend, one of our young poets, who told him that the following day he should set out on his long-intended tour.

"So you are going away again!" said the clerk. "You are a

very free and happy being; we others are chained by the leg and held fast to our desk."

"Yes; but it is a chain, friend, which ensures you the blessed bread of existence," answered the poet. "You need feel no care for the coming morrow: when you are old, you receive a pension."

"True," said the clerk, shrugging his shoulders; "and yet you are the better off. To sit at one's ease and poetise—that is a pleasure; everybody has something agreeable to say to you, and you are always your own master. No, friend, you should but try what it is to sit from one year's end to the other occupied with and judging the most trivial matters."

The poet shook his head, the copying-clerk did the same. Each one kept to his own opinion, and so they separated.

"It's a strange race, those poets!" said the clerk, who was very fond of soliloquising. "I should like some day, just for a trial, to take such nature upon me, and be a poet myself; I am very sure I should make no such miserable verses as the others. Today, methinks, is a most delicious day for a poet. Nature seems anew to celebrate her awakening into life. The air is so unusually clear, the clouds sail on so buoyantly, and from the green herbage a fragrance is exhaled that fills me with delight. For many a year have I not felt as at this moment."

We see already, by the foregoing effusion, that he is become a poet; to give further proof of it, however, would in most cases be insipid, for it is a most foolish notion to fancy a poet different from other men. Among the latter there may be far more poetical natures than many an acknowledged poet, when examined more closely, could boast of; the difference only is, that the poet possesses a better mental memory, on which account he is able to retain the feeling and the thought till they can be embodied by means of words; a faculty which the others do not possess. But the transition from a commonplace nature to one that is richly endowed, demands always a more or less breakneck leap over a certain abyss which yawns threateningly below; and thus must the sudden change with the clerk strike the reader.

"The sweet air!" continued he of the police-office, in his dreamy imaginings; "how it reminds me of the violets in the garden of my aunt Magdalena! Yes, then I was a little wild boy, who did not go to school very regularly. O heavens! 'tis a long time since I have thought on those times. The good old soul! She lived behind the Exchange. She always had a few twigs or green shoots in water—let the winter rage without as it might. The violets exhaled their sweet breath, whilst I pressed against the windowpanes covered with fantastic frost-work the copper coin I had heated on the stove, and so made peep-holes. What splendid vistas were then opened to my view! What change—what magnificence! Yonder in the canal lay the ships frozen up, and deserted by their whole crews, with a screaming crow for the sole occupant. But when the spring, with a gentle stirring motion, announced her arrival, a new and busy life arose; with songs and hurrahs the ice was sawn asunder, the ships were fresh tarred and rigged, that they might sail away to distant lands. But I have remained here—must always remain here, sitting at my desk in the office, and patiently see other people fetch their passports to go abroad. Such is my fate! Alas!"—sighed he, and was again silent. "Great Heaven! What is come to me! Never have I thought or felt like this before! It must be the summer air that affects me with feelings almost as disquieting as they are refreshing."

He felt in his pocket for the papers. "These police-reports will soon stem the torrent of my ideas, and effectually hinder any rebellious overflowing of the time-worn banks of official duties"; he said to himself consolingly, while his eye ran over the first page. "DAME TIGBRITH, tragedy in five acts." "What is that? And yet it is undeniably my own handwriting. Have I written the tragedy?

"Wonderful, very wonderful!—And this—what have I here?

'INTRIGUE ON THE RAMPARTS; or THE DAY OF REPENTANCE: vaudeville with new songs to the most favourite airs.' The deuce! Where did I get all this rubbish? Some one must have slipped it slyly into my pocket for a joke. There is too a letter to me; a crumpled letter and the seal broken."

Yes; it was not a very polite epistle from the manager of a theatre, in which both pieces were flatly refused.

"Hem! hem!" said the clerk breathlessly, and quite exhausted he seated himself on a bank. His thoughts were so elastic, his heart so tender; and involuntarily he picked one of the nearest flowers. It is a simple daisy, just bursting out of the bud. What the botanist tells us after a number of imperfect lectures, the flower proclaimed in a minute. It related the mythus of its birth, told of the power of the sun-light that spread out its delicate leaves, and forced them to impregnate the air with their incense—and then he thought of the manifold struggles of life, which in like manner awaken the budding flowers of feeling in our bosom. Light and air contend with chivalric emulation for the love of the fair flower that bestowed her chief favours on the latter; full of longing she turned towards the light, and as soon as it vanished, rolled her tender leaves together and slept in the embraces of the air. "It is the light which adorns me," said the flower.

"But 'tis the air which enables thee to breathe," said the poet's voice.

Close by stood a boy who dashed his stick into a wet ditch. The drops of water splashed up to the green leafy roof, and the clerk thought of the million of ephemera which in a single drop were thrown up to a height, that was as great doubtless for their size, as for us if we were to be hurled above the clouds. While he thought of this and of the whole metamorphosis he had undergone, he smiled and said, "I sleep and dream; but it is wonderful how one can dream so naturally, and know besides so exactly that it is but a dream. If only tomorrow on awaking, I could again call all to mind so vividly! I seem in unusually good spirits; my perception of things is clear, I feel as light and cheerful as though I were in heaven; but I know for a certainty, that if tomorrow a dim remembrance of it should swim before my mind, it will then seem nothing but stupid nonsense, as I have often experienced already—especially before I enlisted under the banner of the police, for that dispels like a whirlwind all the visions of an unfettered imagination. All we hear or say in a dream that is fair and beautiful is like the gold of the subterranean spirits; it is rich and splendid when it is given us, but viewed by daylight we find only withered leaves. Alas!" he sighed quite sorrowful, and gazed at the chirping birds that hopped contentedly from branch to branch, "they are much better off than I! To fly must be a heavenly art; and happy do I prize that creature in which it is innate. Yes! Could I exchange my nature with any other creature, I fain would be such a happy little lark!"

He had hardly uttered these hasty words when the skirts and sleeves of his coat folded themselves together into wings; the clothes became feathers, and the galoshes claws. He observed it perfectly, and laughed in his heart. "Now then, there is no doubt that I am dreaming; but I never before was aware of such mad freaks as these." And up he flew into the green roof and sang; but in the song there was no poetry, for the spirit of the poet was gone. The Shoes, as is the case with anybody who does what he has to do properly, could only attend to one thing at a time. He wanted to be a poet, and he was one; he now wished to be a merry chirping bird: but when he was metamorphosed into one, the former peculiarities ceased immediately. "It is really pleasant enough," said he: "the whole day long I sit in the office amid the driest law-papers, and at night I fly in my dream as a lark in the gardens of Fredericksburg; one might really write a very pretty comedy upon it." He now fluttered down into the grass, turned his head gracefully on every side, and with his bill pecked the pliant blades of grass, which, in comparison to his present size, seemed as majestic as the palm-branches of northern Africa.

Unfortunately the pleasure lasted but a moment. Presently black night overshadowed our enthusiast, who had so entirely missed his part of copying-clerk at a police-office; some vast object seemed to be thrown over him. It was a large oil-skin cap, which a sailor-boy of the quay had thrown over the struggling bird; a coarse hand sought its way carefully in under the broad rim, and seized the clerk over the back and wings. In the first moment of fear, he called, indeed, as loud as he could—"You impudent little blackguard! I am a copying-clerk at the police-office; and you know you cannot insult any belonging to the constabulary force without a chastisement. Besides, you good-for-nothing rascal, it is strictly forbidden to catch birds in the royal gardens of Fredericksburg; but your blue uniform betrays where you come from." This fine tirade sounded, however, to the ungodly sailor-boy like a mere "Pippi-pi." He gave the noisy bird a knock on his beak, and walked on.

He was soon met by two schoolboys of the upper class—that is to say as individuals, for with regard to learning they were in the lowest class in the school; and they bought the stupid bird. So the copying-clerk came to Copenhagen as guest, or rather as prisoner in a family living in Gother Street.

"'Tis well that I'm dreaming," said the clerk, "or I really should get angry. First I was a poet; now sold for a few pence as a lark; no doubt it was that accursed poetical nature which has metamorphosed me into such a poor harmless little creature. It is really pitiable, particularly when one gets into the hands of a little blackguard, perfect in all sorts of cruelty to animals: all I should like to know is, how the story will end."

The two schoolboys, the proprietors now of the transformed clerk, carried him into an elegant room. A stout stately dame received them with a smile; but she expressed much dissatisfaction that a common field-bird, as she called the lark, should appear in such high society. For today, however, she would allow it; and they must shut him in the empty cage that was standing in the window. "Perhaps he will amuse my good Polly," added the lady, looking with a benignant smile at a large green parrot that swung himself backwards and forwards most comfortably in his ring, inside a magnificent brass-wired cage. "Today is Polly's birthday," said she with stupid simplicity: "and the little brown field-bird must wish him joy."

Mr. Polly uttered not a syllable in reply, but swung to and fro with dignified condescension; while a pretty canary, as yellow as gold, that had lately been brought from his sunny fragrant home, began to sing aloud.

"Noisy creature! Will you be quiet!" screamed the lady of the house, covering the cage with an embroidered white pocket handkerchief.

"Chirp, chirp!" sighed he. "That was a dreadful snowstorm"; and he sighed again, and was silent.

The copying-clerk, or, as the lady said, the brown field-bird, was put into a small cage, close to the Canary, and not far from "my good Polly." The only human sounds that the Parrot could bawl out were, "Come, let us be men!"

Everything else that he said was as unintelligible to everybody as the chirping of the Canary, except to the clerk, who was now a bird too: he understood his companion perfectly.

"I flew about beneath the green palms and the blossoming almond-trees," sang the Canary; "I flew around, with my brothers and sisters, over the beautiful flowers, and over the glassy lakes, where the bright water-plants nodded to me from below. There, too, I saw many splendidly-dressed paroquets, that told the drollest stories, and the wildest fairy tales without end."

"Oh! those were uncouth birds," answered the Parrot. "They had no education, and talked of whatever came into their head.

"If my mistress and all her friends can laugh at what I say, so may you too, I should think. It is a great fault to have no taste for what is witty or amusing—come, let us be men."

"Ah, you have no remembrance of love for the charming maidens that danced beneath the outspread tents beside the bright fragrant flowers? Do you no longer remember the sweet fruits, and the cooling juice in the wild plants of our never-to-be-forgotten home?" said the former inhabitant of the Canary Isles, continuing his dithyrambic.

"Oh, yes," said the Parrot; "but I am far better off here. I am well fed, and get friendly treatment. I know I am a clever fellow; and that is all I care about. Come, let us be men. You are of a poetical nature, as it is called—I, on the contrary, possess profound knowledge and inexhaustible wit. You have genius; but clear-sighted, calm discretion does not take such lofty flights, and utter such high natural tones. For this they have covered you over—they never do the like to me; for I cost more. Besides, they are afraid of my beak; and I have always a witty answer at hand. Come, let us be men!"

"O warm spicy land of my birth," sang the Canary bird; "I will sing of thy dark-green bowers, of the calm bays where the pendent boughs kiss the surface of the water; I will sing of the rejoicing of all my brothers and sisters where the cactus grows in wanton luxuriance."

"Spare us your elegiac tones," said the Parrot giggling. "Rather speak of something at which one may laugh heartily. Laughing is an infallible sign of the highest degree of mental development. Can a dog, or a horse laugh? No, but they can cry. The gift of laughing was given to man alone. Ha! ha! ha!" screamed Polly, and added his stereotype witticism. "Come, let us be men!"

"Poor little Danish grey-bird," said the Canary; "you have been caught too. It is, no doubt, cold enough in your woods, but there at least is the breath of liberty; therefore fly away. In the hurry they have forgotten to shut your cage, and the upper window is open. Fly, my friend; fly away. Farewell!"

Instinctively the Clerk obeyed; with a few strokes of his wings he was out of the cage; but at the same moment the door, which was only ajar, and which led to the next room, began to creak, and supple and creeping came the large tomcat into the room, and began to pursue him. The frightened Canary fluttered about in his cage; the Parrot flapped his wings, and cried, "Come, let us be men!" The Clerk felt a mortal fright, and flew through the window, far away over the houses and streets. At last he was forced to rest a little.

The neighbouring house had a something familiar about it; a window stood open; he flew in; it was his own room. He perched upon the table.

"Come, let us be men!" said he, involuntarily imitating the chatter of the Parrot, and at the same moment he was again a copying-clerk; but he was sitting in the middle of the table.

"Heaven help me!" cried he. "How did I get up here—and so buried in sleep, too? After all, that was a very unpleasant, disagreeable dream that haunted me! The whole story is nothing but silly, stupid nonsense!"

VI.
The Best That the Galoshes Gave

The following day, early in the morning, while the Clerk was still in bed, someone knocked at his door. It was his neighbour, a young Divine, who lived on the same floor. He walked in.

"Lend me your Galoshes," said he; "it is so wet in the garden, though the sun is shining most invitingly. I should like to go out a little."

He got the Galoshes, and he was soon below in a little duodecimo garden, where between two immense walls a plumtree and an apple-tree were standing. Even such a little garden as this was considered in the metropolis of Copenhagen as a great luxury.

The young man wandered up and down the narrow paths, as well as the prescribed limits would allow; the clock struck six; without was heard the horn of a post-boy.

"To travel! to travel!" exclaimed he, overcome by most painful and passionate remembrances. "That is the happiest thing in the world! That is the highest aim of all my wishes! Then at last would the agonising restlessness be allayed, which destroys my existence! But it must be far, far away! I would behold magnificent Switzerland; I would travel to Italy, and—"

It was a good thing that the power of the Galoshes worked as instantaneously as lightning in a powder-magazine would do, otherwise the poor man with his overstrained wishes would have travelled about the world too much for himself as well as for us. In short, he was travelling. He was in the middle of Switzerland, but packed up with eight other passengers in the inside of an eternally-creaking diligence; his head ached till it almost split, his weary neck could hardly bear the heavy load, and his feet, pinched by his torturing boots, were terribly swollen. He was in an intermediate state between sleeping and waking; at variance with himself, with his company, with the country, and with the government. In his right pocket he had his letter of credit, in the left, his passport, and in a small leathern purse some double louis d'or, carefully sewn up in the bosom of his waistcoat. Every dream proclaimed that one or the other of these valuables was lost; wherefore he started up as in a fever; and the first movement which his hand made, described a magic triangle from the right pocket to the left, and then up towards the bosom, to feel if he had them all safe or not. From the roof inside the carriage, umbrellas, walking-sticks, hats, and sundry other articles were depending, and hindered the view, which was particularly imposing. He now endeavoured as well as he was able to dispel his gloom, which was caused by outward chance circumstances merely, and on the bosom of nature imbibe the milk of purest human enjoyment.

Grand, solemn, and dark was the whole landscape around. The gigantic pine-forests, on the pointed crags, seemed almost like little tufts of heather, coloured by the surrounding clouds. It began to snow, a cold wind blew and roared as though it were seeking a bride.

"Augh!" sighed he, "were we only on the other side the Alps, then we should have summer, and I could get my letters of credit cashed. The anxiety I feel about them prevents me enjoying Switzerland. Were I but on the other side!"

And so saying he was on the other side in Italy, between Florence and Rome. Lake Thracymene, illumined by the evening sun, lay like flaming gold between the dark-blue mountain-ridges; here, where Hannibal defeated Flaminius, the rivers now held each other in their green embraces; lovely, half-naked children tended a herd of black swine, beneath a group of fragrant laurel-trees, hard by the road-side. Could we render this inimitable picture properly, then would everybody exclaim, "Beautiful, unparalleled Italy!" But neither the young Divine said so, nor anyone of his grumbling companions in the coach of the vetturino.

The poisonous flies and gnats swarmed around by thousands; in vain one waved myrtle-branches about like mad; the audacious insect population did not cease to sting; nor was there a single person in the well-crammed carriage whose face was not swollen and sore from their ravenous bites. The poor horses, tortured almost to death, suffered most from this truly Egyptian plague; the flies alighted upon them in large disgusting swarms; and if the coachman got down and scraped them off, hardly a minute elapsed before they were there again. The sun now set: a freezing cold, though of short duration pervaded the whole creation; it was like a horrid gust coming from a burial-vault on a warm summer's day—but all around the mountains retained that wonderful green tone which we see in some old pictures, and which, should we not have seen a similar play of colour in the

South, we declare at once to be unnatural. It was a glorious prospect; but the stomach was empty, the body tired; all that the heart cared and longed for was good night-quarters; yet how would they be? For these one looked much more anxiously than for the charms of nature, which everywhere were so profusely displayed.

The road led through an olive-grove, and here the solitary inn was situated. Ten or twelve crippled beggars had encamped outside. The healthiest of them resembled, to use an expression of Marryat's, "Hunger's eldest son when he had come of age"; the others were either blind, had withered legs and crept about on their hands, or withered arms and fingerless hands. It was the most wretched misery, dragged from among the filthiest rags. "*Excellenza, miserabili!*" sighed they, thrusting forth their deformed limbs to view. Even the hostess, with bare feet, uncombed hair, and dressed in a garment of doubtful colour, received the guests grumblingly. The doors were fastened with a loop of string; the floor of the rooms presented a stone paving half torn up; bats fluttered wildly about the ceiling; and as to the smell therein—no—that was beyond description.

"You had better lay the cloth below in the stable," said one of the travellers; "there, at all events, one knows what one is breathing."

The windows were quickly opened, to let in a little fresh air. Quicker, however, than the breeze, the withered, sallow arms of the beggars were thrust in, accompanied by the eternal whine of "*Miserabili, miserabili, excellenza!*"

On the walls were displayed innumerable inscriptions, written in nearly every language of Europe, some in verse, some in prose, most of them not very laudatory of "*bella Italia*."

The meal was served. It consisted of a soup of salted water, seasoned with pepper and rancid oil. The last ingredient played a very prominent part in the salad; stale eggs and roasted cocks'-

combs furnished the grand dish of the repast; the wine even was not without a disgusting taste—it was like a medicinal draught.

At night the boxes and other effects of the passengers were placed against the rickety doors. One of the travellers kept watch while the others slept. The sentry was our young Divine. How close it was in the chamber! The heat oppressive to suffocation—the gnats hummed and stung unceasingly—the "*miserabili*" without whined and moaned in their sleep.

"Travelling would be agreeable enough," said he groaning, "if one only had no body, or could send it to rest while the spirit went on its pilgrimage unhindered, whither the voice within might call it. Wherever I go, I am pursued by a longing that is insatiable—that I cannot explain to myself, and that tears my very heart. I want something better than what is but what is fled in an instant. But what is it, and where is it to be found? Yet, I know in reality what it is I wish for. Oh! most happy were I, could I but reach one aim—could but reach the happiest of all!"

And as he spoke the word he was again in his home; the long white curtains hung down from the windows, and in the middle of the floor stood the black coffin; in it he lay in the sleep of death. His wish was fulfilled—the body rested, while the spirit went unhindered on its pilgrimage. "Let no one deem himself happy before his end," were the words of Solon; and here was a new and brilliant proof of the wisdom of the old apothegm.

Every corpse is a sphynx of immortality; here too on the black coffin the sphynx gave us no answer to what he who lay within had written two days before:

> "O mighty Death! thy silence teaches nought,
> Thou leadest only to the near grave's brink;
> Is broken now the ladder of my thoughts?
> Do I instead of mounting only sink?

> Our heaviest grief the world oft seeth not,
> Our sorest pain we hide from stranger eyes:
> And for the sufferer there is nothing left
> But the green mound that o'er the coffin lies."

Two figures were moving in the chamber. We knew them both; it was the fairy of Care, and the emissary of Fortune. They both bent over the corpse.

"Do you now see," said Care, "what happiness your Galoshes have brought to mankind?"

"To him, at least, who slumbers here, they have brought an imperishable blessing," answered the other.

"Ah no!" replied Care. "He took his departure himself; he was not called away. His mental powers here below were not strong enough to reach the treasures lying beyond this life, and which his destiny ordained he should obtain. I will now confer a benefit on him."

And she took the Galoshes from his feet; his sleep of death was ended; and he who had been thus called back again to life arose from his dread couch in all the vigor of youth. Care vanished, and with her the Galoshes. She has no doubt taken them for herself, to keep them to all eternity.

The Fir Tree

Out in the woods stood a nice little Fir Tree. The place he had was a very good one: the sun shone on him: as to fresh air, there was enough of that, and round him grew many large-sized comrades, pines as well as firs. But the little Fir wanted so very much to be a grown-up tree.

He did not think of the warm sun and of the fresh air; he did not care for the little cottage children that ran about and prattled when they were in the woods looking for wild-strawberries. The children often came with a whole pitcher full of berries, or a long row of them threaded on a straw, and sat down near the young tree and said, "Oh, how pretty he is! What a nice little fir!" But this was what the Tree could not bear to hear.

At the end of a year he had shot up a good deal, and after another year he was another long bit taller; for with fir trees one can always tell by the shoots how many years old they are.

"Oh! Were I but such a high tree as the others are," sighed he. "Then I should be able to spread out my branches, and with the tops to look into the wide world! Then would the birds build nests among my branches: and when there was a breeze, I could bend with as much stateliness as the others!"

Neither the sunbeams, nor the birds, nor the red clouds which morning and evening sailed above him, gave the little Tree any pleasure.

In winter, when the snow lay glittering on the ground, a hare would often come leaping along, and jump right over the little Tree. Oh, that made him so angry! But two winters were past, and in the third the Tree was so large that the hare was obliged to go round it. "To grow and grow, to get older and be tall," thought the Tree—"that, after all, is the most delightful thing in the world!"

In autumn the wood-cutters always came and felled some of the largest trees. This happened every year; and the young Fir Tree, that had now grown to a very comely size, trembled at the sight; for the magnificent great trees fell to the earth with noise and cracking, the branches were lopped off, and the trees looked long and bare; they were hardly to be recognised; and then they were laid in carts, and the horses dragged them out of the wood.

Where did they go to? What became of them?

In spring, when the swallows and the storks came, the Tree asked them, "Don't you know where they have been taken? Have you not met them anywhere?"

The swallows did not know anything about it; but the Stork looked musing, nodded his head, and said, "Yes; I think I know; I met many ships as I was flying hither from Egypt; on the ships were magnificent masts, and I venture to assert that it was they that smelt so of fir. I may congratulate you, for they lifted themselves on high most majestically!"

"Oh, were I but old enough to fly across the sea! But how does the sea look in reality? What is it like?"

"That would take a long time to explain," said the Stork, and with these words off he went.

"Rejoice in thy growth!" said the Sunbeams. "Rejoice in thy vigorous growth, and in the fresh life that moveth within thee!"

And the Wind kissed the Tree, and the Dew wept tears over him; but the Fir understood it not.

When Christmas came, quite young trees were cut down: trees which often were not even as large or of the same age as this Fir Tree, who could never rest, but always wanted to be off. These young trees, and they were always the finest looking, retained their branches; they were laid on carts, and the horses drew them out of the wood.

"Where are they going to?" asked the Fir. "They are not taller than I; there was one indeed that was considerably shorter; and why do they retain all their branches? Whither are they taken?"

"We know! We know!" chirped the Sparrows. "We have peeped in at the windows in the town below! We know whither they are taken! The greatest splendour and the greatest magnificence one can imagine await them. We peeped through the windows, and saw them planted in the middle of the warm room and ornamented with the most splendid things, with gilded apples, with gingerbread, with toys, and many hundred lights!"

"And then?" asked the Fir Tree, trembling in every bough. "And then? What happens then?"

"We did not see anything more: it was incomparably beautiful."

"I would fain know if I am destined for so glorious a career," cried the Tree, rejoicing. "That is still better than to cross the sea! What a longing do I suffer! Were Christmas but come! I am now tall, and my branches spread like the others that were carried off last year! Oh! were I but already on the cart! Were I in the warm room with all the splendour and magnificence! Yes; then something better, something still grander, will surely follow, or wherefore should they thus ornament me? Something better, something still grander must follow—but what? Oh, how I long, how I suffer! I do not know myself what is the matter with me!"

"Rejoice in our presence!" said the Air and the Sunlight. "Rejoice in thy own fresh youth!"

But the Tree did not rejoice at all; he grew and grew, and was green both winter and summer. People that saw him said, "What a fine tree!" and towards Christmas he was one of the first that was cut down. The axe struck deep into the very pith; the Tree fell to the earth with a sigh; he felt a pang—it was like a swoon; he could not think of happiness, for he was sorrowful at being separated from his home, from the place where he had sprung up. He well knew that he should never see his dear old comrades, the little bushes and flowers around him, anymore; perhaps not even the birds! The departure was not at all agreeable.

The Tree only came to himself when he was unloaded in a

court-yard with the other trees, and heard a man say, "That one is splendid! We don't want the others." Then two servants came in rich livery and carried the Fir Tree into a large and splendid drawing-room. Portraits were hanging on the walls, and near the white porcelain stove stood two large Chinese vases with lions on the covers. There, too, were large easy-chairs, silken sofas, large tables full of picture-books and full of toys, worth hundreds and hundreds of crowns—at least the children said so. And the Fir Tree was stuck upright in a cask that was filled with sand; but no one could see that it was a cask, for green cloth was hung all round it, and it stood on a large gaily-coloured carpet. Oh! how the Tree quivered! What was to happen? The servants, as well as the young ladies, decorated it. On one branch there hung little nets cut out of coloured paper, and each net was filled with sugarplums; and among the other boughs gilded apples and walnuts were suspended, looking as though they had grown there, and little blue and white tapers were placed among the leaves. Dolls that looked for all the world like men—the Tree had never beheld such before—were seen among the foliage, and at the very top a large star of gold tinsel was fixed. It was really splendid—beyond description splendid.

"This evening!" they all said. "How it will shine this evening!"

"Oh!" thought the Tree. "If the evening were but come! If the tapers were but lighted! And then I wonder what will happen! Perhaps the other trees from the forest will come to look at me! Perhaps the sparrows will beat against the windowpanes! I wonder if I shall take root here, and winter and summer stand covered with ornaments!"

He knew very much about the matter—but he was so impatient that for sheer longing he got a pain in his back, and this with trees is the same thing as a headache with us.

The candles were now lighted—what brightness! What splendour! The Tree trembled so in every bough that one of the tapers set fire to the foliage. It blazed up famously.

"Help! Help!" cried the young ladies, and they quickly put out the fire.

Now the Tree did not even dare tremble. What a state he was in! He was so uneasy lest he should lose something of his splendour, that he was quite bewildered amidst the glare and brightness; when suddenly both folding-doors opened and a troop of children rushed in as if they would upset the Tree. The older persons followed quietly; the little ones stood quite still. But it was only for a moment; then they shouted that the whole place re-echoed with their rejoicing; they danced round the Tree, and one present after the other was pulled off.

"What are they about?" thought the Tree. "What is to happen now!" And the lights burned down to the very branches, and as they burned down they were put out one after the other, and then the children had permission to plunder the Tree. So they fell upon it with such violence that all its branches cracked; if it had not been fixed firmly in the ground, it would certainly have tumbled down.

The children danced about with their beautiful playthings; no one looked at the Tree except the old nurse, who peeped between the branches; but it was only to see if there was a fig or an apple left that had been forgotten.

"A story! A story!" cried the children, drawing a little fat man towards the Tree. He seated himself under it and said, "Now we are in the shade, and the Tree can listen too. But I shall tell only one story. Now which will you have; that about Ivedy-Avedy, or about Humpy-Dumpy, who tumbled downstairs, and yet after all came to the throne and married the princess?"

"Ivedy-Avedy," cried some; "Humpy-Dumpy," cried the others. There was such a bawling and screaming—the Fir Tree alone was silent, and he thought to himself, "Am I not to bawl with the rest? Am I to do nothing whatever?" for he was one of the company, and had done what he had to do.

And the man told about Humpy-Dumpy that tumbled down, who notwithstanding came to the throne, and at last married the princess. And the children clapped their hands, and cried. "Oh, go on! Do go on!" They wanted to hear about Ivedy-Avedy too, but the little man only told them about Humpy-Dumpy. The Fir Tree stood quite still and absorbed in thought; the birds in the wood had never related the like of this. "Humpy-Dumpy fell downstairs, and yet he married the princess! Yes, yes! That's the way of the world!" thought the Fir Tree, and believed it all, because the man who told the story was so good-looking. "Well, well! who knows, perhaps I may fall downstairs, too, and get a princess as wife! And he looked forward with joy to the morrow, when he hoped to be decked out again with lights, playthings, fruits, and tinsel.

"I won't tremble tomorrow!" thought the Fir Tree. "I will enjoy to the full all my splendour! Tomorrow I shall hear again the story of Humpy-Dumpy, and perhaps that of Ivedy-Avedy too." And the whole night the Tree stood still and in deep thought.

In the morning the servant and the housemaid came in.

"Now then the splendour will begin again," thought the Fir. But they dragged him out of the room, and up the stairs into the loft: and here, in a dark corner, where no daylight could enter, they left him. "What's the meaning of this?" thought the Tree. "What am I to do here? What shall I hear now, I wonder?" And he leaned against the wall lost in reverie. Time enough had he too for his reflections; for days and nights passed on, and nobody came up; and when at last somebody did come, it was only to put some great trunks in a corner, out of the way. There stood the Tree quite hidden; it seemed as if he had been entirely forgotten.

"'Tis now winter out-of-doors!" thought the Tree. "The earth is hard and covered with snow; men cannot plant me now, and therefore I have been put up here under shelter till the springtime comes! How thoughtful that is! How kind man is, after all! If it only were not so dark here, and so terribly lonely! Not even a hare! And out in the woods it was so pleasant, when the snow was on the ground, and the hare leaped by; yes—even when he jumped over me; but I did not like it then! It is really terribly lonely here!"

"Squeak! Squeak!" said a little Mouse, at the same moment, peeping out of his hole. And then another little one came. They snuffed about the Fir Tree, and rustled among the branches.

"It is dreadfully cold," said the Mouse. "But for that, it would be delightful here, old Fir, wouldn't it?"

"I am by no means old," said the Fir Tree. "There's many a one considerably older than I am."

"Where do you come from," asked the Mice; "and what can you do?" They were so extremely curious. "Tell us about the most beautiful spot on the earth. Have you never been there? Were you never in the larder, where cheeses lie on the shelves, and hams hang from above; where one dances about on tallow candles: that place where one enters lean, and comes out again fat and portly?"

"I know no such place," said the Tree. "But I know the wood, where the sun shines and where the little birds sing." And then he told all about his youth; and the little Mice had never heard the like before; and they listened and said,

"Well, to be sure! How much you have seen! How happy you must have been!"

"I!" said the Fir Tree, thinking over what he had himself related. "Yes, in reality those were happy times." And then he told about Christmas-eve, when he was decked out with cakes and candles.

"Oh," said the little Mice, "how fortunate you have been, old Fir Tree!"

"I am by no means old," said he. "I came from the wood this winter; I am in my prime, and am only rather short for my age."

"What delightful stories you know," said the Mice: and the next night they came with four other little Mice, who were to hear what the Tree recounted: and the more he related, the more he remembered himself; and it appeared as if those times had really been happy times. "But they may still come—they may still come! Humpy-Dumpy fell downstairs, and yet he got a princess!" and he thought at the moment of a nice little Birch Tree growing out in the woods: to the Fir, that would be a real charming princess.

"Who is Humpy-Dumpy?" asked the Mice. So then the Fir Tree told the whole fairy tale, for he could remember every single word of it; and the little Mice jumped for joy up to the very top of the Tree. Next night two more Mice came, and on Sunday two Rats even; but they said the stories were not interesting, which vexed the little Mice; and they, too, now began to think them not so very amusing either.

"Do you know only one story?" asked the Rats.

"Only that one," answered the Tree. "I heard it on my happiest evening; but I did not then know how happy I was."

"It is a very stupid story! Don't you know one about bacon and tallow candles? Can't you tell any larder stories?"

"No," said the Tree.

"Then good-bye," said the Rats; and they went home.

At last the little Mice stayed away also; and the Tree sighed: "After all, it was very pleasant when the sleek little Mice sat round me, and listened to what I told them. Now that too is over. But I will take good care to enjoy myself when I am brought out again."

But when was that to be? Why, one morning there came a quantity of people and set to work in the loft. The trunks were moved, the tree was pulled out and thrown—rather hard, it is true—down on the floor, but a man drew him towards the stairs, where the daylight shone.

"Now a merry life will begin again," thought the Tree. He

felt the fresh air, the first sunbeam—and now he was out in the courtyard. All passed so quickly, there was so much going on around him, the Tree quite forgot to look to himself. The court adjoined a garden, and all was in flower; the roses hung so fresh and odorous over the balustrade, the lindens were in blossom, the Swallows flew by, and said, "Quirre-vit! My husband is come!" but it was not the Fir Tree that they meant.

"Now, then, I shall really enjoy life," said he exultingly, and spread out his branches; but, alas, they were all withered and yellow! It was in a corner that he lay, among weeds and nettles. The golden star of tinsel was still on the top of the Tree, and glittered in the sunshine.

In the court-yard some of the merry children were playing who had danced at Christmas round the Fir Tree, and were so glad at the sight of him. One of the youngest ran and tore off the golden star.

"Only look what is still on the ugly old Christmas tree!" said he, trampling on the branches, so that they all cracked beneath his feet.

And the Tree beheld all the beauty of the flowers, and the freshness in the garden; he beheld himself, and wished he had remained in his dark corner in the loft; he thought of his first youth in the wood, of the merry Christmas-eve, and of the little Mice who had listened with so much pleasure to the story of Humpy-Dumpy.

"'Tis over—'tis past!" said the poor Tree. "Had I but rejoiced when I had reason to do so! But now 'tis past, 'tis past!"

And the gardener's boy chopped the Tree into small pieces; there was a whole heap lying there. The wood flamed up splendidly under the large brewing copper, and it sighed so deeply! Each sigh was like a shot.

The boys played about in the court, and the youngest wore the gold star on his breast which the Tree had had on the happiest evening of his life. However, that was over now—the Tree gone, the story at an end. All, all was over—every tale must end at last.

The Snow Queen

First Story

(Which Treats of a Mirror and of the Splinters)

Now then, let us begin. When we are at the end of the story, we shall know more than we know now: but to begin.

Once upon a time there was a wicked sprite, indeed he was the most mischievous of all sprites. One day he was in a very good humour, for he had made a mirror with the power of causing all that was good and beautiful when it was reflected therein, to look poor and mean; but that which was good-for-nothing and looked ugly was shown magnified and increased in ugliness. In this mirror the most beautiful landscapes looked like boiled spinach, and the best persons were turned into frights, or appeared to stand on their heads; their faces were so distorted that they were not to be recognised; and if anyone had a mole, you might be sure that it would be magnified and spread over both nose and mouth.

"That's glorious fun!" said the sprite. If a good thought passed through a man's mind, then a grin was seen in the mirror, and the sprite laughed heartily at his clever discovery. All the little sprites who went to his school—for he kept a sprite school—told each other that a miracle had happened; and that now only, as they thought, it would be possible to see how the world really looked. They ran about with the mirror; and at last there was not a land or a person who was not represented distorted in the mirror. So then they thought they would fly up to the sky, and have a joke there. The higher they flew with the mirror, the more terribly it grinned: they could hardly hold it fast. Higher and higher still they flew, nearer and nearer to the stars, when suddenly the mirror shook so terribly with grinning, that it flew out of their hands and fell to the earth, where it was dashed in a hundred million and more pieces. And now it worked much more evil than before; for some of these pieces were hardly so large as a grain of sand, and they flew about in the wide world, and when they got into people's eyes, there they stayed; and then people saw everything perverted, or only had an eye for that which was evil. This happened because the very smallest bit had the same power which the whole mirror had possessed. Some persons even got a splinter in their heart, and then it made one shudder, for their heart became like a lump of ice. Some of the broken pieces were so large that they were used for window-panes, through which one could not see one's friends. Other pieces were put in spectacles; and that was a sad affair when people put on their glasses to see well and rightly. Then the wicked sprite laughed till he almost choked, for all this tickled his fancy. The fine splinters still flew about in the air: and now we shall hear what happened next.

Second Story

(A Little Boy and a Little Girl)

In a large town, where there are so many houses, and so many people, that there is no roof left for everybody to have a little garden; and where, on this account, most persons are obliged to content themselves with flowers in pots; there lived two little children, who had a garden somewhat larger than a flower-pot. They were not brother and sister; but they cared for each other as much as if they were. Their parents lived exactly opposite. They inhabited two garrets; and where the roof of the one house joined that of the other, and the gutter ran along the extreme end of it, there was to each house a small window: one needed only to step over the gutter to get from one window to the other.

The children's parents had large wooden boxes there, in which vegetables for the kitchen were planted, and little rose-trees besides: there was a rose in each box, and they grew splendidly. They now thought of placing the boxes across the gutter, so that they nearly reached from one window to the other, and looked just like two walls of flowers. The tendrils of the peas hung down over the boxes; and the rose-trees shot up long branches, twined round the windows, and then bent towards each other: it was almost like a triumphant arch of foliage and flowers. The boxes were very high, and the children knew that they must not creep over them; so they often obtained permission to get out of the windows to each other, and to sit on their little stools among the roses, where they could play delightfully. In winter there was an end of this pleasure. The windows were often frozen over; but then they heated copper farthings on the stove, and laid the hot farthing on the windowpane, and then they had a capital peep-hole, quite nicely rounded; and out of each peeped a gentle friendly eye—it was the little boy and the little girl who were looking out. His name was Kay, hers was Gerda. In summer, with one jump, they could get to each other; but in winter they were obliged first to go down the long stairs, and then up the long stairs again: and out-of-doors there was quite a snow-storm.

"It is the white bees that are swarming," said Kay's old grandmother.

"Do the white bees choose a queen?" asked the little boy; for he knew that the honey-bees always have one.

"Yes," said the grandmother, "she flies where the swarm hangs in the thickest clusters. She is the largest of all; and she can never remain quietly on the earth, but goes up again into the black clouds. Many a winter's night she flies through the streets of the town, and peeps in at the windows; and they then freeze in so wondrous a manner that they look like flowers."

"Yes, I have seen it," said both the children; and so they knew that it was true.

"Can the Snow Queen come in?" said the little girl.

"Only let her come in!" said the little boy. "Then I'd put her on the stove, and she'd melt."

And then his grandmother patted his head and told him other stories.

In the evening, when little Kay was at home, and half undressed, he climbed up on the chair by the window, and peeped out of the little hole. A few snow-flakes were falling, and one, the largest of all, remained lying on the edge of a flower-pot.

The flake of snow grew larger and larger; and at last it was like a young lady, dressed in the finest white gauze, made of a million little flakes like stars. She was so beautiful and delicate, but she was of ice, of dazzling, sparkling ice; yet she lived; her eyes gazed fixedly, like two stars; but there was neither quiet nor repose in them. She nodded towards the window, and beckoned with her hand. The little boy was frightened, and jumped down from the chair; it seemed to him as if, at the same moment, a large bird flew past the window.

The next day it was a sharp frost—and then the spring came; the sun shone, the green leaves appeared, the swallows built their nests, the windows were opened, and the little children again sat in their pretty garden, high up on the leads at the top of the house.

That summer the roses flowered in unwonted beauty. The little girl had learned a hymn, in which there was something about roses; and then she thought of her own flowers; and she sang the verse to the little boy, who then sang it with her:

"The rose in the valley is blooming so sweet,
And angels descend there the children to greet."

And the children held each other by the hand, kissed the roses, looked up at the clear sunshine, and spoke as though they really saw angels there. What lovely summer-days those were! How delightful to be out in the air, near the fresh rose-bushes, that seem as if they would never finish blossoming!

Kay and Gerda looked at the picture-book full of beasts and of birds; and it was then—the clock in the church-tower was just striking five—that Kay said, "Oh! I feel such a sharp pain in my heart; and now something has got into my eye!"

The little girl put her arms around his neck. He winked his eves; now there was nothing to be seen.

"I think it is out now," said he; but it was not. It was just one of those pieces of glass from the magic mirror that had got into his eye; and poor Kay had got another piece right in his heart. It will soon become like ice. It did not hurt any longer, but there it was.

"What are you crying for?" asked he. "You look so ugly! There's nothing the matter with me. Ah," said he at once, "that rose is cankered! And look, this one is quite crooked! After all, these roses are very ugly! They are just like the box they are planted in!" And then he gave the box a good kick with his foot, and pulled both the roses up.

"What are you doing?" cried the little girl; and as he perceived her fright, he pulled up another rose, got in at the window, and hastened off from dear little Gerda.

Afterwards, when she brought her picture-book, he asked, "What horrid beasts have you there?" And if his grandmother told them stories, he always interrupted her; besides, if he could manage it, he would get behind her, put on her spectacles, and imitate her way of speaking; he copied all her ways, and then everybody laughed at him. He was soon able to imitate the gait and manner of everyone in the street. Everything that was peculiar and displeasing in them—that Kay knew how to imitate: and at such times all the people said, "The boy is certainly very clever!" But it was the glass he had got in his eye; the glass that was sticking in his heart, which made him tease even little Gerda, whose whole soul was devoted to him.

His games now were quite different to what they had formerly been, they were so very knowing. One winter's day, when the flakes of snow were flying about, he spread the skirts of his blue coat, and caught the snow as it fell.

"Look through this glass, Gerda," said he. And every flake seemed larger, and appeared like a magnificent flower, or beautiful star; it was splendid to look at!

"Look, how clever!" said Kay. "That's much more interesting than real flowers! They are as exact as possible; there is not a fault in them, if they did not melt!"

It was not long after this, that Kay came one day with large gloves on, and his little sledge at his back, and bawled right into Gerda's ears, "I have permission to go out into the square where the others are playing"; and off he was in a moment.

There, in the market-place, some of the boldest of the boys used to tie their sledges to the carts as they passed by, and so they were pulled along, and got a good ride. It was so capital! Just as they were in the very height of their amusement, a large sledge passed by: it was painted quite white, and there was someone in it wrapped up in a rough white mantle of fur, with a rough white fur cap on his head. The sledge drove round the square twice, and Kay tied on his sledge as quickly as he could, and off he drove with it. On they went quicker and quicker into the next street; and the person who drove turned round to Kay, and nodded to him in a friendly manner, just as if they knew each other. Every time he was going to untie his sledge, the person nodded to him, and then Kay sat quiet; and so on they went till they came outside the gates of the town. Then the snow began to fall so thickly that the little boy could not see an arm's length before him, but still on he went: when suddenly he let go the string he held in his hand in order to get loose from the sledge, but it was of no use; still the little vehicle rushed on with the quickness of the wind. He then cried as loud as he could, but no one beard him; the snow drifted and the sledge flew on, and sometimes it gave a jerk as though they were driving over hedges and ditches. He was quite frightened, and he tried to repeat the Lord's Prayer; but he was only able to remember the multiplication table.

The snow-flakes grew larger and larger, till at last they looked just like great white fowls. Suddenly they flew on one side; the large sledge stopped, and the person who drove rose up. It was a lady; her cloak and cap were of snow. She was tall and of slender figure, and of a dazzling whiteness. It was the Snow Queen.

"We have travelled fast," said she; "but it is freezingly cold. Come under my bearskin." And she put him in the sledge beside her, wrapped the fur round him, and he felt as though he were sinking in a snow-wreath.

"Are you still cold?" asked she; and then she kissed his forehead. Ah! it was colder than ice; it penetrated to his very heart, which was already almost a frozen lump; it seemed to him as if he were about to die—but a moment more and it was quite congenial to him, and he did not remark the cold that was around him.

"My sledge! Do not forget my sledge!" It was the first thing he thought of. It was there tied to one of the white chickens, who flew along with it on his back behind the large sledge. The Snow Queen kissed Kay once more, and then he forgot little Gerda, grandmother, and all whom he had left at his home.

"Now you will have no more kisses," said she, "or else I should kiss you to death!"

Kay looked at her. She was very beautiful; a more clever, or a more lovely countenance he could not fancy to himself; and she no longer appeared of ice as before, when she sat outside the window, and beckoned to him; in his eyes she was perfect, he did not fear her at all, and told her that he could calculate in his head and with fractions, even; that he knew the number of square miles there were in the different countries, and how many inhabitants they contained; and she smiled while he spoke. It then seemed to him as if what he knew was not enough, and he looked upwards in the huge empty space above him, and on she flew with him; flew high over the black clouds, while the storm moaned and whistled as though it were singing some old tune. On they flew over woods and lakes, over seas, and many lands; and beneath them the chilling storm rushed fast, the wolves howled, the snow crackled; above them flew large screaming crows, but higher up appeared the moon, quite large and bright; and it was on it that Kay gazed during the long long winter's night; while by day he slept at the feet of the Snow Queen.

Third Story

(Of the Flower-Garden At the Old Woman's Who Understood Witchcraft)

But what became of little Gerda when Kay did not return? Where could he be?

Nobody knew; nobody could give any intelligence. All the boys knew was, that they had seen him tie his sledge to another large and splendid one, which drove down the street and out of the town. Nobody knew where he was; many sad tears were shed, and little Gerda wept long and bitterly; at last she said he must be dead; that he had been drowned in the river which flowed close to the town. Oh! those were very long and dismal winter evenings!

At last spring came, with its warm sunshine.

"Kay is dead and gone!" said little Gerda.

"That I don't believe," said the Sunshine.

"Kay is dead and gone!" said she to the Swallows.

"That I don't believe," said they: and at last little Gerda did not think so any longer either.

"I'll put on my red shoes," said she, one morning; "Kay has never seen them, and then I'll go down to the river and ask there."

It was quite early; she kissed her old grandmother, who was still asleep, put on her red shoes, and went alone to the river.

"Is it true that you have taken my little playfellow? I will make you a present of my red shoes, if you will give him back to me."

And, as it seemed to her, the blue waves nodded in a strange manner; then she took off her red shoes, the most precious things she possessed, and threw them both into the river. But they fell close to the bank, and the little waves bore them immediately to land; it was as if the stream would not take what was dearest to her; for in reality it had not got little Kay; but Gerda thought that she had not thrown the shoes out far enough, so she clambered into a boat which lay among the rushes, went to the farthest end, and threw out the shoes. But the boat was not fastened, and the motion which she occasioned, made it drift from the shore. She observed this, and hastened to get back; but before she could do so, the boat was more than a yard from the land, and was gliding quickly onward.

Little Gerda was very frightened, and began to cry; but no one heard her except the sparrows, and they could not carry her to land; but they flew along the bank, and sang as if to comfort her, "Here we are! Here we are!" The boat drifted with the stream, little Gerda sat quite still without shoes, for they were swimming behind the boat, but she could not reach them, because the boat went much faster than they did.

The banks on both sides were beautiful; lovely flowers, venerable trees, and slopes with sheep and cows, but not a human being was to be seen.

"Perhaps the river will carry me to little Kay," said she; and then she grew less sad. She rose, and looked for many hours at the beautiful green banks. Presently she sailed by a large cherry-orchard, where was a little cottage with curious red and blue windows; it was thatched, and before it two wooden soldiers stood sentry, and presented arms when anyone went past.

Gerda called to them, for she thought they were alive; but they, of course, did not answer. She came close to them, for the stream drifted the boat quite near the land.

Gerda called still louder, and an old woman then came out of the cottage, leaning upon a crooked stick. She had a large broad-brimmed hat on, painted with the most splendid flowers.

"Poor little child!" said the old woman. "How did you get upon the large rapid river, to be driven about so in the wide world!" And then the old woman went into the water, caught hold of the boat with her crooked stick, drew it to the bank, and lifted little Gerda out.

And Gerda was so glad to be on dry land again; but she was rather afraid of the strange old woman.

"But come and tell me who you are, and how you came here," said she.

And Gerda told her all; and the old woman shook her head and said, "A-hem! a-hem!" and when Gerda had told her everything, and asked her if she had not seen little Kay, the woman answered that he had not passed there, but he no doubt would come; and she told her not to be cast down, but taste her cherries, and look at her flowers, which were finer than any in a picture-book, each of which could tell a whole story. She then took Gerda by the hand, led her into the little cottage, and locked the door.

The windows were very high up; the glass was red, blue, and green, and the sunlight shone through quite wondrously in all sorts of colours. On the table stood the most exquisite cherries, and Gerda ate as many as she chose, for she had permission to do so. While she was eating, the old woman combed her hair with a golden comb, and her hair curled and shone with a lovely golden colour around that sweet little face, which was so round and so like a rose.

"I have often longed for such a dear little girl," said the old woman. "Now you shall see how well we agree together"; and while she combed little Gerda's hair, the child forgot her foster-brother Kay more and more, for the old woman understood magic; but she was no evil being, she only practised witchcraft a little for her own private amusement, and now she wanted very much to keep little Gerda. She therefore went out in the garden, stretched out her crooked stick towards the rose-bushes, which, beautifully as they were blowing, all sank into the earth and no one could tell where they had stood. The old woman feared that if Gerda should see the roses, she would then think of her own, would remember little Kay, and run away from her.

She now led Gerda into the flower-garden. Oh, what odour and what loveliness was there! Every flower that one could think of, and of every season, stood there in fullest bloom; no picture-book could be gayer or more beautiful. Gerda jumped for joy, and played till the sun set behind the tall cherry-tree; she then had a pretty bed, with a red silken coverlet filled with blue violets. She fell asleep, and had as pleasant dreams as ever a queen on her wedding-day.

The next morning she went to play with the flowers in the warm sunshine, and thus passed away a day. Gerda knew every flower; and, numerous as they were, it still seemed to Gerda that one was wanting, though she did not know which. One day while she was looking at the hat of the old woman painted with flowers, the most beautiful of them all seemed to her to be a rose. The old woman had forgotten to take it from her hat when she made the others vanish in the earth. But so it is when one's thoughts are not collected. "What!" said Gerda. "Are there no roses here?" and she ran about amongst the flowerbeds, and looked, and looked, but there was not one to be found. She then sat down and wept; but her hot tears fell just where a rose-bush had sunk; and when her warm tears watered the ground, the tree shot up suddenly as fresh and blooming as when it had been swallowed up. Gerda kissed the roses, thought of her own dear roses at home, and with them of little Kay.

"Oh, how long I have stayed!" said the little girl. "I intended to look for Kay! Don't you know where he is?" she asked of the roses. "Do you think he is dead and gone?"

"Dead he certainly is not," said the Roses. "We have been in the earth where all the dead are, but Kay was not there."

"Many thanks!" said little Gerda; and she went to the other flowers, looked into their cups, and asked, "Don't you know where little Kay is?"

But every flower stood in the sunshine, and dreamed its own fairy tale or its own story: and they all told her very many things, but not one knew anything of Kay.

Well, what did the Tiger-Lily say?

"Hearest thou not the drum? Boom! Boom! Those are the only two tones. Always boom! Boom! Hark to the plaintive song of the old woman, to the call of the priests! The Hindoo woman in her long robe stands upon the funeral pile; the flames rise around her and her dead husband, but the Hindoo woman thinks on the living one in the surrounding circle; on him whose eyes burn hotter than the flames—on him, the fire of whose eyes pierces her heart more than the flames which soon will burn her body to ashes. Can the heart's flame die in the flame of the funeral pile?"

"I don't understand that at all," said little Gerda.

"That is my story," said the Lily.

What did the Convolvulus say?

"Projecting over a narrow mountain-path there hangs an old feudal castle. Thick evergreens grow on the dilapidated walls, and around the altar, where a lovely maiden is standing: she bends over the railing and looks out upon the rose. No fresher rose hangs on the branches than she; no appleblossom carried away by the wind is more buoyant! How her silken robe is rustling!

"'Is he not yet come?'"

"Is it Kay that you mean?" asked little Gerda.

"I am speaking about my story—about my dream," answered the Convolvulus.

What did the Snowdrops say?

"Between the trees a long board is hanging—it is a swing. Two little girls are sitting in it, and swing themselves backwards and forwards; their frocks are as white as snow, and long green silk ribands flutter from their bonnets. Their brother, who is older than they are, stands up in the swing; he twines his arms round the cords to hold himself fast, for in one hand he has a little cup, and in the other a clay-pipe. He is blowing soap-bubbles. The swing moves, and the bubbles float in charming changing colours: the last is still hanging to the end of the pipe, and rocks in the breeze. The swing moves. The little black dog, as light as a soap-bubble, jumps up on his hind legs to try to get into the swing. It moves, the dog falls down, barks, and is angry. They tease him; the bubble bursts! A swing, a bursting bubble—such is my song!"

"What you relate may be very pretty, but you tell it in so melancholy a manner, and do not mention Kay."

What do the Hyacinths say?

"There were once upon a time three sisters, quite transparent, and very beautiful. The robe of the one was red, that of the second blue, and that of the third white. They danced hand in hand beside the calm lake in the clear moonshine. They were not elfin maidens, but mortal children. A sweet fragrance was smelt, and the maidens vanished in the wood; the fragrance grew stronger—three coffins, and in them three lovely maidens, glided out of the forest and across the lake: the shining glow-worms flew around like little floating lights. Do the dancing maidens sleep, or are they dead? The odour of the flowers says they are corpses; the evening bell tolls for the dead!"

"You make me quite sad," said little Gerda. "I cannot help thinking of the dead maidens. Oh! is little Kay really dead? The Roses have been in the earth, and they say no."

"Ding, dong!" sounded the Hyacinth bells. "We do not toll for little Kay; we do not know him. That is our way of singing, the only one we have."

And Gerda went to the Ranunculuses, that looked forth from among the shining green leaves.

"You are a little bright sun!" said Gerda. "Tell me if you know where I can find my playfellow."

And the Ranunculus shone brightly, and looked again at Gerda. What song could the Ranunculus sing? It was one that said nothing about Kay either.

"In a small court the bright sun was shining in the first days of spring. The beams glided down the white walls of a neighbour's house, and close by the fresh yellow flowers were growing, shining like gold in the warm sun-rays. An old grandmother was sitting in the air; her grand-daughter, the poor and lovely servant just come for a short visit. She knows her grandmother. There was gold, pure virgin gold in that blessed kiss. There, that is my little story," said the Ranunculus.

"My poor old grandmother!" sighed Gerda. "Yes, she is longing for me, no doubt: she is sorrowing for me, as she did for little Kay. But I will soon come home, and then I will bring Kay with me. It is of no use asking the flowers; they only know their own old rhymes, and can tell me nothing." And she tucked up her frock, to enable her to run quicker; but the Narcissus gave her a knock on the leg, just as she was going to jump over it. So she stood still, looked at the long yellow flower, and asked, "You perhaps know something?" and she bent down to the Narcissus. And what did it say?

"I can see myself—I can see myself! Oh, how odorous I am! Up in the little garret there stands, half-dressed, a little Dancer. She stands now on one leg, now on both; she despises the whole world; yet she lives only in imagination. She pours water out of the teapot over a piece of stuff which she holds in her hand; it is the bodice; cleanliness is a fine thing. The white dress is hanging on the hook; it was washed in the teapot, and dried on the roof. She puts it on, ties a saffron-coloured kerchief round her neck, and then the gown looks whiter. I can see myself—I can see myself!"

"That's nothing to me," said little Gerda. "That does not concern me." And then off she ran to the further end of the garden.

The gate was locked, but she shook the rusted bolt till it was loosened, and the gate opened; and little Gerda ran off barefooted into the wide world. She looked round her thrice, but no one followed her. At last she could run no longer; she sat down on a large stone, and when she looked about her, she saw that the summer had passed; it was late in the autumn, but that one could not remark in the beautiful garden, where there was always sunshine, and where there were flowers the whole year round.

"Dear me, how long I have stayed!" said Gerda. "Autumn is come. I must not rest any longer." And she got up to go further.

Oh, how tender and wearied her little feet were! All around it looked so cold and raw: the long willow-leaves were quite yellow, and the fog dripped from them like water; one leaf fell after the other: the sloes only stood full of fruit, which set one's teeth on edge. Oh, how dark and comfortless it was in the dreary world!

Fourth Story

(The Prince and Princess)

Gerda was obliged to rest herself again, when, exactly opposite to her, a large Raven came hopping over the white snow. He had long been looking at Gerda and shaking his head; and now he said, "Caw! Caw! Good day! Good day!"

He could not say it better; but he felt a sympathy for the little girl, and asked her where she was going all alone. The word "alone" Gerda understood quite well, and felt how much was expressed by it; so she told the Raven her whole history, and asked if he had not seen Kay.

The Raven nodded very gravely, and said, "It may be—it may be!"

"What, do you really think so?" cried the little girl; and she nearly squeezed the Raven to death, so much did she kiss him.

"Gently, gently," said the Raven. "I think I know; I think that it may be little Kay. But now he has forgotten you for the Princess."

"Does he live with a Princess?" asked Gerda.

"Yes—listen," said the Raven; "but it will be difficult for me to speak your language. If you understand the Raven language I can tell you better."

"No, I have not learnt it," said Gerda; "but my grandmother understands it, and she can speak gibberish too. I wish I had learnt it."

"No matter," said the Raven; "I will tell you as well as I can; however, it will be bad enough." And then he told all he knew.

"In the kingdom where we now are there lives a Princess, who is extraordinarily clever; for she has read all the newspapers in the whole world, and has forgotten them again—so clever is she. She was lately, it is said, sitting on her throne—which is not very amusing after all—when she began humming an old tune, and it was just, 'Oh, why should I not be married?'

"'That song is not without its meaning,' said she, and so then she was determined to marry; but she would have a husband who knew how to give an answer when he was spoken to—not one who looked only as if he were a great personage, for that is so tiresome. She then had all the ladies of the court drummed together; and when they heard her intention, all were very pleased, and said, 'We are very glad to hear it; it is the very thing we were thinking of.' You may believe every word I say," said the Raven; "for I have a tame sweetheart that hops about in the palace quite free, and it was she who told me all this.

"The newspapers appeared forthwith with a border of hearts and the initials of the Princess; and therein you might read that every good-looking young man was at liberty to come to the palace and speak to the Princess; and he who spoke in such wise as showed he felt himself at home there, that one the Princess would choose for her husband.

"Yes, Yes," said the Raven, "you may believe it; it is as true as I am sitting here. People came in crowds; there was a crush and a hurry, but no one was successful either on the first or second day. They could all talk well enough when they were out in the street; but as soon as they came inside the palace gates, and saw the guard richly dressed in silver, and the lackeys in gold on the staircase, and the large illuminated saloons, then they were abashed; and when they stood before the throne on which the Princess was sitting, all they could do was to repeat the last word they had uttered, and to hear it again did not interest her very much. It was just as if the people within were under a charm, and had fallen into a trance till they came out again into the street; for then—oh, then—they could chatter enough. There was a whole row of them standing from the town-gates to the palace. I was there myself to look," said the Raven. "They grew hungry and thirsty; but from the palace they got nothing whatever, not even a glass of water. Some of the cleverest, it is true, had taken bread and butter with them: but none shared it with his neighbour, for each thought, 'Let him look hungry, and then the Princess won't have him.'"

"But Kay—little Kay," said Gerda, "when did he come? Was he among the number?"

"Patience, patience; we are just come to him. It was on the third day when a little personage without horse or equipage, came marching right boldly up to the palace; his eyes shone like yours, he had beautiful long hair, but his clothes were very shabby."

"That was Kay," cried Gerda, with a voice of delight. "Oh, now I've found him!" and she clapped her hands for joy.

"He had a little knapsack at his back," said the Raven.

"No, that was certainly his sledge," said Gerda; "for when he went away he took his sledge with him."

"That may be," said the Raven; "I did not examine him so minutely; but I know from my tame sweetheart, that when he came into the court-yard of the palace, and saw the body-guard in silver, the lackeys on the staircase, he was not the least abashed; he nodded, and said to them, 'It must be very tiresome to stand on the stairs; for my part, I shall go in.' The saloons were gleaming with lustres—privy councillors and excellencies were walking about barefooted, and wore gold keys; it was enough to make any one feel uncomfortable. His boots creaked, too, so loudly, but still he was not at all afraid."

"That's Kay for certain," said Gerda. "I know he had on new boots; I have heard them creaking in grandmama's room."

"Yes, they creaked," said the Raven. "And on he went boldly up to the Princess, who was sitting on a pearl as large as a spinning-wheel. All the ladies of the court, with their attendants and attendants' attendants, and all the cavaliers, with their gentlemen and gentlemen's gentlemen, stood round; and the nearer they stood to the door, the prouder they looked. It was hardly possible to look at the gentleman's gentleman, so very haughtily did he stand in the doorway."

"It must have been terrible," said little Gerda. "And did Kay get the Princess?"

"Were I not a Raven, I should have taken the Princess myself, although I am promised. It is said he spoke as well as I speak when I talk Raven language; this I learned from my tame sweetheart. He was bold and nicely behaved; he had not come to woo the Princess, but only to hear her wisdom. She pleased him, and he pleased her."

"Yes, yes; for certain that was Kay," said Gerda. "He was so clever; he could reckon fractions in his head. Oh, won't you take me to the palace?"

"That is very easily said," answered the Raven. "But how are we to manage it? I'll speak to my tame sweetheart about it: she must advise us; for so much I must tell you, such a little girl as you are will never get permission to enter."

"Oh, yes I shall," said Gerda; "when Kay hears that I am here, he will come out directly to fetch me."

"Wait for me here on these steps," said the Raven. He moved his head backwards and forwards and flew away.

The evening was closing in when the Raven returned. "Caw—caw!" said he. "She sends you her compliments; and here is a roll for you. She took it out of the kitchen, where there is bread enough. You are hungry, no doubt. It is not possible for you to enter the palace, for you are barefooted: the guards in silver, and the lackeys in gold, would not allow it; but do not cry, you shall come in still. My sweetheart knows a little back stair that leads to the bedchamber, and she knows where she can get the key of it."

And they went into the garden in the large avenue, where one leaf was falling after the other; and when the lights in the palace had all gradually disappeared, the Raven led little Gerda to the back door, which stood half open.

Oh, how Gerda's heart beat with anxiety and longing! It was just as if she had been about to do something wrong; and yet she only wanted to know if little Kay was there. Yes, he must be there. She called to mind his intelligent eyes, and his long hair, so vividly, she could quite see him as he used to laugh when they were sitting under the roses at home. "He will, no doubt, be glad to see you—to hear what a long way you have come for his sake; to know how unhappy all at home were when he did not come back."

Oh, what a fright and a joy it was!

They were now on the stairs. A single lamp was burning there; and on the floor stood the tame Raven, turning her head on every side and looking at Gerda, who bowed as her grandmother had taught her to do.

"My intended has told me so much good of you, my dear young lady," said the tame Raven. "Your tale is very affecting. If you will take the lamp, I will go before. We will go straight on, for we shall meet no one."

"I think there is somebody just behind us," said Gerda; and something rushed past: it was like shadowy figures on the wall; horses with flowing manes and thin legs, huntsmen, ladies and gentlemen on horseback.

"They are only dreams," said the Raven. "They come to fetch the thoughts of the high personages to the chase; 'tis well, for now you can observe them in bed all the better. But let me find, when you enjoy honour and distinction, that you possess a grateful heart."

"Tut! That's not worth talking about," said the Raven of the woods.

They now entered the first saloon, which was of rose-coloured satin, with artificial flowers on the wall. Here the dreams were rushing past, but they hastened by so quickly that Gerda could not see the high personages. One hall was more magnificent than the other; one might indeed well be abashed; and at last they came into the bedchamber. The ceiling of the room resembled a large palm-tree with leaves of glass, of costly glass; and in the middle, from a thick golden stem, hung two beds, each of which resembled a lily. One was white, and in this lay the Princess; the other was red, and it was here that Gerda was to look for little Kay. She bent back one of the red leaves, and saw a brown neck. Oh! that was Kay! She called him quite loud by name, held the lamp towards him—the dreams rushed back again into the chamber—he awoke, turned his head, and—

it was not little Kay!

The Prince was only like him about the neck; but he was young and handsome. And out of the white lily leaves the Princess peeped, too, and asked what was the matter. Then little Gerda cried, and told her her whole history, and all that the Ravens had done for her.

"Poor little thing!" said the Prince and the Princess. They praised the Ravens very much, and told them they were not at all angry with them, but they were not to do so again. However, they should have a reward. "Will you fly about here at liberty," asked the Princess; "or would you like to have a fixed appointment as court ravens, with all the broken bits from the kitchen?"

And both the Ravens nodded, and begged for a fixed appointment; for they thought of their old age, and said, "It is a good thing to have a provision for our old days."

And the Prince got up and let Gerda sleep in his bed, and more than this he could not do. She folded her little hands and thought, "How good men and animals are!" and she then fell asleep and slept soundly. All the dreams flew in again, and they now looked like the angels; they drew a little sledge, in which little Kay sat and nodded his head; but the whole was only a dream, and therefore it all vanished as soon as she awoke.

The next day she was dressed from head to foot in silk and velvet. They offered to let her stay at the palace, and lead a happy life; but she begged to have a little carriage with a horse in front, and for a small pair of shoes; then, she said, she would again go forth in the wide world and look for Kay.

Shoes and a muff were given her; she was, too, dressed very nicely; and when she was about to set off, a new carriage stopped before the door. It was of pure gold, and the arms of the Prince and Princess shone like a star upon it; the coachman, the footmen, and the outriders, for outriders were there, too, all wore golden crowns. The Prince and the Princess assisted her into the carriage themselves, and wished her all success. The

Raven of the woods, who was now married, accompanied her for the first three miles. He sat beside Gerda, for he could not bear riding backwards; the other Raven stood in the doorway, and flapped her wings; she could not accompany Gerda, because she suffered from headache since she had had a fixed appointment and ate so much. The carriage was lined inside with sugar-plums, and in the seats were fruits and gingerbread.

"Farewell! Farewell!" cried Prince and Princess; and Gerda wept, and the Raven wept. Thus passed the first miles; and then the Raven bade her farewell, and this was the most painful separation of all. He flew into a tree, and beat his black wings as long as he could see the carriage, that shone from afar like a sunbeam.

Fifth Story

(The Little Robber Maiden)

They drove through the dark wood; but the carriage shone like a torch, and it dazzled the eyes of the robbers, so that they could not bear to look at it.

"'Tis gold! 'Tis gold!" they cried; and they rushed forward, seized the horses, knocked down the little postilion, the coachman, and the servants, and pulled little Gerda out of the carriage.

"How plump, how beautiful she is! She must have been fed on nut-kernels," said the old female robber, who had a long, scrubby beard, and bushy eyebrows that hung down over her eyes. "She is as good as a fatted lamb! How nice she will be!" And then she drew out a knife, the blade of which shone so that it was quite dreadful to behold.

"Oh!" cried the woman at the same moment. She had been bitten in the ear by her own little daughter, who hung at her back; and who was so wild and unmanageable, that it was quite amusing to see her. "You naughty child!" said the mother: and now she had not time to kill Gerda.

"She shall play with me," said the little robber child. "She shall give me her muff, and her pretty frock; she shall sleep in my bed!" And then she gave her mother another bite, so that she jumped, and ran round with the pain; and the Robbers laughed, and said, "Look, how she is dancing with the little one!"

"I will go into the carriage," said the little robber maiden; and she would have her will, for she was very spoiled and very headstrong. She and Gerda got in; and then away they drove over the stumps of felled trees, deeper and deeper into the woods. The little robber maiden was as tall as Gerda, but stronger, broader-shouldered, and of dark complexion; her eyes were quite black; they looked almost melancholy. She embraced little Gerda, and said, "They shall not kill you as long as I am not displeased with you. You are, doubtless, a Princess?"

"No," said little Gerda; who then related all that had happened to her, and how much she cared about little Kay.

The little robber maiden looked at her with a serious air, nodded her head slightly, and said, "They shall not kill you, even if I am angry with you: then I will do it myself"; and she dried Gerda's eyes, and put both her hands in the handsome muff, which was so soft and warm.

At length the carriage stopped. They were in the midst of the court-yard of a robber's castle. It was full of cracks from top to bottom; and out of the openings magpies and rooks were flying; and the great bull-dogs, each of which looked as if he could swallow a man, jumped up, but they did not bark, for that was forbidden.

In the midst of the large, old, smoking hall burnt a great fire on the stone floor. The smoke disappeared under the stones, and had to seek its own egress. In an immense caldron soup was boiling; and rabbits and hares were being roasted on a spit.

"You shall sleep with me tonight, with all my animals," said the little robber maiden. They had something to eat and drink; and then went into a corner, where straw and carpets were lying. Beside them, on laths and perches, sat nearly a hundred pigeons, all asleep, seemingly; but yet they moved a little when the robber maiden came. "They are all mine," said she, at the same time seizing one that was next to her by the legs and shaking it so that its wings fluttered. "Kiss it," cried the little girl, and flung the pigeon in Gerda's face. "Up there is the rabble of the wood," continued she, pointing to several laths which were fastened before a hole high up in the wall; "that's the rabble; they would all fly away immediately, if they were not well fastened in. And here is my dear old Bac"; and she laid hold of the horns of a reindeer, that had a bright copper ring round its neck, and was tethered to the spot. "We are obliged to lock this fellow in too, or he would make his escape. Every evening I tickle his neck with my sharp knife; he is so frightened at it!" and the little girl drew forth a long knife, from a crack in the wall, and let it glide over the Reindeer's neck. The poor animal kicked; the girl laughed, and pulled Gerda into bed with her.

"Do you intend to keep your knife while you sleep?" asked Gerda; looking at it rather fearfully.

"I always sleep with the knife," said the little robber maiden. "There is no knowing what may happen. But tell me now, once more, all about little Kay; and why you have started off in the wide world alone." And Gerda related all, from the very beginning: the Wood-pigeons cooed above in their cage, and the others slept. The little robber maiden wound her arm round Gerda's neck, held the knife in the other hand, and snored so loud that everybody could hear her; but Gerda could not close her eyes, for she did not know whether she was to live or die. The robbers sat round the fire, sang and drank; and the old female robber jumped about so, that it was quite dreadful for Gerda to see her.

Then the Wood-pigeons said, "Coo! Coo! We have seen little Kay! A white hen carries his sledge; he himself sat in the carriage of the Snow Queen, who passed here, down just over the wood, as we lay in our nest. She blew upon us young ones; and all died except we two. Coo! Coo!"

"What is that you say up there?" cried little Gerda. "Where did the Snow Queen go to? Do you know anything about it?"

"She is no doubt gone to Lapland; for there is always snow and ice there. Only ask the Reindeer, who is tethered there."

"Ice and snow is there! There it is, glorious and beautiful!" said the Reindeer. "One can spring about in the large shining valleys! The Snow Queen has her summer-tent there; but her fixed abode is high up towards the North Pole, on the Island called Spitzbergen."

"Oh, Kay! Poor little Kay!" sighed Gerda.

"Do you choose to be quiet?" said the robber maiden. "If you don't, I shall make you."

In the morning Gerda told her all that the Wood-pigeons had said; and the little maiden looked very serious, but she nodded her head, and said, "That's no matter—that's no matter. Do you know where Lapland lies!" she asked of the Reindeer.

"Who should know better than I?" said the animal; and his eyes rolled in his head. "I was born and bred there—there I leapt about on the fields of snow.

"Listen," said the robber maiden to Gerda. "You see that the men are gone; but my mother is still here, and will remain. However, towards morning she takes a draught out of the large flask, and then she sleeps a little: then I will do something for you." She now jumped out of bed, flew to her mother; with her arms round her neck, and pulling her by the beard, said, "Good morrow, my own sweet nanny-goat of a mother." And her mother took hold of her nose, and pinched it till it was red and blue; but this was all done out of pure love.

When the mother had taken a sup at her flask, and was having a nap, the little robber maiden went to the Reindeer, and said, "I should very much like to give you still many a tickling with the sharp knife, for then you are so amusing; however, I will untether you, and help you out, so that you may go back to Lapland. But you must make good use of your legs; and take this little girl for me to the palace of the Snow Queen, where her playfellow is. You have heard, I suppose, all she said; for she spoke loud enough, and you were listening."

The Reindeer gave a bound for joy. The robber maiden lifted up little Gerda, and took the precaution to bind her fast on the Reindeer's back; she even gave her a small cushion to sit on. "Here are your worsted leggins, for it will be cold; but the muff I shall keep for myself, for it is so very pretty. But I do not wish you to be cold. Here is a pair of lined gloves of my mother's; they just reach up to your elbow. On with them! Now you look about the hands just like my ugly old mother!"

And Gerda wept for joy.

"I can't bear to see you fretting," said the little robber maiden. "This is just the time when you ought to look pleased. Here are two loaves and a ham for you, so that you won't starve." The bread and the meat were fastened to the Reindeer's back; the little maiden opened the door, called in all the dogs, and then with her knife cut the rope that fastened the animal, and said to him, "Now, off with you; but take good care of the little girl!"

And Gerda stretched out her hands with the large wadded gloves towards the robber maiden, and said, "Farewell!" and the Reindeer flew on over bush and bramble through the great wood, over moor and heath, as fast as he could go.

"Ddsa! Ddsa!" was heard in the sky. It was just as if somebody was sneezing.

"These are my old northern-lights," said the Reindeer, "look how they gleam!"

And on he now sped still quicker—day and night on he went: the loaves were consumed, and the ham too; and now they were in Lapland.

Sixth Story

(The Lapland Woman and the Finland Woman)

Suddenly they stopped before a little house, which looked very miserable. The roof reached to the ground; and the door was so low, that the family were obliged to creep upon their stomachs when they went in or out. Nobody was at home except an old Lapland woman, who was dressing fish by the light of an oil lamp. And the Reindeer told her the whole of Gerda's history, but first of all his own; for that seemed to him of much greater importance. Gerda was so chilled that she could not speak.

"Poor thing," said the Lapland woman, "you have far to run still. You have more than a hundred miles to go before you get to Finland; there the Snow Queen has her country-house, and burns blue lights every evening. I will give you a few words from me, which I will write on a dried haberdine, for paper I have none; this you can take with you to the Finland woman, and she will be able to give you more information than I can."

When Gerda had warmed herself, and had eaten and drunk, the Lapland woman wrote a few words on a dried haberdine, begged Gerda to take care of them, put her on the Reindeer, bound her fast, and away sprang the animal. "Ddsa! Ddsa!" was again heard in the air; the most charming blue lights burned the whole night in the sky, and at last they came to Finland. They knocked at the chimney of the Finland woman; for as to a door, she had none.

There was such a heat inside that the Finland woman herself went about almost naked. She was diminutive and dirty. She immediately loosened little Gerda's clothes, pulled off her thick gloves and boots; for otherwise the heat would have been too great—and after laying a piece of ice on the Reindeer's head, read what was written on the fish-skin. She read it three times: she then knew it by heart; so she put the fish into the cupboard—for it might very well be eaten, and she never threw anything away.

Then the Reindeer related his own story first, and afterwards that of little Gerda; and the Finland woman winked her eyes, but said nothing.

"You are so clever," said the Reindeer; "you can, I know, twist all the winds of the world together in a knot. If the seaman loosens one knot, then he has a good wind; if a second, then it blows pretty stiffly; if he undoes the third and fourth, then it rages so that the forests are upturned. Will you give the little maiden a potion, that she may possess the strength of twelve men, and vanquish the Snow Queen?"

"The strength of twelve men!" said the Finland woman. "Much good that would be!" Then she went to a cupboard, and drew out a large skin rolled up. When she had unrolled it, strange characters were to be seen written thereon; and the Finland woman read at such a rate that the perspiration trickled down her forehead.

But the Reindeer begged so hard for little Gerda, and Gerda looked so imploringly with tearful eyes at the Finland woman, that she winked, and drew the Reindeer aside into a corner, where they whispered together, while the animal got some fresh ice put on his head.

"'Tis true little Kay is at the Snow Queen's, and finds everything there quite to his taste; and he thinks it the very best place in the world; but the reason of that is, he has a splinter of glass in his eye, and in his heart. These must be got out first; otherwise he will never go back to mankind, and the Snow Queen will retain her power over him."

"But can you give little Gerda nothing to take which will endue her with power over the whole?"

"I can give her no more power than what she has already.

Don't you see how great it is? Don't you see how men and animals are forced to serve her; how well she gets through the world barefooted? She must not hear of her power from us; that power lies in her heart, because she is a sweet and innocent child! If she cannot get to the Snow Queen by herself, and rid little Kay of the glass, we cannot help her. Two miles hence the garden of the Snow Queen begins; thither you may carry the little girl. Set her down by the large bush with red berries, standing in the snow; don't stay talking, but hasten back as fast as possible." And now the Finland woman placed little Gerda on the Reindeer's back, and off he ran with all imaginable speed.

"Oh! I have not got my boots! I have not brought my gloves!" cried little Gerda. She remarked she was without them from the cutting frost; but the Reindeer dared not stand still; on he ran till he came to the great bush with the red berries, and there he set Gerda down, kissed her mouth, while large bright tears flowed from the animal's eyes, and then back he went as fast as possible. There stood poor Gerda now, without shoes or gloves, in the very middle of dreadful icy Finland.

She ran on as fast as she could. There then came a whole regiment of snow-flakes, but they did not fall from above, and they were quite bright and shining from the Aurora Borealis. The flakes ran along the ground, and the nearer they came the larger they grew. Gerda well remembered how large and strange the snow-flakes appeared when she once saw them through a magnifying-glass; but now they were large and terrific in another manner—they were all alive. They were the outposts of the Snow Queen. They had the most wondrous shapes; some looked like large ugly porcupines; others like snakes knotted together, with their heads sticking out; and others, again, like small fat bears, with the hair standing on end: all were of dazzling whiteness—all were living snow-flakes.

Little Gerda repeated the Lord's Prayer. The cold was so intense that she could see her own breath, which came like smoke out of her mouth. It grew thicker and thicker, and took the form of little angels, that grew more and more when they touched the earth. All had helms on their heads, and lances and shields in their hands; they increased in numbers; and when Gerda had finished the Lord's Prayer, she was surrounded by a whole legion. They thrust at the horrid snow-flakes with their spears, so that they flew into a thousand pieces; and little Gerda walked on bravely and in security. The angels patted her hands and feet; and then she felt the cold less, and went on quickly towards the palace of the Snow Queen.

But now we shall see how Kay fared. He never thought of Gerda, and least of all that she was standing before the palace.

Seventh Story

(What Took Place in the Palace of the Snow Queen, and What Happened Afterward)

The walls of the palace were of driving snow, and the windows and doors of cutting winds. There were more than a hundred halls there, according as the snow was driven by the winds. The largest was many miles in extent; all were lighted up by the powerful Aurora Borealis, and all were so large, so empty, so icy cold, and so resplendent! Mirth never reigned there; there was never even a little bear-ball, with the storm for music, while the polar bears went on their hind legs and showed off their steps. Never a little tea-party of white young lady foxes; vast, cold, and empty were the halls of the Snow Queen. The northern-lights shone with such precision that one could tell exactly when they were at their highest or lowest degree of brightness. In the middle of the empty, endless hall of snow, was a frozen lake; it was cracked in a thousand pieces, but each piece was so like the other, that it seemed the work of a cunning artificer. In the middle of this lake sat the Snow Queen when she was at home; and then she said she was sitting in the Mirror of Understanding, and that this was the only one and the best thing in the world.

Little Kay was quite blue, yes nearly black with cold; but he did not observe it, for she had kissed away all feeling of cold from his body, and his heart was a lump of ice. He was dragging along some pointed flat pieces of ice, which he laid together in all possible ways, for he wanted to make something with them; just as we have little flat pieces of wood to make geometrical figures with, called the Chinese Puzzle. Kay made all sorts of figures, the most complicated, for it was an ice-puzzle for the understanding. In his eyes the figures were extraordinarily beautiful, and of the utmost importance; for the bit of glass which was in his eye caused this. He found whole figures which represented a written word; but he never could manage to represent just the word he wanted—that word was "eternity"; and the Snow Queen had said, "If you can discover that figure, you shall be your own master, and I will make you a present of the whole world and a pair of new skates." But he could not find it out.

"I am going now to warm lands," said the Snow Queen. "I must have a look down into the black caldrons." It was the volcanoes Vesuvius and Etna that she meant. "I will just give them a coating of white, for that is as it ought to be; besides, it is good for the oranges and the grapes." And then away she flew, and Kay sat quite alone in the empty halls of ice that were miles long, and looked at the blocks of ice, and thought and thought till his skull was almost cracked. There he sat quite benumbed and motionless; one would have imagined he was frozen to death.

Suddenly little Gerda stepped through the great portal into the palace. The gate was formed of cutting winds; but Gerda repeated her evening prayer, and the winds were laid as though they slept; and the little maiden entered the vast, empty, cold halls. There she beheld Kay: she recognised him, flew to embrace him, and cried out, her arms firmly holding him the while, "Kay, sweet little Kay! Have I then found you at last?"

But he sat quite still, benumbed and cold. Then little Gerda shed burning tears; and they fell on his bosom, they penetrated to his heart, they thawed the lumps of ice, and consumed the splinters of the looking-glass; he looked at her, and she sang the hymn:

> "The rose in the valley is blooming so sweet,
> And angels descend there the children to greet."

Hereupon Kay burst into tears; he wept so much that the splinter rolled out of his eye, and he recognised her, and shouted, "Gerda, sweet little Gerda! Where have you been so long? And where have I been?" He looked round him. "How cold it is here!" said he. "How empty and cold!" And he held fast by Gerda, who laughed and wept for joy. It was so beautiful, that even the blocks of ice danced about for joy; and when they were tired and laid themselves down, they formed exactly the letters which the Snow Queen had told him to find out; so now he was his own master, and he would have the whole world and a pair of new skates into the bargain.

Gerda kissed his cheeks, and they grew quite blooming; she kissed his eyes, and they shone like her own; she kissed his hands and feet, and he was again well and merry. The Snow Queen might come back as soon as she liked; there stood his discharge written in resplendent masses of ice.

They took each other by the hand, and wandered forth out of the large hall; they talked of their old grandmother, and of the roses upon the roof; and wherever they went, the winds ceased raging, and the sun burst forth. And when they reached the bush with the red berries, they found the Reindeer waiting for them. He had brought another, a young one, with him, whose udder was filled with milk, which he gave to the little ones, and kissed their lips. They then carried Kay and Gerda—first to the Finland woman, where they warmed themselves in the warm room, and learned what they were to do on their journey home; and they went to the Lapland woman, who made some new clothes for them and repaired their sledges.

The Reindeer and the young hind leaped along beside them, and accompanied them to the boundary of the country. Here the first vegetation peeped forth; here Kay and Gerda took leave of the Lapland woman. "Farewell! Farewell!" they all said. And the first green buds appeared, the first little birds began to chirrup; and out of the wood came, riding on a magnificent horse, which Gerda knew (it was one of the leaders in the golden carriage), a young damsel with a bright-red cap on her head, and armed with pistols. It was the little robber maiden, who, tired of being at home, had determined to make a journey to the north; and afterwards in another direction, if that did not please her. She recognised Gerda immediately, and Gerda knew her too. It was a joyful meeting.

"You are a fine fellow for tramping about," said she to little Kay; "I should like to know, faith, if you deserve that one should run from one end of the world to the other for your sake?"

But Gerda patted her cheeks, and inquired for the Prince and Princess.

"They are gone abroad," said the other.

"But the Raven?" asked little Gerda.

"Oh! The Raven is dead," she answered. "His tame sweetheart is a widow, and wears a bit of black worsted round her leg; she laments most piteously, but it's all mere talk and stuff! Now tell me what you've been doing and how you managed to catch him."

And Gerda and Kay both told their story.

And "Schnipp-schnapp-schnurre-basselurre," said the robber maiden; and she took the hands of each, and promised that if she should some day pass through the town where they lived, she would come and visit them; and then away she rode. Kay and Gerda took each other's hand: it was lovely spring weather, with abundance of flowers and of verdure. The church-bells rang, and the children recognised the high towers, and the large town; it was that in which they dwelt. They entered and hastened up to their grandmother's room, where everything was standing as formerly. The clock said "tick! tock!" and the finger moved round; but as they entered, they remarked that they were now grown up. The roses on the leads hung blooming in at the open window; there stood the little children's chairs, and Kay and Gerda sat down on them, holding each other by the hand; they both had forgotten the cold empty splendour of the Snow Queen, as though it had been a dream. The grandmother sat in the bright sunshine, and read aloud from the Bible: "Unless ye become as little children, ye cannot enter the kingdom of heaven."

And Kay and Gerda looked in each other's eyes, and all at once they understood the old hymn:

> "The rose in the valley is blooming so sweet,
> And angels descend there the children to greet."

There sat the two grown-up persons; grown-up, and yet children; children at least in heart; and it was summer-time; summer, glorious summer!

The Leap Frog

A Flea, a Grasshopper, and a Leap-frog once wanted to see which could jump highest; and they invited the whole world, and everybody else besides who chose to come to see the festival. Three famous jumpers were they, as everyone would say, when they all met together in the room.

"I will give my daughter to him who jumps highest," exclaimed the King; "for it is not so amusing where there is no prize to jump for."

The Flea was the first to step forward. He had exquisite manners, and bowed to the company on all sides; for he had noble blood, and was, moreover, accustomed to the society of man alone; and that makes a great difference.

Then came the Grasshopper. He was considerably heavier, but he was well-mannered, and wore a green uniform, which he had by right of birth; he said, moreover, that he belonged to a very ancient Egyptian family, and that in the house where he then was, he was thought much of. The fact was, he had been just brought out of the fields, and put in a pasteboard house, three stories high, all made of court-cards, with the coloured side inwards; and doors and windows cut out of the body of the Queen of Hearts. "I sing so well," said he, "that sixteen native grasshoppers who have chirped from infancy, and yet got no house built of cards to live in, grew thinner than they were before for sheer vexation when they heard me."

It was thus that the Flea and the Grasshopper gave an account of themselves, and thought they were quite good enough to marry a Princess.

The Leap-frog said nothing; but people gave it as their opinion, that he therefore thought the more; and when the housedog snuffed at him with his nose, he confessed the Leap-frog was of good family. The old councillor, who had had three orders given him to make him hold his tongue, asserted that the Leap-frog was a prophet; for that one could see on his back, if there would be a severe or mild winter, and that was what one could not see even on the back of the man who writes the almanac.

"I say nothing, it is true," exclaimed the King; "but I have my own opinion, notwithstanding."

Now the trial was to take place. The Flea jumped so high that nobody could see where he went to; so they all asserted he had not jumped at all; and that was dishonourable.

The Grasshopper jumped only half as high; but he leaped into the King's face, who said that was ill-mannered.

The Leap-frog stood still for a long time lost in thought; it was believed at last he would not jump at all.

"I only hope he is not unwell," said the house-dog; when, pop! he made a jump all on one side into the lap of the Princess, who was sitting on a little golden stool close by.

Hereupon the King said, "There is nothing above my daughter; therefore to bound up to her is the highest jump that can be made; but for this, one must possess understanding, and the Leap-frog has shown that he has understanding. He is brave and intellectual."

And so he won the Princess.

"It's all the same to me," said the Flea. "She may have the old Leap-frog, for all I care. I jumped the highest; but in this world merit seldom meets its reward. A fine exterior is what people look at now-a-days."

The Flea then went into foreign service, where, it is said, he was killed.

The Grasshopper sat without on a green bank, and reflected on worldly things; and he said too, "Yes, a fine exterior is everything—a fine exterior is what people care about." And then he began chirping his peculiar melancholy song, from which we have taken this history; and which may, very possibly, be all untrue, although it does stand here printed in black and white.

The Elderbush

Once upon a time there was a little boy who had taken cold. He had gone out and got his feet wet; though nobody could imagine how it had happened, for it was quite dry weather. So his mother undressed him, put him to bed, and had the tea-pot brought in, to make him a good cup of Elderflower tea. Just at that moment the merry old man came in who lived up a-top of the house all alone; for he had neither wife nor children—but he liked children very much, and knew so many fairy tales, that it was quite delightful.

"Now drink your tea," said the boy's mother; "then, perhaps, you may hear a fairy tale."

"If I had but something new to tell," said the old man. "But how did the child get his feet wet?"

"That is the very thing that nobody can make out," said his mother.

"Am I to hear a fairy tale?" asked the little boy.

"Yes, if you can tell me exactly—for I must know that first—how deep the gutter is in the little street opposite, that you pass through in going to school."

"Just up to the middle of my boot," said the child; "but then I must go into the deep hole."

"Ah, ah! That's where the wet feet came from," said the old man. "I ought now to tell you a story; but I don't know any more."

"You can make one in a moment," said the little boy. "My mother says that all you look at can be turned into a fairy tale: and that you can find a story in everything."

"Yes, but such tales and stories are good for nothing. The right sort come of themselves; they tap at my forehead and say, 'Here we are.'"

"Won't there be a tap soon?" asked the little boy. And his mother laughed, put some Elder-flowers in the tea-pot, and poured boiling water upon them.

"Do tell me something! Pray do!"

"Yes, if a fairy tale would come of its own accord; but they are proud and haughty, and come only when they choose. Stop!" said he, all on a sudden. "I have it! Pay attention! There is one in the tea-pot!"

And the little boy looked at the tea-pot. The cover rose more and more; and the Elder-flowers came forth so fresh and white, and shot up long branches. Out of the spout even did they spread themselves on all sides, and grew larger and larger; it was a splendid Elderbush, a whole tree; and it reached into the very bed, and pushed the curtains aside. How it bloomed! And what an odour! In the middle of the bush sat a friendly-looking old woman in a most strange dress. It was quite green, like the leaves of the elder, and was trimmed with large white Elder-flowers; so that at first one could not tell whether it was a stuff, or a natural green and real flowers.

"What's that woman's name?" asked the little boy.

"The Greeks and Romans," said the old man, "called her a Dryad; but that we do not understand. The people who live in the New Booths* have a much better name for her; they call her 'old Granny'—and she it is to whom you are to pay attention. Now listen, and look at the beautiful Elderbush.

"Just such another large blooming Elder Tree stands near the New Booths. It grew there in the corner of a little miserable court-yard; and under it sat, of an afternoon, in the most splendid sunshine, two old people; an old, old seaman, and his old, old wife. They had great-grand-children, and were soon to celebrate the fiftieth anniversary of their marriage; but they could not exactly recollect the date: and old Granny sat in the tree, and

* A row of buildings for seamen in Copenhagen.

looked as pleased as now. 'I know the date,' said she; but those below did not hear her, for they were talking about old times.

"'Yes, can't you remember when we were very little,' said the old seaman, 'and ran and played about? It was the very same court-yard where we now are, and we stuck slips in the ground, and made a garden.'

"'I remember it well,' said the old woman; 'I remember it quite well. We watered the slips, and one of them was an Elderbush. It took root, put forth green shoots, and grew up to be the large tree under which we old folks are now sitting.'

"'To be sure,' said he. 'And there in the corner stood a water-pail, where I used to sail my boats.'

"'True; but first we went to school to learn somewhat,' said she; 'and then we were confirmed. We both cried; but in the afternoon we went up the Round Tower, and looked down on Copenhagen, and far, far away over the water; then we went to Friedericksberg, where the King and the Queen were sailing about in their splendid barges.'

"'But I had a different sort of sailing to that, later; and that, too, for many a year; a long way off, on great voyages.'

"'Yes, many a time have I wept for your sake,' said she. 'I thought you were dead and gone, and lying down in the deep waters. Many a night have I got up to see if the wind had not changed: and changed it had, sure enough; but you never came. I remember so well one day, when the rain was pouring down in torrents, the scavengers were before the house where I was in service, and I had come up with the dust, and remained standing at the door—it was dreadful weather—when just as I was there, the postman came and gave me a letter. It was from you! What a tour that letter had made! I opened it instantly and read: I laughed and wept. I was so happy. In it I read that you were in warm lands where the coffee-tree grows. What a blessed land that must be! You related so much, and I saw it all the while the rain was pouring down, and I standing there with the dust-box.

At the same moment came someone who embraced me.'

"'Yes; but you gave him a good box on his ear that made it tingle!'

"'But I did not know it was you. You arrived as soon as your letter, and you were so handsome—that you still are—and had a long yellow silk handkerchief round your neck, and a brand new hat on; oh, you were so dashing! Good heavens! What weather it was, and what a state the street was in!'

"'And then we married,' said he. 'Don't you remember? And then we had our first little boy, and then Mary, and Nicholas, and Peter, and Christian.'

"'Yes, and how they all grew up to be honest people, and were beloved by everybody.'

"'And their children also have children,' said the old sailor; 'yes, those are our grand-children, full of strength and vigor. It was, methinks about this season that we had our wedding.'

"'Yes, this very day is the fiftieth anniversary of the marriage,' said old Granny, sticking her head between the two old people; who thought it was their neighbour who nodded to them. They looked at each other and held one another by the hand. Soon after came their children, and their grand-children; for they knew well enough that it was the day of the fiftieth anniversary, and had come with their congratulations that very morning; but the old people had forgotten it, although they were able to remember all that had happened many years ago. And the Elderbush sent forth a strong odour in the sun, that was just about to set, and shone right in the old people's faces. They both looked so rosy-cheeked; and the youngest of the grandchildren danced around them, and called out quite delighted, that there was to be something very splendid that evening—they were all to have hot potatoes. And old Nanny nodded in the bush, and shouted 'hurrah!' with the rest."

"But that is no fairy tale," said the little boy, who was listening to the story.

"The thing is, you must understand it," said the narrator; "let us ask old Nanny."

"That was no fairy tale, 'tis true," said old Nanny; "but now it's coming. The most wonderful fairy tales grow out of that which is reality; were that not the case, you know, my magnificent Elderbush could not have grown out of the tea-pot." And then she took the little boy out of bed, laid him on her bosom, and the branches of the Elder Tree, full of flowers, closed around her. They sat in an aerial dwelling, and it flew with them through the air. Oh, it was wondrous beautiful! Old Nanny had grown all of a sudden a young and pretty maiden; but her robe was still the same green stuff with white flowers, which she had worn before. On her bosom she had a real Elderflower, and in her yellow waving hair a wreath of the flowers; her eyes were so large and blue that it was a pleasure to look at them; she kissed the boy, and now they were of the same age and felt alike.

Hand in hand they went out of the bower, and they were standing in the beautiful garden of their home. Near the green lawn papa's walking-stick was tied, and for the little ones it seemed to be endowed with life; for as soon as they got astride it, the round polished knob was turned into a magnificent neighing head, a long black mane fluttered in the breeze, and four slender yet strong legs shot out. The animal was strong and handsome, and away they went at full gallop round the lawn.

"Huzza! Now we are riding miles off," said the boy. "We are riding away to the castle where we were last year!"

And on they rode round the grass-plot; and the little maiden, who, we know, was no one else but old Nanny, kept on crying out, "Now we are in the country! Don't you see the farmhouse yonder? And there is an Elder Tree standing beside it; and the cock is scraping away the earth for the hens, look, how he struts! And now we are close to the church. It lies high upon the hill, between the large oak-trees, one of which is half decayed. And now we are by the smithy, where the fire is blazing, and where the half-naked men are banging with their hammers till the sparks fly about. Away! away! To the beautiful country-seat!"

And all that the little maiden, who sat behind on the stick, spoke of, flew by in reality. The boy saw it all, and yet they were only going round the grass-plot. Then they played in a side avenue, and marked out a little garden on the earth; and they took Elder-blossoms from their hair, planted them, and they grew just like those the old people planted when they were children, as related before. They went hand in hand, as the old people had done when they were children; but not to the Round Tower, or to Friedericksberg; no, the little damsel wound her arms round the boy, and then they flew far away through all Denmark. And spring came, and summer; and then it was autumn, and then winter; and a thousand pictures were reflected in the eye and in the heart of the boy; and the little girl always sang to him, "This you will never forget." And during their whole flight the Elder Tree smelt so sweet and odorous; he remarked the roses and the fresh beeches, but the Elder Tree had a more wondrous fragrance, for its flowers hung on the breast of the little maiden; and there, too, did he often lay his head during the flight.

"It is lovely here in spring!" said the young maiden. And they stood in a beech-wood that had just put on its first green, where the woodroof* at their feet sent forth its fragrance, and the pale-red anemony looked so pretty among the verdure. "Oh, would it were always spring in the sweetly-smelling Danish beech-forests!"

"It is lovely here in summer!" said she. And she flew past old castles of by-gone days of chivalry, where the red walls and the embattled gables were mirrored in the canal, where the swans were swimming, and peered up into the old cool avenues. In the fields the corn was waving like the sea; in the

* Asperula odorata.

ditches red and yellow flowers were growing; while wild-drone flowers, and blooming convolvuluses were creeping in the hedges; and towards evening the moon rose round and large, and the haycocks in the meadows smelt so sweetly. "This one never forgets!"

"It is lovely here in autumn!" said the little maiden. And suddenly the atmosphere grew as blue again as before; the forest grew red, and green, and yellow-coloured. The dogs came leaping along, and whole flocks of wild-fowl flew over the cairn, where blackberry-bushes were hanging round the old stones. The sea was dark blue, covered with ships full of white sails; and in the barn old women, maidens, and children were sitting picking hops into a large cask; the young sang songs, but the old told fairy tales of mountain-sprites and soothsayers. Nothing could be more charming.

"It is delightful here in winter!" said the little maiden. And all the trees were covered with hoar-frost; they looked like white corals; the snow crackled under foot, as if one had new boots on; and one falling star after the other was seen in the sky. The Christmas-tree was lighted in the room; presents were there, and good-humour reigned. In the country the violin sounded in the room of the peasant; the newly-baked cakes were attacked; even the poorest child said, "It is really delightful here in winter!"

Yes, it was delightful; and the little maiden showed the boy everything; and the Elder Tree still was fragrant, and the red flag, with the white cross, was still waving: the flag under which the old seaman in the New Booths had sailed. And the boy grew up to be a lad, and was to go forth in the wide world—far, far away to warm lands, where the coffee-tree grows; but at his departure the little maiden took an Elder-blossom from her bosom, and gave it him to keep; and it was placed between the leaves of his Prayer-Book; and when in foreign lands he opened the book, it was always at the place where the keepsake-flower lay; and the more he looked at it, the fresher it became; he felt as it were, the fragrance of the Danish groves; and from among the leaves of the flowers he could distinctly see the little maiden, peeping forth with her bright blue eyes—and then she whispered, "It is delightful here in Spring, Summer, Autumn, and Winter"; and a hundred visions glided before his mind.

Thus passed many years, and he was now an old man, and sat with his old wife under the blooming tree. They held each other by the hand, as the old grand-father and grand-mother yonder in the New Booths did, and they talked exactly like them of old times, and of the fiftieth anniversary of their wedding. The little maiden, with the blue eyes, and with Elder-blossoms in her hair, sat in the tree, nodded to both of them, and said, "Today is the fiftieth anniversary!" And then she took two flowers out of her hair, and kissed them. First, they shone like silver, then like gold; and when they laid them on the heads of the old people, each flower became a golden crown. So there they both sat, like a king and a queen, under the fragrant tree, that looked exactly like an elder: the old man told his wife the story of "Old Nanny," as it had been told him when a boy. And it seemed to both of them it contained much that resembled their own history; and those parts that were like it pleased them best.

"Thus it is," said the little maiden in the tree, "some call me 'Old Nanny,' others a 'Dryad,' but, in reality, my name is 'Remembrance'; 'tis I who sit in the tree that grows and grows! I can remember; I can tell things! Let me see if you have my flower still?"

And the old man opened his Prayer-Book. There lay the Elder-blossom, as fresh as if it had been placed there but a short time before; and Remembrance nodded, and the old people, decked with crowns of gold, sat in the flush of the evening sun. They closed their eyes, and—and—! Yes, that's the end of the story!

The little boy lay in his bed; he did not know if he had dreamed or not, or if he had been listening while someone told him the story. The tea-pot was standing on the table, but no Elder Tree was growing out of it! And the old man, who had been talking, was just on the point of going out at the door, and he did go.

"How splendid that was!" said the little boy. "Mother, I have been to warm countries."

"So I should think," said his mother. "When one has drunk two good cupfuls of Elder-flower tea, 'tis likely enough one goes into warm climates"; and she tucked him up nicely, lest he should take cold. "You have had a good sleep while I have been sitting here, and arguing with him whether it was a story or a fairy tale."

"And where is old Nanny?" asked the little boy.

"In the tea-pot," said his mother; "and there she may remain."

The Bell

People said "The Evening Bell is sounding, the sun is setting." For a strange wondrous tone was heard in the narrow streets of a large town. It was like the sound of a church-bell: but it was only heard for a moment, for the rolling of the carriages and the voices of the multitude made too great a noise.

Those persons who were walking outside the town, where the houses were farther apart, with gardens or little fields between them, could see the evening sky still better, and heard the sound of the bell much more distinctly. It was as if the tones came from a church in the still forest; people looked thitherward, and felt their minds attuned most solemnly.

A long time passed, and people said to each other—"I wonder if there is a church out in the wood? The bell has a tone that is wondrous sweet; let us stroll thither, and examine the matter nearer." And the rich people drove out, and the poor walked, but the way seemed strangely long to them; and when they came to a clump of willows which grew on the skirts of the forest, they sat down, and looked up at the long branches, and fancied they were now in the depth of the green wood. The confectioner of the town came out, and set up his booth there; and soon after came another confectioner, who hung a bell over his stand, as a sign or ornament, but it had no clapper, and it was tarred over to preserve it from the rain. When all the people returned home, they said it had been very romantic, and that it was quite a different sort of thing to a pic-nic or tea-party. There were three persons who asserted they had penetrated to the end of the forest, and that they had always heard the wonderful sounds of the bell, but it had seemed to them as if it had come from the town. One wrote a whole poem about it, and said the bell sounded like the voice of a mother to a good dear child, and that no melody was sweeter than the tones of the bell. The king of the country was also observant of it, and vowed that he who could discover whence the sounds proceeded, should have the title of "Universal Bell-ringer," even if it were not really a bell.

Many persons now went to the wood, for the sake of getting the place, but one only returned with a sort of explanation; for nobody went far enough, not even he. However, he said that the sound proceeded from a very large owl, in a hollow tree; a sort of learned owl, that continually knocked its head against the branches. But whether the sound came from his head or from the hollow tree, that no one could say with certainty. So now he got the place of "Universal Bell-ringer," and wrote yearly a short treatise "On the Owl"; but no-one was any the wiser.

It was the day of confirmation. The clergyman had spoken so touchingly, the children who were confirmed had been greatly moved; it was an eventful day for them; from children they become all at once grown-up-persons; it was as if their infant souls were now to fly all at once into persons with more understanding. The sun was shining gloriously; the children that had been confirmed went out of the town; and from the wood was borne towards them the sounds of the unknown bell with wonderful distinctness. They all immediately felt a wish to go thither; all except three. One of them had to go home to try on a ball-dress; for it was just the dress and the ball which had caused her to be confirmed this time, for otherwise she would not have come; the other was a poor boy, who had borrowed his coat and boots to be confirmed in from the innkeeper's son, and he was to give them back by a certain hour; the third said that he never went to a strange place if his parents were not with him—that he had always been a good boy hitherto, and would still be so now that he was confirmed, and that one ought not to laugh at him for it: the others, however, did make fun of him, after all.

There were three, therefore, that did not go; the others hastened on. The sun shone, the birds sang, and the children sang too, and each held the other by the hand; for as yet they had none of them any high office, and were all of equal rank in the eye of God.

But two of the youngest soon grew tired, and both returned to town; two little girls sat down, and twined garlands, so they did not go either; and when the others reached the willow-tree, where the confectioner was, they said, "Now we are there! In reality the bell does not exist; it is only a fancy that people have taken into their heads!"

At the same moment the bell sounded deep in the wood, so clear and solemnly that five or six determined to penetrate somewhat further. It was so thick, and the foliage so dense, that it was quite fatiguing to proceed. Woodroof and anemonies grew almost too high; blooming convolvuluses and blackberry-bushes hung in long garlands from tree to tree, where the nightingale sang and the sunbeams were playing: it was very beautiful, but it was no place for girls to go; their clothes would get so torn. Large blocks of stone lay there, overgrown with moss of every colour; the fresh spring bubbled forth, and made a strange gurgling sound.

"That surely cannot be the bell," said one of the children, lying down and listening. "This must be looked to." So he remained, and let the others go on without him.

They afterwards came to a little house, made of branches and the bark of trees; a large wild apple-tree bent over it, as if it would shower down all its blessings on the roof, where roses were blooming. The long stems twined round the gable, on which there hung a small bell.

Was it that which people had heard? Yes, everybody was unanimous on the subject, except one, who said that the bell was too small and too fine to be heard at so great a distance, and besides it was very different tones to those that could move a human heart in such a manner. It was a king's son who spoke;

whereon the others said, "Such people always want to be wiser than everybody else."

They now let him go on alone; and as he went, his breast was filled more and more with the forest solitude; but he still heard the little bell with which the others were so satisfied, and now and then, when the wind blew, he could also hear the people singing who were sitting at tea where the confectioner had his tent; but the deep sound of the bell rose louder; it was almost as if an organ were accompanying it, and the tones came from the left hand, the side where the heart is placed. A rustling was heard in the bushes, and a little boy stood before the King's Son, a boy in wooden shoes, and with so short a jacket that one could see what long wrists he had. Both knew each other: the boy was that one among the children who could not come because he had to go home and return his jacket and boots to the innkeeper's son. This he had done, and was now going on in wooden shoes and in his humble dress, for the bell sounded with so deep a tone, and with such strange power, that proceed he must.

"Why, then, we can go together," said the King's Son. But the poor child that had been confirmed was quite ashamed; he looked at his wooden shoes, pulled at the short sleeves of his jacket, and said that he was afraid he could not walk so fast; besides, he thought that the bell must be looked for to the right; for that was the place where all sorts of beautiful things were to be found.

"But there we shall not meet," said the King's Son, nodding at the same time to the poor boy, who went into the darkest, thickest part of the wood, where thorns tore his humble dress, and scratched his face and hands and feet till they bled. The King's Son got some scratches too; but the sun shone on his path, and it is him that we will follow, for he was an excellent and resolute youth.

"I must and will find the bell," said he, "even if I am obliged to go to the end of the world."

The ugly apes sat upon the trees, and grinned. "Shall we thrash him?" said they. "Shall we thrash him? He is the son of a king!"

But on he went, without being disheartened, deeper and deeper into the wood, where the most wonderful flowers were growing. There stood white lilies with blood-red stamina, sky-blue tulips, which shone as they waved in the winds, and apple-trees, the apples of which looked exactly like large soapbubbles: so only think how the trees must have sparkled in the sunshine! Around the nicest green meads, where the deer were playing in the grass, grew magnificent oaks and beeches; and if the bark of one of the trees was cracked, there grass and long creeping plants grew in the crevices. And there were large calm lakes there too, in which white swans were swimming, and beat the air with their wings. The King's Son often stood still and listened. He thought the bell sounded from the depths of these still lakes; but then he remarked again that the tone proceeded not from there, but farther off, from out the depths of the forest.

The sun now set: the atmosphere glowed like fire. It was still in the woods, so very still; and he fell on his knees, sung his evening hymn, and said: "I cannot find what I seek; the sun is going down, and night is coming—the dark, dark night. Yet perhaps I may be able once more to see the round red sun before he entirely disappears. I will climb up yonder rock."

And he seized hold of the creeping-plants, and the roots of trees—climbed up the moist stones where the water-snakes were writhing and the toads were croaking—and he gained the summit before the sun had quite gone down. How magnificent was the sight from this height! The sea—the great, the glorious sea, that dashed its long waves against the coast—was stretched out before him. And yonder, where sea and sky meet, stood the sun, like a large shining altar, all melted together in the most glowing colours. And the wood and the sea sang a song of rejoicing, and his heart sang with the rest: all nature was a vast holy church, in which the trees and the buoyant clouds were the pillars, flowers and grass the velvet carpeting, and heaven itself the large cupola. The red colours above faded away as the sun vanished, but a million stars were lighted, a million lamps shone; and the King's Son spread out his arms towards heaven, and wood, and sea; when at the same moment, coming by a path to the right, appeared, in his wooden shoes and jacket, the poor boy who had been confirmed with him. He had followed his own path, and had reached the spot just as soon as the son of the king had done. They ran towards each other, and stood together hand in hand in the vast church of nature and of poetry, while over them sounded the invisible holy bell: blessed spirits floated around them, and lifted up their voices in a rejoicing hallelujah!

THE OLD HOUSE

In the street, up there, was an old, a very old house—it was almost three hundred years old, for that might be known by reading the great beam on which the date of the year was carved: together with tulips and hop-binds there were whole verses spelled as in former times, and over every window was a distorted face cut out in the beam. The one story stood forward a great way over the other; and directly under the eaves was a leaden spout with a dragon's head; the rain-water should have run out of the mouth, but it ran out of the belly, for there was a hole in the spout.

All the other houses in the street were so new and so neat, with large window panes and smooth walls, one could easily see that they would have nothing to do with the old house: they certainly thought, "How long is that old decayed thing to stand here as a spectacle in the street? And then the projecting windows stand so far out, that no one can see from our windows what happens in that direction! The steps are as broad as those of a palace, and as high as to a church tower. The iron railings look just like the door to an old family vault, and then they have brass tops—that's so stupid!"

On the other side of the street were also new and neat houses, and they thought just as the others did; but at the window opposite the old house there sat a little boy with fresh rosy cheeks and bright beaming eyes: he certainly liked the old house best, and that both in sunshine and moonshine. And when he looked across at the wall where the mortar had fallen out, he could sit and find out there the strangest figures imaginable; exactly as the street had appeared before, with steps, projecting windows, and pointed gables; he could see soldiers with halberds, and spouts where the water ran, like dragons and serpents. That was a house to look at; and there lived an old man, who wore plush breeches; and he had a coat with large brass buttons, and a wig that one could see was a real wig. Every morning there came an old fellow to him who put his rooms in order, and went on errands; otherwise, the old man in the plush breeches was quite alone in the old house. Now and then he came to the window and looked out, and the little boy nodded to him, and the old man nodded again, and so they became acquaintances, and then they were friends, although they had never spoken to each other—but that made no difference. The little boy heard his parents say, "The old man opposite is very well off, but he is so very, very lonely!"

The Sunday following, the little boy took something, and wrapped it up in a piece of paper, went downstairs, and stood in the doorway; and when the man who went on errands came past, he said to him—

"I say, master! will you give this to the old man over the way from me? I have two pewter soldiers—this is one of them, and he shall have it, for I know he is so very, very lonely."

And the old errand man looked quite pleased, nodded, and took the pewter soldier over to the old house. Afterwards there came a message; it was to ask if the little boy himself had not a wish to come over and pay a visit; and so he got permission of his parents, and then went over to the old house.

And the brass balls on the iron railings shone much brighter than ever; one would have thought they were polished on account of the visit; and it was as if the carved-out trumpeters—for there were trumpeters, who stood in tulips, carved out on the door—blew with all their might, their cheeks appeared so much rounder than before. Yes, they blew—"Trateratra! The little boy comes! Trateratra!"—and then the door opened.

The whole passage was hung with portraits of knights in armour, and ladies in silken gowns; and the armour rattled, and the silken gowns rustled! And then there was a flight of stairs which went a good way upwards, and a little way downwards, and then one came on a balcony which was in a very dilapidated state, sure enough, with large holes and long crevices, but grass grew there and leaves out of them altogether, for the whole balcony outside, the yard, and the walls, were overgrown with so much green stuff, that it looked like a garden; though it was only a balcony. Here stood old flower-pots with faces and asses' ears, and the flowers grew just as they liked. One of the pots was quite overrun on all sides with pinks, that is to say, with the green part; shoot stood by shoot, and it said quite distinctly, "The air has cherished me, the sun has kissed me, and promised me a little flower on Sunday, a little flower on Sunday!"

And then they entered a chamber where the walls were covered with hog's leather, and printed with gold flowers.

'The gilding decays,
But hog's leather stays!'

said the walls.

And there stood easy-chairs, with such high backs, and so carved out, and with arms on both sides. "Sit down! sit down!" said they. "Ugh! how I creak; now I shall certainly get the gout, like the old clothespress, ugh!"

And then the little boy came into the room where the projecting windows were, and where the old man sat.

"I thank you for the pewter soldier, my little friend!" said the old man. "And I thank you because you come over to me."

"Thankee! thankee!" or "cranky! cranky!" sounded from all the furniture; there was so much of it, that each article stood in the other's way, to get a look at the little boy.

In the middle of the wall hung a picture representing a beautiful lady, so young, so glad, but dressed quite as in former times, with clothes that stood quite stiff, and with powder in her hair; she neither said "thankee, thankee!" nor "cranky, cranky!"

but looked with her mild eyes at the little boy, who directly asked the old man, "Where did you get her?"

"Yonder, at the broker's," said the old man, "where there are so many pictures hanging. No one knows or cares about them, for they are all of them buried; but I knew her in by-gone days, and now she has been dead and gone these fifty years!"

Under the picture, in a glazed frame, there hung a bouquet of withered flowers; they were almost fifty years old; they looked so very old!

The pendulum of the great clock went to and fro, and the hands turned, and everything in the room became still older; but they did not observe it.

"They say at home," said the little boy, "that you are so very, very lonely!"

"Oh!" said he. "The old thoughts, with what they may bring with them, come and visit me, and now you also come! I am very well off!"

Then he took a book with pictures in it down from the shelf; there were whole long processions and pageants, with the strangest characters, which one never sees now-a-days; soldiers like the knave of clubs, and citizens with waving flags: the tailors had theirs, with a pair of shears held by two lions—and the shoemakers theirs, without boots, but with an eagle that had two heads, for the shoemakers must have everything so that they can say, it is a pair! Yes, that was a picture book!

The old man now went into the other room to fetch preserves, apples, and nuts—yes, it was delightful over there in the old house.

"I cannot bear it any longer!" said the pewter soldier, who sat on the drawers. "It is so lonely and melancholy here! But when one has been in a family circle one cannot accustom oneself to this life! I cannot bear it any longer! The whole day is so long, and the evenings are still longer! Here it is not at all as it is over the way at your home, where your father and mother spoke so pleasantly, and where you and all your sweet children made such a delightful noise. Nay, how lonely the old man is—do you think that he gets kisses? Do you think he gets mild eyes, or a Christmas tree? He will get nothing but a grave! I can bear it no longer!"

"You must not let it grieve you so much," said the little boy. "I find it so very delightful here, and then all the old thoughts, with what they may bring with them, they come and visit here."

"Yes, it's all very well, but I see nothing of them, and I don't know them!" said the pewter soldier. "I cannot bear it!"

"But you must!" said the little boy.

Then in came the old man with the most pleased and happy face, the most delicious preserves, apples, and nuts, and so the little boy thought no more about the pewter soldier.

The little boy returned home happy and pleased, and weeks and days passed away, and nods were made to the old house, and from the old house, and then the little boy went over there again.

The carved trumpeters blew, "Trateratra! There is the little boy! Trateratra!" and the swords and armour on the knights' portraits rattled, and the silk gowns rustled; the hog's leather spoke, and the old chairs had the gout in their legs and rheumatism in their backs: Ugh! it was exactly like the first time, for over there one day and hour was just like another.

"I cannot bear it!" said the pewter soldier. "I have shed pewter tears! It is too melancholy! Rather let me go to the wars and lose arms and legs! It would at least be a change. I cannot bear it longer! Now, I know what it is to have a visit from one's old thoughts, with what they may bring with them! I have had a visit from mine, and you may be sure it is no pleasant thing in the end; I was at last about to jump down from the drawers.

"I saw you all over there at home so distinctly, as if you really were here; it was again that Sunday morning; all you children stood before the table and sung your Psalms, as you do every morning. You stood devoutly with folded hands; and father and mother were just as pious; and then the door was opened, and little sister Mary, who is not two years old yet, and who always dances when she hears music or singing, of whatever kind it may be, was put into the room—though she ought not to have been there—and then she began to dance, but could not keep time, because the tones were so long; and then she stood, first on the one leg, and bent her head forwards, and then on the other leg, and bent her head forwards—but all would not do. You stood very seriously all together, although it was difficult enough; but I laughed to myself, and then I fell off the table, and got a bump, which I have still—for it was not right of me to laugh. But the whole now passes before me again in thought, and everything that I have lived to see; and these are the old thoughts, with what they may bring with them.

"Tell me if you still sing on Sundays? Tell me something about little Mary! And how my comrade, the other pewter soldier, lives! Yes, he is happy enough, that's sure! I cannot bear it any longer!"

"You are given away as a present!" said the little boy. "You must remain. Can you not understand that?"

The old man now came with a drawer, in which there was much to be seen, both "tin boxes" and "balsam boxes," old cards, so large and so gilded, such as one never sees them now. And several drawers were opened, and the piano was opened; it had landscapes on the inside of the lid, and it was so hoarse when the old man played on it! and then he hummed a song.

"Yes, she could sing that!" said he, and nodded to the portrait, which he had bought at the broker's, and the old man's eyes shone so bright!

"I will go to the wars! I will go to the wars!" shouted the pewter soldier as loud as he could, and threw himself off the drawers right down on the floor. What became of him? The old man sought, and the little boy sought; he was away, and he stayed away.

"I shall find him!" said the old man; but he never found him. The floor was too open—the pewter soldier had fallen through a crevice, and there he lay as in an open tomb.

That day passed, and the little boy went home, and that week passed, and several weeks too. The windows were quite frozen, the little boy was obliged to sit and breathe on them to get a peep-hole over to the old house, and there the snow had been blown into all the carved work and inscriptions; it lay quite up over the steps, just as if there was no one at home—nor was there any one at home—the old man was dead!

In the evening there was a hearse seen before the door, and he was borne into it in his coffin: he was now to go out into the country, to lie in his grave. He was driven out there, but no one followed; all his friends were dead, and the little boy kissed his hand to the coffin as it was driven away.

Some days afterwards there was an auction at the old house, and the little boy saw from his window how they carried the old knights and the old ladies away, the flower-pots with the long ears, the old chairs, and the old clothes-presses. Something came here, and something came there; the portrait of her who had been found at the broker's came to the broker's again; and there it hung, for no one knew her more—no one cared about the old picture.

In the spring they pulled the house down, for, as people said, it was a ruin. One could see from the street right into the room with the hog's-leather hanging, which was slashed and torn; and the green grass and leaves about the balcony hung quite wild about the falling beams. And then it was put to rights.

"That was a relief," said the neighbouring houses.

A fine house was built there, with large windows, and smooth white walls; but before it, where the old house had in fact stood, was a little garden laid out, and a wild grapevine ran up the wall of the neighbouring house. Before the garden there was a large iron railing with an iron door, it looked quite splendid, and people stood still and peeped in, and the sparrows hung by scores in the vine, and chattered away at each other as well as they could, but it was not about the old house, for they could not remember it, so many years had passed—so many that the little boy had grown up to a whole man, yes, a clever man, and a pleasure to his parents; and he had just been married, and, together with his little wife, had come to live in the house here, where the garden was; and he stood by her there whilst she planted a field-flower that she found so pretty; she planted it with her little hand, and pressed the earth around it with her fingers. Oh! what was that? She had stuck herself. There sat something pointed, straight out of the soft mould.

It was—yes, guess! It was the pewter soldier, he that was lost up at the old man's, and had tumbled and turned about amongst the timber and the rubbish, and had at last laid for many years in the ground.

The young wife wiped the dirt off the soldier, first with a green leaf, and then with her fine handkerchief—it had such a delightful smell, that it was to the pewter soldier just as if he had awaked from a trance.

"Let me see him," said the young man. He laughed, and then shook his head. "Nay, it cannot be he; but he reminds me of a story about a pewter soldier which I had when I was a little boy!" And then he told his wife about the old house, and the old man, and about the pewter soldier that he sent over to him because he was so very, very lonely; and he told it as correctly as it had really been, so that the tears came into the eyes of his young wife, on account of the old house and the old man.

"It may possibly be, however, that it is the same pewter soldier!" said she. "I will take care of it, and remember all that you have told me; but you must show me the old man's grave!"

"But I do not know it," said he, "and no one knows it! All his friends were dead, no one took care of it, and I was then a little boy!"

"How very, very lonely he must have been!" said she.

"Very, very lonely!" said the pewter soldier. "But it is delightful not to be forgotten!"

"Delightful!" shouted something close by; but no one, except the pewter soldier, saw that it was a piece of the hog's-leather hangings; it had lost all its gilding, it looked like a piece of wet clay, but it had an opinion, and it gave it:

"The gilding decays,
But hog's leather stays!"

This the pewter soldier did not believe.

The Happy Family

Really, the largest green leaf in this country is a dockleaf; if one holds it before one, it is like a whole apron, and if one holds it over one's head in rainy weather, it is almost as good as an umbrella, for it is so immensely large. The burdock never grows alone, but where there grows one there always grow several: it is a great delight, and all this delightfulness is snails' food. The great white snails which persons of quality in former times made fricassees of, ate, and said, "Hem, hem! how delicious!" for they thought it tasted so delicate—lived on dockleaves, and therefore burdock seeds were sown.

Now, there was an old manor-house, where they no longer ate snails, they were quite extinct; but the burdocks were not extinct, they grew and grew all over the walks and all the beds; they could not get the mastery over them—it was a whole forest of burdocks. Here and there stood an apple and a plum-tree, or else one never would have thought that it was a garden; all was burdocks, and there lived the two last venerable old snails.

They themselves knew not how old they were, but they could remember very well that there had been many more; that they were of a family from foreign lands, and that for them and theirs the whole forest was planted. They had never been outside it, but they knew that there was still something more in the world, which was called the manor-house, and that there they were boiled, and then they became black, and were then placed on a silver dish; but what happened further they knew not; or, in fact, what it was to be boiled, and to lie on a silver dish, they could not possibly imagine; but it was said to be delightful, and particularly genteel. Neither the chafers, the toads, nor the earth-worms, whom they asked about it could give them any information—none of them had been boiled or laid on a silver dish.

The old white snails were the first persons of distinction in the world, that they knew; the forest was planted for their sake, and the manor-house was there that they might be boiled and laid on a silver dish.

Now they lived a very lonely and happy life; and as they had no children themselves, they had adopted a little common snail, which they brought up as their own; but the little one would not grow, for he was of a common family; and the old ones, especially Dame Mother Snail, thought they could observe how he increased in size, and she begged father, if he could not see it, that he would at least feel the little snail's shell; and then he felt it, and found the good dame was right.

One day there was a heavy storm of rain.

"Hear how it beats like a drum on the dock-leaves!" said Father Snail.

"There are also raindrops!" said Mother Snail. "And now the rain pours right down the stalk! You will see that it will be wet here! I am very happy to think that we have our good house, and the little one has his also! There is more done for us than for all other creatures, sure enough; but can you not see that we are folks of quality in the world? We are provided with a house from our birth, and the burdock forest is planted for our sakes! I should like to know how far it extends, and what there is outside!"

"There is nothing at all," said Father Snail. "No place can be better than ours, and I have nothing to wish for!"

"Yes," said the dame. "I would willingly go to the manor-house, be boiled, and laid on a silver dish; all our forefathers have been treated so; there is something extraordinary in it, you may be sure!"

"The manor-house has most likely fallen to ruin!" said Father Snail. "Or the burdocks have grown up over it, so that they cannot come out. There need not, however, be any haste about that; but you are always in such a tremendous hurry, and the little one is beginning to be the same. Has he not been creeping up that stalk these three days? It gives me a headache when I look up to him!"

"You must not scold him," said Mother Snail. "He creeps so carefully; he will afford us much pleasure—and we have nothing but him to live for! But have you not thought of it? Where shall we get a wife for him? Do you not think that there are some of our species at a great distance in the interior of the burdock forest?"

"Black snails, I dare say, there are enough of," said the old one. "Black snails without a house—but they are so common, and so conceited. But we might give the ants a commission to look out for us; they run to and fro as if they had something to do, and they certainly know of a wife for our little snail!"

"I know one, sure enough—the most charming one!" said one of the ants. "But I am afraid we shall hardly succeed, for she is a queen!"

"That is nothing!" said the old folks. "Has she a house?"

"She has a palace!" said the ant. "The finest ant's palace, with seven hundred passages!"

"I thank you!" said Mother Snail. "Our son shall not go into an ant-hill; if you know nothing better than that, we shall give the commission to the white gnats. They fly far and wide, in rain and sunshine; they know the whole forest here, both within and without."

"We have a wife for him," said the gnats. "At a hundred human paces from here there sits a little snail in her house, on a gooseberry bush; she is quite lonely, and old enough to be married. It is only a hundred human paces!"

"Well, then, let her come to him!" said the old ones. "He has a whole forest of burdocks, she has only a bush!"

And so they went and fetched little Miss Snail. It was a

whole week before she arrived; but therein was just the very best of it, for one could thus see that she was of the same species.

And then the marriage was celebrated. Six earth-worms shone as well as they could. In other respects the whole went off very quietly, for the old folks could not bear noise and merriment; but old Dame Snail made a brilliant speech. Father Snail could not speak, he was too much affected; and so they gave them as a dowry and inheritance, the whole forest of burdocks, and said—what they had always said—that it was the best in the world; and if they lived honestly and decently, and increased and multiplied, they and their children would once in the course of time come to the manor-house, be boiled black, and laid on silver dishes. After this speech was made, the old ones crept into their shells, and never more came out. They slept; the young couple governed in the forest, and had a numerous progeny, but they were never boiled, and never came on the silver dishes; so from this they concluded that the manor-house had fallen to ruins, and that all the men in the world were extinct; and as no one contradicted them, so, of course it was so. And the rain beat on the dock-leaves to make drum-music for their sake, and the sun shone in order to give the burdock forest a colour for their sakes; and they were very happy, and the whole family was happy; indeed they were.

The Story of a Mother

A mother sat there with her little child. She was so downcast, so afraid that it should die! It was so pale, the small eyes had closed themselves, and it drew its breath so softly, now and then, with a deep respiration, as if it sighed; and the mother looked still more sorrowfully on the little creature.

Then a knocking was heard at the door, and in came a poor old man wrapped up as in a large horse-cloth, for it warms one, and he needed it, as it was the cold winter season! Everything out-of-doors was covered with ice and snow, and the wind blew so that it cut the face.

As the old man trembled with cold, and the little child slept a moment, the mother went and poured some ale into a pot and set it on the stove, that it might be warm for him; the old man sat and rocked the cradle, and the mother sat down on a chair close by him, and looked at her little sick child that drew its breath so deep, and raised its little hand.

"Do you not think that I shall save him?" said she. "Our Lord will not take him from me!"

And the old man—it was Death himself—he nodded so strangely, it could just as well signify yes as no. And the mother looked down in her lap, and the tears ran down over her cheeks; her head became so heavy—she had not closed her eyes for three days and nights; and now she slept, but only for a minute, when she started up and trembled with cold.

"What is that?" said she, and looked on all sides; but the old man was gone, and her little child was gone—he had taken it with him; and the old clock in the corner burred, and burred, the great leaden weight ran down to the floor, bump! and then the clock also stood still.

But the poor mother ran out of the house and cried aloud for her child.

Out there, in the midst of the snow, there sat a woman in long, black clothes; and she said, "Death has been in thy chamber, and I saw him hasten away with thy little child; he goes faster than the wind, and he never brings back what he takes!"

"Oh, only tell me which way he went!" said the mother. "Tell me the way, and I shall find him!"

"I know it!" said the woman in the black clothes. "But before I tell it, thou must first sing for me all the songs thou hast sung for thy child! I am fond of them. I have heard them before; I am Night; I saw thy tears whilst thou sang'st them!"

"I will sing them all, all!" said the mother. "But do not stop me now—I may overtake him—I may find my child!"

But Night stood still and mute. Then the mother wrung her hands, sang and wept, and there were many songs, but yet many more tears; and then Night said, "Go to the right, into the dark pine forest; thither I saw Death take his way with thy little child!"

The roads crossed each other in the depths of the forest, and she no longer knew whither she should go! Then there stood a thorn-bush; there was neither leaf nor flower on it, it was also in the cold winter season, and ice-flakes hung on the branches.

"Hast thou not seen Death go past with my little child?" said the mother.

"Yes," said the thorn-bush; "but I will not tell thee which way he took, unless thou wilt first warm me up at thy heart. I am freezing to death; I shall become a lump of ice!"

And she pressed the thorn-bush to her breast, so firmly, that it might be thoroughly warmed, and the thorns went right into her flesh, and her blood flowed in large drops, but the thornbush shot forth fresh green leaves, and there came flowers on it in the cold winter night, the heart of the afflicted mother was so warm; and the thorn-bush told her the way she should go.

She then came to a large lake, where there was neither ship nor boat. The lake was not frozen sufficiently to bear her; neither was it open, nor low enough that she could wade through it; and across it she must go if she would find her child! Then she lay down to drink up the lake, and that was an impossibility for a human being, but the afflicted mother thought that a miracle might happen nevertheless.

"Oh, what would I not give to come to my child!" said the weeping mother; and she wept still more, and her eyes sunk down in the depths of the waters, and became two precious pearls; but the water bore her up, as if she sat in a swing, and she flew in the rocking waves to the shore on the opposite side, where there stood a mile-broad, strange house, one knew not if it were a mountain with forests and caverns, or if it were built up; but the poor mother could not see it; she had wept her eyes out.

"Where shall I find Death, who took away my little child?" said she.

"He has not come here yet!" said the old grave woman, who was appointed to look after Death's great greenhouse. "How have you been able to find the way hither? And who has helped you?"

"Our Lord has helped me," said she. "He is merciful, and you will also be so! Where shall I find my little child?"

"Nay, I know not," said the woman, "and you cannot see! Many flowers and trees have withered this night; Death will soon come and plant them over again! You certainly know that every person has his or her life's tree or flower, just as everyone happens to be settled; they look like other plants, but they have pulsations of the heart. Children's hearts can also beat; go after yours, perhaps you may know your child's; but what will you give me if I tell you what you shall do more?"

"I have nothing to give," said the afflicted mother, "but I will go to the world's end for you!"

"Nay, I have nothing to do there!" said the woman. "But you

can give me your long black hair; you know yourself that it is fine, and that I like! You shall have my white hair instead, and that's always something!"

"Do you demand nothing else?" said she. "That I will gladly give you!" And she gave her her fine black hair, and got the old woman's snow-white hair instead.

So they went into Death's great greenhouse, where flowers and trees grew strangely into one another. There stood fine hyacinths under glass bells, and there stood strong-stemmed peonies; there grew water plants, some so fresh, others half sick, the water-snakes lay down on them, and black crabs pinched their stalks. There stood beautiful palm-trees, oaks, and plantains; there stood parsley and flowering thyme: every tree and every flower had its name; each of them was a human life, the human still lived—one in China, and another in Greenland—others round about in the world. There were large trees in small pots, so that they stood so stunted in growth, and ready to burst the pots; in other places, there was a little dull flower in rich mould, with moss round about it, and it was so petted and nursed. But the distressed mother bent down over all the smallest plants, and heard within them how the human heart beat; and amongst millions she knew her child's.

"There it is!" cried she, and stretched her hands out over a little blue crocus, that hung quite sickly on one side.

"Don't touch the flower!" said the old woman. "But place yourself here, and when Death comes—I expect him every moment—do not let him pluck the flower up, but threaten him that you will do the same with the others. Then he will be afraid! He is responsible for them to Our Lord, and no one dares to pluck them up before HE gives leave."

All at once an icy cold rushed through the great hall, and the blind mother could feel that it was Death that came.

"How hast thou been able to find thy way hither?" he asked. "How couldst thou come quicker than I?"

"I am a mother," said she.

And Death stretched out his long hand towards the fine little flower, but she held her hands fast around his, so tight, and yet afraid that she should touch one of the leaves. Then Death blew on her hands, and she felt that it was colder than the cold wind, and her hands fell down powerless.

"Thou canst not do anything against me!" said Death.

"But Our Lord can!" said she.

"I only do His bidding!" said Death. "I am His gardener, I take all His flowers and trees, and plant them out in the great garden of Paradise, in the unknown land; but how they grow there, and how it is there I dare not tell thee."

"Give me back my child!" said the mother, and she wept and prayed. At once she seized hold of two beautiful flowers close by, with each hand, and cried out to Death, "I will tear all thy flowers off, for I am in despair."

"Touch them not!" said Death. "Thou say'st that thou art so unhappy, and now thou wilt make another mother equally unhappy."

"Another mother!" said the poor woman, and directly let go her hold of both the flowers.

"There, thou hast thine eyes," said Death; "I fished them up from the lake, they shone so bright; I knew not they were thine. Take them again, they are now brighter than before; now look down into the deep well close by; I shall tell thee the names of the two flowers thou wouldst have torn up, and thou wilt see their whole future life—their whole human existence: and see what thou wast about to disturb and destroy."

And she looked down into the well; and it was a happiness to see how the one became a blessing to the world, to see how much happiness and joy were felt everywhere. And she saw the other's life, and it was sorrow and distress, horror, and wretchedness.

"Both of them are God's will!" said Death.

"Which of them is Misfortune's flower and which is that of Happiness?" asked she.

"That I will not tell thee," said Death; "but this thou shalt know from me, that the one flower was thy own child! it was thy child's fate thou saw'st—thy own child's future life!"

Then the mother screamed with terror, "Which of them was my child? Tell it me! Save the innocent! Save my child from all that misery! Rather take it away! Take it into God's kingdom! Forget my tears, forget my prayers, and all that I have done!"

"I do not understand thee!" said Death. "Wilt thou have thy child again, or shall I go with it there, where thou dost not know!"

Then the mother wrung her hands, fell on her knees, and prayed to our Lord: "Oh, hear me not when I pray against Thy will, which is the best! hear me not! hear me not!"

And she bowed her head down in her lap, and Death took her child and went with it into the unknown land.

THE FALSE COLLAR

There was once a fine gentleman, all of whose moveables were a boot-jack and a hair-comb: but he had the finest false collars in the world; and it is about one of these collars that we are now to hear a story.

It was so old, that it began to think of marriage; and it happened that it came to be washed in company with a garter.

"Nay!" said the collar. "I never did see anything so slender and so fine, so soft and so neat. May I not ask your name?"

"That I shall not tell you!" said the garter.

"Where do you live?" asked the collar.

But the garter was so bashful, so modest, and thought it was a strange question to answer.

"You are certainly a girdle," said the collar; "that is to say an inside girdle. I see well that you are both for use and ornament, my dear young lady."

"I will thank you not to speak to me," said the garter. "I think I have not given the least occasion for it."

"Yes! When one is as handsome as you," said the collar, "that is occasion enough."

"Don't come so near me, I beg of you!" said the garter. "You look so much like those men-folks."

"I am also a fine gentleman," said the collar. "I have a boot-jack and a hair-comb."

But that was not true, for it was his master who had them: but he boasted.

"Don't come so near me," said the garter: "I am not accustomed to it."

"Prude!" exclaimed the collar; and then it was taken out of the washing-tub. It was starched, hung over the back of a chair in the sunshine, and was then laid on the ironing-blanket; then came the warm box-iron. "Dear lady!" said the collar. "Dear widow-lady! I feel quite hot. I am quite changed. I begin to unfold myself. You will burn a hole in me. Oh! I offer you my hand."

"Rag!" said the box-iron; and went proudly over the collar: for she fancied she was a steam-engine, that would go on the railroad and draw the waggons. "Rag!" said the box-iron.

The collar was a little jagged at the edge, and so came the long scissors to cut off the jagged part. "Oh!" said the collar. "You are certainly the first opera dancer. How well you can stretch your legs out! It is the most graceful performance I have ever seen. No one can imitate you."

"I know it," said the scissors.

"You deserve to be a baroness," said the collar. "All that I have is a fine gentleman, a boot-jack, and a hair-comb. If I only had the barony!"

"Do you seek my hand?" said the scissors; for she was angry; and without more ado, she *cut him*, and then he was condemned.

"I shall now be obliged to ask the hair-comb. It is surprising how well you preserve your teeth, Miss," said the collar. "Have you never thought of being betrothed?"

"Yes, of course! you may be sure of that," said the hair-comb. "I *am* betrothed—to the boot-jack!"

"Betrothed!" exclaimed the collar. Now there was no other to court, and so he despised courting.

A long time passed away, then the collar came into the rag chest at the paper mill; there was a large company of rags, the fine by themselves, and the coarse by themselves, just as it should be. They all had much to say, but the collar the most; for he was a real boaster.

"I have had such an immense number of sweethearts!" said the collar. "I could not be in peace! It is true, I was always a fine starched-up gentleman! I had both a boot-jack and a hair-comb, which I never used! You should have seen me then, you should have seen me when I lay down! I shall never forget MY FIRST LOVE—she was a girdle, so fine, so soft, and so charming, she threw herself into a tub of water for my sake! There was also a widow, who became glowing hot, but I left her standing till she got black again; there was also the first opera dancer, she gave me that cut which I now go with, she was so ferocious! My own hair-comb was in love with me, she lost all her teeth from the heart-ache; yes, I have lived to see much of that sort of thing; but I am extremely sorry for the garter—I mean the girdle—that went into the water-tub. I have much on my conscience, I want to become white paper!"

And it became so, all the rags were turned into white paper; but the collar came to be just this very piece of white paper we here see, and on which the story is printed; and that was because it boasted so terribly afterwards of what had never happened to it. It would be well for us to beware, that we may not act in a similar manner, for we can never know if we may not, in the course of time, also come into the rag chest, and be made into white paper, and then have our whole life's history printed on it, even the most secret, and be obliged to run about and tell it ourselves, just like this collar.

The Shadow

It is in the hot lands that the sun burns, sure enough! There the people become quite a mahogany brown, ay, and in the hottest lands they are burnt black. But now it was to the hot lands that a learned man had come from the cold; there he thought that he could run about just as when at home, but he soon found out his mistake.

He, and all sensible folks, were obliged to stay within doors—the window-shutters and doors were closed the whole day; it looked as if the whole house slept, or there was no one at home.

The narrow street with the high houses was built so that the sunshine must fall there from morning till evening—it was really not to be borne.

The learned man from the cold lands—he was a young man, and seemed to be a clever man—sat in a glowing oven; it took effect on him, he became quite meagre—even his shadow shrunk in, for the sun had also an effect on it. It was first towards evening when the sun was down, that they began to freshen up again.

In the warm lands every window has a balcony, and the people came out on all the balconies in the street—for one must have air, even if one be accustomed to be mahogany-coloured! It was lively both up and down the street. Tailors, and shoemakers, and all the folks, moved out into the street—chairs and tables were brought forth—and candles burnt—yes, above a thousand lights were burning—and the one talked and the other sang; and people walked and church-bells rang, and asses went along with a dingle-dingle-dong! for they too had bells on. The street boys were screaming and hooting, and shouting and shooting, with devils and detonating balls—and there came corpse bearers and hood wearers—for there were funerals with psalm and hymn—and then the din of carriages driving and company arriving: yes, it was, in truth, lively enough down in the street. Only in that single house, which stood opposite that in which the learned foreigner lived, it was quite still; and yet some one lived there, for there stood flowers in the balcony—they grew so well in the sun's heat! and that they could not do unless they were watered—and some one must water them—there must be somebody there. The door opposite was also opened late in the evening, but it was dark within, at least in the front room; further in there was heard the sound of music. The learned foreigner thought it quite marvellous, but now—it might be that he only imagined it—for he found everything marvellous out there, in the warm lands, if there had only been no sun. The stranger's landlord said that he didn't know who had taken the house opposite, one saw no person about, and as to the music, it appeared to him to be extremely tiresome. "It is as if someone sat there, and practised a piece that he could not master—always the same piece. 'I shall master it!' says he; but yet he cannot master it, however long he plays."

The word mahogany can be understood, in Danish, as having two meanings. In general, it means the reddish-brown wood itself; but in jest, it signifies "excessively fine," which arose from an anecdote of Nyboder, in Copenhagen, (the seamen's quarter.) A sailor's wife, who was always proud and fine, in her way, came to her neighbour, and complained that she had got a splinter in her finger. "What of?" asked the neighbour's wife.

"It is a mahogany splinter," said the other.

"Mahogany! It cannot be less with you!" exclaimed the woman—and thence the proverb, "It is so mahogany!"—(that is, so excessively fine)—is derived.

One night the stranger awoke—he slept with the doors of the balcony open—the curtain before it was raised by the wind, and he thought that a strange lustre came from the opposite neighbour's house; all the flowers shone like flames, in the most beautiful colours, and in the midst of the flowers stood a slender, graceful maiden—it was as if she also shone; the light really hurt his eyes. He now opened them quite wide—yes, he was quite awake; with one spring he was on the floor; he crept gently behind the curtain, but the maiden was gone; the flowers shone no longer, but there they stood, fresh and blooming as ever; the door was ajar, and, far within, the music sounded so soft and delightful, one could really melt away in sweet thoughts from it. Yet it was like a piece of enchantment. And who lived there? Where was the actual entrance? The whole of the ground-floor was a row of shops, and there people could not always be running through.

One evening the stranger sat out on the balcony. The light burnt in the room behind him; and thus it was quite natural that his shadow should fall on his opposite neighbour's wall. Yes! there it sat, directly opposite, between the flowers on the balcony; and when the stranger moved, the shadow also moved: for that it always does.

"I think my shadow is the only living thing one sees over there," said the learned man. "See, how nicely it sits between the flowers. The door stands half-open: now the shadow should be cunning, and go into the room, look about, and then come and tell me what it had seen. Come, now! Be useful, and do me a service," said he, in jest. "Have the kindness to step in. Now! Art thou going?" and then he nodded to the shadow, and the shadow nodded again. "Well then, go! But don't stay away."

The stranger rose, and his shadow on the opposite neighbour's balcony rose also; the stranger turned round and the shadow also turned round. Yes! if anyone had paid particular attention to it, they would have seen, quite distinctly, that the shadow went in through the half-open balcony-door of their opposite neighbour, just as the stranger went into his own room, and let the long curtain fall down after him.

Next morning, the learned man went out to drink coffee and read the newspapers.

"What is that?" said he, as he came out into the sunshine. "I have no shadow! So then, it has actually gone last night, and not come again. How tiresome!"

This annoyed him: not so much because the shadow was gone, but because he knew there was a story about a man without a shadow.* It was known to everybody at home, in the cold lands; and if the learned man now came there and told his story, they would say that he was imitating it, and that he had no need to do. He would, therefore, not talk about it at all; and that was wisely thought.

In the evening he went out again on the balcony. He had placed the light directly behind him, for he knew that the shadow would always have its master for a screen, but he could not entice it. He made himself little; he made himself great: but no shadow came. He said, "Hem! hem!" but it was of no use.

This was vexatious; but in the warm lands everything grows so quickly; and after the lapse of eight days he observed, to his great joy, that a new shadow came in the sunshine. In the course of three weeks he had a very fair shadow, which, when he set out for his home in the northern lands, grew more and more in the journey, so that at last it was so long and so large, that it was more than sufficient.

The learned man then came home, and he wrote books about what was true in the world, and about what was good and what was beautiful; and there passed days and years—yes! many years passed.

One evening, as he was sitting in his room, there was a gentle knocking at the door.

"Come in!" said he; but no one came in; so he opened the

*Peter Schlemihl, the shadowless man.

door, and there stood before him such an extremely lean man, that he felt quite strange. As to the rest, the man was very finely dressed—he must be a gentleman.

"Whom have I the honour of speaking to?" asked the learned man.

"Yes! I thought as much," said the fine man. "I thought you would not know me. I have got so much body. I have even got flesh and clothes. You certainly never thought of seeing me so well off. Do you not know your old shadow? You certainly thought I should never more return. Things have gone well with me since I was last with you. I have, in all respects, become very well off. Shall I purchase my freedom from service? If so, I can do it"; and then he rattled a whole bunch of valuable seals that hung to his watch, and he stuck his hand in the thick gold chain he wore around his neck—nay! how all his fingers glittered with diamond rings; and all were real gems.

"Nay; I cannot recover from my surprise!" said the learned man. "What is the meaning of all this?"

"Something uncommon, is it not?" said the shadow. "But you yourself do not belong to the common order; and I, as you know well, have from childhood followed in your footsteps. As soon as you found I was capable of going out alone in the world, I went my own way. I am in the most brilliant circumstances, but there came a sort of desire over me to see you once more before you die; you will die, I suppose? I also wished to see this land again—for you know we always love our native land. I know you have got another shadow again; have I anything to pay to it or you? If so, you will oblige me by saying what it is."

"Nay, is it really thou?" said the learned man. "It is most remarkable: I never imagined that one's old shadow could come again as a man."

"Tell me what I have to pay," said the shadow; "for I don't like to be in any sort of debt."

"How canst thou talk so?" said the learned man. "What debt

is there to talk about? Make thyself as free as anyone else. I am extremely glad to hear of thy good fortune: sit down, old friend, and tell me a little how it has gone with thee, and what thou hast seen at our opposite neighbour's there—in the warm lands."

"Yes, I will tell you all about it," said the shadow, and sat down: "but then you must also promise me that, wherever you may meet me, you will never say to anyone here in the town that I have been your shadow. I intend to get betrothed, for I can provide for more than one family."

"Be quite at thy ease about that," said the learned man; "I shall not say to anyone who thou actually art: here is my hand—I promise it, and a man's bond is his word."

"A word is a shadow," said the shadow, "and as such it must speak."

It was really quite astonishing how much of a man it was. It was dressed entirely in black, and of the very finest cloth; it had patent leather boots, and a hat that could be folded together, so that it was bare crown and brim; not to speak of what we already know it had—seals, gold neck-chain, and diamond rings; yes, the shadow was well-dressed, and it was just that which made it quite a man.

"Now I shall tell you my adventures," said the shadow; and then he sat, with the polished boots, as heavily as he could, on the arm of the learned man's new shadow, which lay like a poodle at his feet. Now this was perhaps from arrogance; and the shadow on the ground kept itself so still and quiet, that it might hear all that passed: it wished to know how it could get free, and work its way up, so as to become its own master.

"Do you know who lived in our opposite neighbour's house?" said the shadow. "It was the most charming of all beings, it was poetry! I was there for three weeks, and that has as much effect as if one had lived three thousand years, and read all that was composed and written; that is what I say, and it is right. I have seen everything and I know everything!"

"Poetry!" cried the learned man. "Yes, yes, she often dwells a recluse in large cities! Poetry! Yes, I have seen her—a single short moment, before sleep came into my eyes! She stood on the balcony and shone as the Aurora Borealis shines. Go on, go on—thou wert on the balcony, and went through the doorway, and then—"

"Then I was in the antechamber," said the shadow. "You always sat and looked over to the antechamber. There was no light; there was a sort of twilight, but the one door stood open directly opposite the other through a long row of rooms and halls, and there it was lit up. I should have been completely killed if I had gone over to the maiden; but I was circumspect, I took time to think, and that one must always do."

"And what didst thou then see?" asked the learned man.

"I saw everything, and I shall tell all to you: but—it is no pride on my part—as a free man, and with the knowledge I have, not to speak of my position in life, my excellent circumstances—I certainly wish that you would say *you** to me!"

"I beg your pardon," said the learned man; "it is an old habit with me. *You* are perfectly right, and I shall remember it; but now you must tell me all *you* saw!"

"Everything!" said the shadow. "For I saw everything, and I know everything!"

"How did it look in the furthest hall?" asked the learned

*It is the custom in Denmark for intimate acquaintances to use the second person singular, "Du," (thou) when speaking to each other. When a friendship is formed between men, they generally affirm it, when occasion offers, either in public or private, by drinking to each other and exclaiming, "thy health," at the same time striking their glasses together. This is called drinking "Duus": they are then, "Duus Brodre," (thou brothers) and ever afterwards use the pronoun "thou," to each other, it being regarded as more familiar than "De," (you). Father and mother, sister and brother say thou to one another—without regard to age or rank. Master and mistress say thou to their servants the superior to the inferior. But servants and inferiors do not use the same term to their masters, or superiors—nor is it ever used when speaking to a stranger, or anyone with whom they are but slightly acquainted—they then say as in English—you.

man. "Was it there as in the fresh woods? Was it there as in a holy church? Were the halls like the star-lit firmament when we stand on the high mountains?"

"Everything was there!" said the shadow. "I did not go quite in, I remained in the foremost room, in the twilight, but I stood there quite well; I saw everything, and I know everything! I have been in the antechamber at the court of Poetry."

"But *what did* you see? Did all the gods of the olden times pass through the large halls? Did the old heroes combat there? Did sweet children play there, and relate their dreams?"

"I tell you I was there, and you can conceive that I saw everything there was to be seen. Had you come over there, you would not have been a man; but I became so! And besides, I learned to know my inward nature, my innate qualities, the relationship I had with Poetry. At the time I was with you, I thought not of that, but always—you know it well—when the sun rose, and when the sun went down, I became so strangely great; in the moonlight I was very near being more distinct than yourself; at that time I did not understand my nature; it was revealed to me in the antechamber! I became a man! I came out matured; but you were no longer in the warm lands; as a man I was ashamed to go as I did. I was in want of boots, of clothes, of the whole human varnish that makes a man perceptible. I took my way—I tell it to you, but you will not put it in any book—I took my way to the cake woman—I hid myself behind her; the woman didn't think how much she concealed. I went out first in the evening; I ran about the streets in the moonlight; I made myself long up the walls—it tickles the back so delightfully! I ran up, and ran down, peeped into the highest windows, into the halls, and on the roofs, I peeped in where no one could peep, and I saw what no one else saw, what no one else should see! This is, in fact, a base world! I would not be a man if it were not now once accepted and regarded as something to be so! I saw the most unimaginable things with the women, with the men, with parents, and with the sweet, matchless children; I saw," said the shadow, "what no human being must know, but what they would all so willingly know—what is bad in their neighbour. Had I written a newspaper, it would have been read! But I wrote directly to the persons themselves, and there was consternation in all the towns where I came. They were so afraid of me, and yet they were so excessively fond of me. The professors made a professor of me; the tailors gave me new clothes—I am well furnished; the master of the mint struck new coin for me, and the women said I was so handsome! And so I became the man I am. And I now bid you farewell. Here is my card—I live on the sunny side of the street, and am always at home in rainy weather!" And so away went the shadow. "That was most extraordinary!" said the learned man. Days and years passed away, then the shadow came again. "How goes it?" said the shadow.

"Alas!" said the learned man. "I write about the true, and the good, and the beautiful, but no one cares to hear such things; I am quite desperate, for I take it so much to heart!"

"But I don't!" said the shadow. "I become fat, and it is that one wants to become! You do not understand the world. You will become ill from it. You must travel! I shall make a tour this summer; will you go with me? I should like to have a travelling companion! Will you go with me, as shadow? It will be a great pleasure for me to have you with me; I shall pay the travelling expenses!"

"Nay, this is too much!" said the learned man.

"It is just as one takes it!" said the shadow. "It will do you much good to travel! Will you be my shadow? You shall have everything free on the journey!"

"Nay, that is too bad!" said the learned man.

"But it is just so with the world!" said the shadow, "and so it will be!" and away it went again.

The learned man was not at all in the most enviable state; grief and torment followed him, and what he said about the true, and the good, and the beautiful, was, to most persons, like roses for a cow! He was quite ill at last.

"You really look like a shadow!" said his friends to him; and the learned man trembled, for he thought of it.

"You must go to a health resort!" said the shadow, who came and visited him. "There is nothing else for it! I will take you with me for old acquaintance' sake; I will pay the travelling expenses, and you write the descriptions—and they shall provide me with a little entertainment on the way! I will go to a health resort—my beard does not grow out as it ought—that is also a sickness—and one must have a beard! Now you be wise and accept the offer; we shall travel as comrades!"

And so they travelled; the shadow was master, and the master was the shadow; they drove with each other, they rode and walked together, side by side, before and behind, just as the sun was; the shadow always took care to keep itself in the master's place. Now the learned man didn't think much about that; he was a very kind-hearted man, and particularly mild and friendly, and so he said one day to the shadow: "As we have now become companions, and in this way have grown up together from childhood, shall we not drink 'thou' together, it is more familiar?"

"You are right," said the shadow, who was now the proper master. "It is said in a very straight-forward and well-meant manner. You, as a learned man, certainly know how strange nature is. Some persons cannot bear to touch grey paper, or they become ill; others shiver in every limb if one rub a pane of glass with a nail: I have just such a feeling on hearing you say thou to me; I feel myself as if pressed to the earth in my first situation with you. You see that it is a feeling; that it is not pride: I cannot allow you to say *thou* to me, but I will willingly say *thou* to you, so it is half done!"

So the shadow said *thou* to its former master.

"This is rather too bad," thought he, "that I must say *you* and he say *thou*," but he was now obliged to put up with it.

So they came to a health resort where there were many strangers, and amongst them was a princess, who was troubled with seeing too well; and that was so alarming!

She directly observed that the stranger who had just come was quite a different sort of person to all the others; "He has come here in order to get his beard to grow, they say, but I see the real cause, he cannot cast a shadow."

She had become inquisitive; and so she entered into conversation directly with the strange gentleman, on their promenades. As the daughter of a king, she needed not to stand upon trifles, so she said, "Your complaint is, that you cannot cast a shadow?"

"Your Royal Highness must be improving considerably," said the shadow, "I know your complaint is, that you see too clearly, but it has decreased, you are cured. I just happen to have a very unusual shadow! Do you not see that person who always goes with me? Other persons have a common shadow, but I do not like what is common to all. We give our servants finer cloth for their livery than we ourselves use, and so I had my shadow trimmed up into a man: yes, you see I have even given him a shadow. It is somewhat expensive, but I like to have something for myself!"

"What!" thought the princess. "Can I really be cured! These baths are the first in the world! In our time water has wonderful powers. But I shall not leave the place, for it now begins to be amusing here. I am extremely fond of that stranger: would that his beard should not grow, for in that case he will leave us!"

In the evening, the princess and the shadow danced together in the large ball-room. She was light, but he was still lighter; she had never had such a partner in the dance. She told him from what land she came, and he knew that land; he had been there, but then she was not at home; he had peeped in at the window, above and below—he had seen both the one and the other, and so he could answer the princess, and make insinuations, so that she was quite astonished; he must be the wisest man in the whole world! She felt such respect for what he knew! So that when they again danced together she fell in love with him; and that the shadow could remark, for she almost pierced him through with her eyes. So they danced once more together; and she was about to declare herself, but she was discreet; she thought of her country and kingdom, and of the many persons she would have to reign over.

"He is a wise man," said she to herself—"It is well; and he dances delightfully—that is also good; but has he solid knowledge? That is just as important! He must be examined."

So she began, by degrees, to question him about the most difficult things she could think of, and which she herself could not have answered; so that the shadow made a strange face.

"You cannot answer these questions?" said the princess.

"They belong to my childhood's learning," said the shadow. "I really believe my shadow, by the door there, can answer them!"

"Your shadow!" said the princess. "That would indeed be marvellous!"

"I will not say for a certainty that he can," said the shadow, "but I think so; he has now followed me for so many years, and listened to my conversation—I should think it possible. But your royal highness will permit me to observe, that he is so proud of passing himself off for a man, that when he is to be in a proper humour—and he must be so to answer well—he must be treated quite like a man."

"Oh! I like that!" said the princess.

So she went to the learned man by the door, and she spoke to him about the sun and the moon, and about persons out of and in the world, and he answered with wisdom and prudence.

"What a man that must be who has so wise a shadow!" thought she. "It will be a real blessing to my people and kingdom if I choose him for my consort—I will do it!"

They were soon agreed, both the princess and the shadow; but no one was to know about it before she arrived in her own kingdom.

"No one—not even my shadow!" said the shadow, and he had his own thoughts about it!

Now they were in the country where the princess reigned when she was at home.

"Listen, my good friend," said the shadow to the learned man. "I have now become as happy and mighty as anyone can be; I will, therefore, do something particular for thee! Thou shalt always live with me in the palace, drive with me in my royal carriage, and have ten thousand pounds a year; but then thou must submit to be called *Shadow* by all and everyone; thou must not say that thou hast ever been a man; and once a year, when I sit on the balcony in the sunshine, thou must lie at my feet, as a shadow shall do! I must tell thee: I am going to marry the king's daughter, and the nuptials are to take place this evening!"

"Nay, this is going too far!" said the learned man. "I will not have it; I will not do it! It is to deceive the whole country and the princess too! I will tell everything! That I am a man, and that thou art a shadow—thou art only dressed up!"

"There is no one who will believe it!" said the shadow. "Be reasonable, or I will call the guard!"

"I will go directly to the princess!" said the learned man.

"But I will go first!" said the shadow. "And thou wilt go to prison!" and that he was obliged to do—for the sentinels obeyed him whom they knew the king's daughter was to marry.

"You tremble!" said the princess, as the shadow came into her chamber. "Has anything happened? You must not be unwell this evening, now that we are to have our nuptials celebrated."

"I have lived to see the most cruel thing that anyone can live to see!" said the shadow. "Only imagine—yes, it is true, such a poor shadow-skull cannot bear much—only think, my shadow has become mad; he thinks that he is a man, and that I—now only think—that I am his shadow!"

"It is terrible!" said the princess; "but he is confined, is he not?"

"That he is. I am afraid that he will never recover."

"Poor shadow!" said the princess. "He is very unfortunate; it would be a real work of charity to deliver him from the little life he has, and, when I think properly over the matter, I am of opinion that it will be necessary to do away with him in all stillness!"

"It is certainly hard," said the shadow, "for he was a faithful servant!" and then he gave a sort of sigh.

"You are a noble character!" said the princess.

The whole city was illuminated in the evening, and the cannons went off with a bum! bum! and the soldiers presented arms. That was a marriage! The princess and the shadow went out on the balcony to show themselves, and get another hurrah!

The learned man heard nothing of all this—for they had deprived him of life.

THE LITTLE MATCH GIRL

Most terribly cold it was; it snowed, and was nearly quite dark, and evening—the last evening of the year. In this cold and darkness there went along the street a poor little girl, bareheaded, and with naked feet. When she left home she had slippers on, it is true; but what was the good of that? They were very large slippers, which her mother had hitherto worn; so large were they; and the poor little thing lost them as she scuffled away across the street, because of two carriages that rolled by dreadfully fast.

One slipper was nowhere to be found; the other had been laid hold of by an urchin, and off he ran with it; he thought it would do capitally for a cradle when he some day or other should have children himself. So the little maiden walked on with her tiny naked feet, that were quite red and blue from cold. She carried a quantity of matches in an old apron, and she held a bundle of them in her hand. Nobody had bought anything of her the whole livelong day; no one had given her a single farthing.

She crept along trembling with cold and hunger—a very picture of sorrow, the poor little thing!

The flakes of snow covered her long fair hair, which fell in beautiful curls around her neck; but of that, of course, she never once now thought. From all the windows the candles were gleaming, and it smelt so deliciously of roast goose, for you know it was New Year's Eve; yes, of that she thought.

In a corner formed by two houses, of which one advanced more than the other, she seated herself down and cowered together. Her little feet she had drawn close up to her, but she grew colder and colder, and to go home she did not venture, for she had not sold any matches and could not bring a farthing of money: from her father she would certainly get blows, and at home it was cold too, for above her she had only the roof, through which the wind whistled, even though the largest cracks were stopped up with straw and rags.

Her little hands were almost numbed with cold. Oh! a match might afford her a world of comfort, if she only dared take a single one out of the bundle, draw it against the wall, and warm her fingers by it. She drew one out. "Rischt!" how it blazed, how it burnt! It was a warm, bright flame, like a candle, as she held her hands over it: it was a wonderful light. It seemed really to the little maiden as though she were sitting before a large iron stove, with burnished brass feet and a brass ornament at top. The fire burned with such blessed influence; it warmed so delightfully. The little girl had already stretched out her feet to warm them too; but—the small flame went out, the stove vanished: she had only the remains of the burnt-out match in her hand.

She rubbed another against the wall: it burned brightly, and where the light fell on the wall, there the wall became transparent like a veil, so that she could see into the room. On the table was spread a snow-white tablecloth; upon it was a splendid porcelain service, and the roast goose was steaming famously with its stuffing of apple and dried plums. And what was still more capital to behold was, the goose hopped down from the dish, reeled about on the floor with knife and fork in its breast, till it came up to the poor little girl; when—the match went out and nothing but the thick, cold, damp wall was left behind. She lighted another match. Now there she was sitting under the most magnificent Christmas tree: it was still larger, and more decorated than the one which she had seen through the glass door in the rich merchant's house.

Thousands of lights were burning on the green branches, and gaily-coloured pictures, such as she had seen in the shop-windows, looked down upon her. The little maiden stretched out her hands towards them when—the match went out. The lights of the Christmas tree rose higher and higher, she saw them now as stars in heaven; one fell down and formed a long trail of fire.

"Someone is just dead!" said the little girl; for her old grandmother, the only person who had loved her, and who was now no more, had told her, that when a star falls, a soul ascends to God.

She drew another match against the wall: it was again light, and in the lustre there stood the old grandmother, so bright and radiant, so mild, and with such an expression of love.

"Grandmother!" cried the little one. "Oh, take me with you! You go away when the match burns out; you vanish like the warm stove, like the delicious roast goose, and like the magnificent Christmas tree!" And she rubbed the whole bundle of matches quickly against the wall, for she wanted to be quite sure of keeping her grandmother near her. And the matches gave such a brilliant light that it was brighter than at noon-day: never formerly had the grandmother been so beautiful and so tall. She took the little maiden, on her arm, and both flew in brightness and in joy so high, so very high, and then above was neither cold, nor hunger, nor anxiety—they were with God.

But in the corner, at the cold hour of dawn, sat the poor girl, with rosy cheeks and with a smiling mouth, leaning against the wall—frozen to death on the last evening of the old year. Stiff and stark sat the child there with her matches, of which one bundle had been burnt. "She wanted to warm herself," people said. No one had the slightest suspicion of what beautiful things she had seen; no one even dreamed of the splendour in which, with her grandmother she had entered on the joys of a new year.

The Dream of little Tuk

Ah! yes, that was little Tuk: in reality his name was not Tuk, but that was what he called himself before he could speak plain: he meant it for Charles, and it is all well enough if one does but know it. He had now to take care of his little sister Augusta, who was much younger than himself, and he was, besides, to learn his lesson at the same time; but these two things would not do together at all. There sat the poor little fellow, with his sister on his lap, and he sang to her all the songs he knew; and he glanced the while from time to time into the geography-book that lay open before him. By the next morning he was to have learnt all the towns in Zealand by heart, and to know about them all that is possible to be known.

His mother now came home, for she had been out, and took little Augusta on her arm. Tuk ran quickly to the window, and read so eagerly that he pretty nearly read his eyes out; for it got darker and darker, but his mother had no money to buy a candle.

"There goes the old washerwoman over the way," said his mother, as she looked out of the window. "The poor woman can hardly drag herself along, and she must now drag the pail home from the fountain. Be a good boy, Tukey, and run across and help the old woman, won't you?"

So Tuk ran over quickly and helped her; but when he came back again into the room it was quite dark, and as to a light, there was no thought of such a thing. He was now to go to bed; that was an old turn-up bedstead; in it he lay and thought about his geography lesson, and of Zealand, and of all that his master had told him. He ought, to be sure, to have read over his lesson again, but that, you know, he could not do. He therefore put his geography-book under his pillow, because he had heard that was a very good thing to do when one wants to learn one's lesson; but one cannot, however, rely upon it entirely. Well, there he lay, and thought and thought, and all at once it was just as if some-one kissed his eyes and mouth: he slept, and yet he did not sleep; it was as though the old washerwoman gazed on him with her mild eyes and said, "It were a great sin if you were not to know your lesson tomorrow morning. You have aided me, I therefore will now help you; and the loving God will do so at all times." And all of a sudden the book under Tuk's pillow began scraping and scratching.

"Kickery-ki! kluk! kluk! kluk!"—that was an old hen who came creeping along, and she was from Kjoge. "I am a Kjoger hen,"* said she, and then she related how many inhabitants there were there, and about the battle that had taken place, and which, after all, was hardly worth talking about.

"Kribledy, krabledy—plump!" down fell somebody: it was a wooden bird, the popinjay used at the shooting-matches at Prastoe. Now he said that there were just as many inhabitants as he had nails in his body; and he was very proud. "Thorwaldsen lived almost next door to me.** Plump! Here I lie capitally."

But little Tuk was no longer lying down: all at once he was on horseback. On he went at full gallop, still galloping on and on. A knight with a gleaming plume, and most magnificently dressed, held him before him on the horse, and thus they rode through the wood to the old town of Bordingborg, and that was

*Kjoge, a town in the bay of Kjoge. "To see the Kjoge hens," is an expression similar to "showing a child London," which is said to be done by taking his head in both hands, and so lifting him off the ground. At the invasion of the English in 1807, an encounter of a no very glorious nature took place between the British troops and the undisciplined Danish militia

**Prastoe, a still smaller town than Kjoge. Some hundred paces from it lies the manor-house Ny Soe, where Thorwaldsen, the famed sculptor, generally sojourned during his stay in Denmark, and where he called many of his immortal works into existence.

a large and very lively town. High towers rose from the castle of the king, and the brightness of many candles streamed from all the windows; within was dance and song, and King Waldemar and the young, richly-attired maids of honour danced together. The morn now came; and as soon as the sun appeared, the whole town and the king's palace crumbled together, and one tower after the other; and at last only a single one remained standing where the castle had been before,* and the town was so small and poor, and the school boys came along with their books under their arms, and said, "2000 inhabitants!" but that was not true, for there were not so many.

And little Tukey lay in his bed: it seemed to him as if he dreamed, and yet as if he were not dreaming; however, somebody was close beside him.

"Little Tukey! Little Tukey!" cried someone near. It was a seaman, quite a little personage, so little as if he were a midshipman; but a midshipman it was not.

"Many remembrances from Corsor.** That is a town that is just rising into importance; a lively town that has steam-boats and stagecoaches: formerly people called it ugly, but that is no longer true. I lie on the sea," said Corsor; "I have high roads and gardens, and I have given birth to a poet who was witty and amusing, which all poets are not. I once intended to equip a ship that was to sail all round the earth; but I did not do it, although I could have done so: and then, too, I smell so deliciously, for close before the gate bloom the most beautiful roses."

Little Tuk looked, and all was red and green before his eyes; but as soon as the confusion of colours was somewhat over, all

*Bordingborg, in the reign of King Waldemar, a considerable place, now an unimportant little town. One solitary tower only, and some remains of a wall, show where the castle once stood.

**Corsor, on the Great Belt, called, formerly, before the introduction of steam-vessels, when travellers were often obliged to wait a long time for a favourable wind, "the most tiresome of towns." The poet Baggesen was born here.

of a sudden there appeared a wooded slope close to the bay, and high up above stood a magnificent old church, with two high pointed towers. From out the hill-side spouted fountains in thick streams of water, so that there was a continual splashing; and close beside them sat an old king with a golden crown upon his white head: that was King Hroar, near the fountains, close to the town of Roeskilde,* as it is now called. And up the slope into the old church went all the kings and queens of Denmark, hand in hand, all with their golden crowns; and the organ played and the fountains rustled. Little Tuk saw all, heard all. "Do not forget the diet," said King Hroar.

Again all suddenly disappeared. Yes, and whither? It seemed to him just as if one turned over a leaf in a book. And now stood there an old peasant-woman, who came from Sorbe,** where grass grows in the market-place. She had an old grey linen apron hanging over her head and back: it was so wet, it certainly must have been raining. "Yes, that it has," said she; and she now related many pretty things out of Holberg's comedies, and about Waldemar and Absalon; but all at once she cowered together, and her head began shaking backwards and forwards, and she looked as she were going to make a spring. "Croak! croak!" said she. "It is wet, it is wet; there is such a pleasant deathlike stillness in Sorbe!" She was now suddenly a frog, "Croak"; and now she was an old woman. "One must dress according to the weather," said she. "It is wet; it is wet. My town is just like a bottle; and one gets in by the neck, and by the neck one must get out again! In former times I had the finest fish, and

*Roeskilde, once the capital of Denmark. The town takes its name from King Hroar, and the many fountains in the neighbourhood. In the beautiful cathedral the greater number of the kings and queens of Denmark are interred. In Roeskilde, too, the members of the Danish Diet assemble.

**Sorbe, a very quiet little town, beautifully situated, surrounded by woods and lakes. Holberg, Denmark's Moliere, founded here an academy for the sons of the nobles. The poets Hauch and Ingemann were appointed professors here. The latter lives there still.

now I have fresh rosy-cheeked boys at the bottom of the bottle, who learn wisdom, Hebrew, Greek—Croak!"

When she spoke it sounded just like the noise of frogs, or as if one walked with great boots over a moor; always the same tone, so uniform and so tiring that little Tuk fell into a good sound sleep, which, by the bye, could not do him any harm.

But even in this sleep there came a dream, or whatever else it was: his little sister Augusta, she with the blue eyes and the fair curling hair, was suddenly a tall, beautiful girl, and without having wings was yet able to fly; and she now flew over Zealand—over the green woods and the blue lakes.

"Do you hear the cock crow, Tukey? Cock-a-doodle-doo! The cocks are flying up from Kjoge! You will have a farm-yard, so large, oh! so very large! You will suffer neither hunger nor thirst! You will get on in the world! You will be a rich and happy man! Your house will exalt itself like King Waldemar's tower, and will be richly decorated with marble statues, like that at Prastoe. You understand what I mean. Your name shall circulate with renown all round the earth, like unto the ship that was to have sailed from Corsor; and in Roeskilde—"

"Do not forget the diet!" said King Hroar.

"Then you will speak well and wisely, little Tukey; and when at last you sink into your grave, you shall sleep as quietly—"

"As if I lay in Soroe," said Tuk, awaking. It was bright day, and he was now quite unable to call to mind his dream; that, however, was not at all necessary, for one may not know what the future will bring.

And out of bed he jumped, and read in his book, and now all at once he knew his whole lesson. And the old washerwoman popped her head in at the door, nodded to him friendly, and said, "Thanks, many thanks, my good child, for your help! May the good ever-loving God fulfil your loveliest dream!"

Little Tukey did not at all know what he had dreamed, but the loving God knew it.

The Naughty Boy

Along time ago, there lived an old poet, a thoroughly kind old poet. As he was sitting one evening in his room, a dreadful storm arose without, and the rain streamed down from heaven; but the old poet sat warm and comfortable in his chimney-corner, where the fire blazed and the roasting apple hissed.

"Those who have not a roof over their heads will be wetted to the skin," said the good old poet.

"Oh let me in! Let me in! I am cold, and I'm so wet!" exclaimed suddenly a child that stood crying at the door and knocking for admittance, while the rain poured down, and the wind made all the windows rattle.

"Poor thing!" said the old poet, as he went to open the door. There stood a little boy, quite naked, and the water ran down from his long golden hair; he trembled with cold, and had he not come into a warm room he would most certainly have perished in the frightful tempest.

"Poor child!" said the old poet, as he took the boy by the hand. "Come in, come in, and I will soon restore thee! Thou shalt have wine and roasted apples, for thou art verily a charming child!" And the boy was really. His eyes were like two bright stars; and although the water trickled down his hair, it waved in beautiful curls. He looked exactly like a little angel, but he was so pale, and his whole body trembled with cold. He had a nice little bow in his hand, but it was quite spoiled by the rain, and the tints of his many-coloured arrows ran one into the other.

The old poet seated himself beside his hearth, and took the little fellow on his lap; he squeezed the water out of his dripping hair, warmed his hands between his own, and boiled for him some sweet wine. Then the boy recovered, his cheeks again rosy, he jumped down from the lap where he was sitting, and danced round the kind old poet.

"You are a merry fellow," said the old man. "What's your name?"

"My name is Cupid," answered the boy. "Don't you know me? There lies my bow; it shoots well, I can assure you! Look, the weather is now clearing up, and the moon is shining clear again through the window."

"Why, your bow is quite spoiled," said the old poet.

"That were sad indeed," said the boy, and he took the bow in his hand and examined it on every side. "Oh, it is dry again, and is not hurt at all; the string is quite tight. I will try it directly." And he bent his bow, took aim, and shot an arrow at the old poet, right into his heart. "You see now that my bow was not spoiled," said he laughing; and away he ran.

The naughty boy, to shoot the old poet in that way; he who had taken him into his warm room, who had treated him so kindly, and who had given him warm wine and the very best apples!

The poor poet lay on the earth and wept, for the arrow had really flown into his heart.

"Fie!" said he. "How naughty a boy Cupid is! I will tell all children about him, that they may take care and not play with him, for he will only cause them sorrow and many a heartache."

And all good children to whom he related this story, took great heed of this naughty Cupid; but he made fools of them still, for he is astonishingly cunning. When the university students come from the lectures, he runs beside them in a black coat, and with a book under his arm. It is quite impossible for them to know him, and they walk along with him arm in arm, as if he, too, were a student like themselves; and then, unperceived, he thrusts an arrow to their bosom. When the young maidens come from being examined by the clergyman, or go to church to be confirmed, there he is again close behind them. Yes, he is forever following people. At the play, he sits in the great chandelier and burns in bright flames, so that people think it is really a flame, but they soon discover it is something else. He roves about in the garden of the palace and upon the ramparts: yes, once he even shot your father and mother right in the heart. Ask them only and you will hear what they'll tell you. Oh, he is a naughty boy, that Cupid; you must never have anything to do with him. He is forever running after everybody. Only think, he shot an arrow once at your old grandmother! But that is a long time ago, and it is all past now; however, a thing of that sort she never forgets. Fie, naughty Cupid! But now you know him, and you know, too, how ill-behaved he is!

The Red Shoes

There was once a little girl who was very pretty and delicate, but in summer she was forced to run about with bare feet, she was so poor, and in winter wear very large wooden shoes, which made her little insteps quite red, and that looked so dangerous!

In the middle of the village lived old Dame Shoemaker; she sat and sewed together, as well as she could, a little pair of shoes out of old red strips of cloth; they were very clumsy, but it was a kind thought. They were meant for the little girl. The little girl was called Karen.

On the very day her mother was buried, Karen received the red shoes, and wore them for the first time. They were certainly not intended for mourning, but she had no others, and with stockingless feet she followed the poor straw coffin in them.

Suddenly a large old carriage drove up, and a large old lady sat in it: she looked at the little girl, felt compassion for her, and then said to the clergyman:

"Here, give me the little girl. I will adopt her!"

And Karen believed all this happened on account of the red shoes, but the old lady thought they were horrible, and they were burnt. But Karen herself was cleanly and nicely dressed; she must learn to read and sew; and people said she was a nice little thing, but the looking-glass said: "Thou art more than nice, thou art beautiful!"

Now the queen once travelled through the land, and she had her little daughter with her. And this little daughter was a princess, and people streamed to the castle, and Karen was there also, and the little princess stood in her fine white dress, in a window, and let herself be stared at; she had neither a train nor a golden crown, but splendid red morocco shoes. They were certainly far handsomer than those Dame Shoemaker had made for little Karen. Nothing in the world can be compared with red shoes.

Now Karen was old enough to be confirmed; she had new clothes and was to have new shoes also. The rich shoemaker in the city took the measure of her little foot. This took place at his house, in his room; where stood large glass-cases, filled with elegant shoes and brilliant boots. All this looked charming, but the old lady could not see well, and so had no pleasure in them. In the midst of the shoes stood a pair of red ones, just like those the princess had worn. How beautiful they were! The shoemaker said also they had been made for the child of a count, but had not fitted.

"That must be patent leather!" said the old lady. "They shine so!"

"Yes, they shine!" said Karen, and they fitted, and were bought, but the old lady knew nothing about their being red, else she would never have allowed Karen to have gone in red shoes to be confirmed. Yet such was the case.

Everybody looked at her feet; and when she stepped through the chancel door on the church pavement, it seemed to her as if the old figures on the tombs, those portraits of old preachers and preachers' wives, with stiff ruffs, and long black dresses, fixed their eyes on her red shoes. And she thought only of them as the clergyman laid his hand upon her head, and spoke of the holy baptism, of the covenant with God, and how she should be now a matured Christian; and the organ pealed so solemnly; the sweet children's voices sang, and the old music-directors sang, but Karen only thought of her red shoes.

In the afternoon, the old lady heard from everyone that the shoes had been red, and she said that it was very wrong of Karen, that it was not at all becoming, and that in future Karen should only go in black shoes to church, even when she should be older.

The next Sunday there was the sacrament, and Karen looked

at the black shoes, looked at the red ones—looked at them again, and put on the red shoes.

The sun shone gloriously; Karen and the old lady walked along the path through the corn; it was rather dusty there.

At the church door stood an old soldier with a crutch, and with a wonderfully long beard, which was more red than white, and he bowed to the ground, and asked the old lady whether he might dust her shoes. And Karen stretched out her little foot.

"See, what beautiful dancing shoes!" said the soldier. "Sit firm when you dance"; and he put his hand out towards the soles.

And the old lady gave the old soldier alms, and went into the church with Karen.

And all the people in the church looked at Karen's red shoes, and all the pictures, and as Karen knelt before the altar, and raised the cup to her lips, she only thought of the red shoes, and they seemed to swim in it; and she forgot to sing her psalm, and she forgot to pray, "Our Father in Heaven!"

Now all the people went out of church, and the old lady got into her carriage. Karen raised her foot to get in after her, when the old soldier said,

"Look, what beautiful dancing shoes!"

And Karen could not help dancing a step or two, and when she began her feet continued to dance; it was just as though the shoes had power over them. She danced round the church corner, she could not leave off; the coachman was obliged to run after and catch hold of her, and he lifted her in the carriage, but her feet continued to dance so that she trod on the old lady dreadfully. At length she took the shoes off, and then her legs had peace.

The shoes were placed in a closet at home, but Karen could not avoid looking at them.

Now the old lady was sick, and it was said she could not recover. She must be nursed and waited upon, and there was no one whose duty it was so much as Karen's. But there was a great ball in the city, to which Karen was invited. She looked at the old lady, who could not recover, she looked at the red shoes, and she thought there could be no sin in it; she put on the red shoes, she might do that also, she thought. But then she went to the ball and began to dance.

When she wanted to dance to the right, the shoes would dance to the left, and when she wanted to dance up the room, the shoes danced back again, down the steps, into the street, and out of the city gate. She danced, and was forced to dance straight out into the gloomy wood.

Then it was suddenly light up among the trees, and she fancied it must be the moon, for there was a face; but it was the old soldier with the red beard; he sat there, nodded his head, and said, "Look, what beautiful dancing shoes!"

Then she was terrified, and wanted to fling off the red shoes, but they clung fast; and she pulled down her stockings, but the shoes seemed to have grown to her feet. And she danced, and must dance, over fields and meadows, in rain and sunshine, by night and day; but at night it was the most fearful.

She danced over the churchyard, but the dead did not dance—they had something better to do than to dance. She wished to seat herself on a poor man's grave, where the bitter tansy grew; but for her there was neither peace nor rest; and when she danced towards the open church door, she saw an angel standing there. He wore long, white garments; he had wings which reached from his shoulders to the earth; his countenance was severe and grave; and in his hand he held a sword, broad and glittering.

"Dance shalt thou!" said he. "Dance in thy red shoes till thou art pale and cold! Till thy skin shrivels up and thou art a skeleton! Dance shalt thou from door to door, and where proud, vain children dwell, thou shalt knock, that they may hear thee and tremble! Dance shalt thou—!"

"Mercy!" cried Karen. But she did not hear the angel's reply, for the shoes carried her through the gate into the fields, across roads and bridges, and she must keep ever dancing.

One morning she danced past a door which she well knew. Within sounded a psalm; a coffin, decked with flowers, was borne forth. Then she knew that the old lady was dead, and felt that she was abandoned by all, and condemned by the angel of God.

She danced, and she was forced to dance through the gloomy night. The shoes carried her over stack and stone; she was torn till she bled; she danced over the heath till she came to a little house. Here, she knew, dwelt the executioner; and she tapped with her fingers at the window, and said, "Come out! Come out! I cannot come in, for I am forced to dance!"

And the executioner said, "Thou dost not know who I am, I fancy? I strike bad people's heads off; and I hear that my axe rings!"

"Don't strike my head off!" said Karen. "Then I can't repent of my sins! But strike off my feet in the red shoes!"

And then she confessed her entire sin, and the executioner struck off her feet with the red shoes, but the shoes danced away with the little feet across the field into the deep wood.

And he carved out little wooden feet for her, and crutches, taught her the psalm criminals always sing; and she kissed the hand which had wielded the axe, and went over the heath.

"Now I have suffered enough for the red shoes!" said she. "Now I will go into the church that people may see me!" And she hastened towards the church door: but when she was near it, the red shoes danced before her, and she was terrified, and turned round. The whole week she was unhappy, and wept many bitter tears; but when Sunday returned, she said, "Well, now I have suffered and struggled enough! I really believe I am as good as many a one who sits in the church, and holds her head so high!"

And away she went boldly; but she had not got farther than the churchyard gate before she saw the red shoes dancing before her; and she was frightened, and turned back, and repented of her sin from her heart.

And she went to the parsonage, and begged that they would take her into service; she would be very industrious, she said, and would do everything she could; she did not care about the wages, only she wished to have a home, and be with good people. And the clergyman's wife was sorry for her and took her into service; and she was industrious and thoughtful. She sat still and listened when the clergyman read the Bible in the evenings. All the children thought a great deal of her; but when they spoke of dress, and grandeur, and beauty, she shook her head.

The following Sunday, when the family was going to church, they asked her whether she would not go with them; but she glanced sorrowfully, with tears in her eyes, at her crutches. The family went to hear the word of God; but she went alone into her little chamber; there was only room for a bed and chair to stand in it; and here she sat down with her Prayer-Book; and whilst she read with a pious mind, the wind bore the strains of the organ towards her, and she raised her tearful countenance, and said, "O God, help me!"

And the sun shone so clearly, and straight before her stood the angel of God in white garments, the same she had seen that night at the church door; but he no longer carried the sharp sword, but in its stead a splendid green spray, full of roses. And he touched the ceiling with the spray, and the ceiling rose so high, and where he had touched it there gleamed a golden star. And he touched the walls, and they widened out, and she saw the organ which was playing; she saw the old pictures of the preachers and the preachers' wives. The congregation sat in cushioned seats, and sang out of their Prayer-Books. For the church itself had come to the poor girl in her narrow chamber, or else she had come into the church. She sat in the pew with the clergyman's family, and when they had ended the psalm and looked up, they nodded and said, "It is right that thou art come!"

"It was through mercy!" she said.

And the organ pealed, and the children's voices in the choir sounded so sweet and soft! The clear sunshine streamed so warmly through the window into the pew where Karen sat! Her heart was so full of sunshine, peace, and joy, that it broke. Her soul flew on the sunshine to God, and there no one asked after the RED SHOES.

THE NIGHTINGALE

In China, you know, the emperor is a Chinese, and all those about him are Chinamen also. The story I am going to tell you happened a great many years ago, so it is well to hear it now before it is forgotten. The emperor's palace was the most beautiful in the world. It was built entirely of porcelain, and very costly, but so delicate and brittle that whoever touched it was obliged to be careful. In the garden could be seen the most singular flowers, with pretty silver bells tied to them, which tinkled so that every one who passed could not help noticing the flowers. Indeed, everything in the emperor's garden was remarkable, and it extended so far that the gardener himself did not know where it ended. Those who travelled beyond its limits knew that there was a noble forest, with lofty trees, sloping down to the deep blue sea, and the great ships sailed under the shadow of its branches. In one of these trees lived a nightingale, who sang so beautifully that even the poor fishermen, who had so many other things to do, would stop and listen. Sometimes, when they went at night to spread their nets, they would hear her sing, and say, "Oh, is not that beautiful?" But when they returned to their fishing, they forgot the bird until the next night. Then they would hear it again, and exclaim, "Oh, how beautiful is the nightingale's song!"

Travellers from every country in the world came to the city of the emperor, which they admired very much, as well as the palace and gardens; but when they heard the nightingale, they all declared it to be the best of all. And the travellers, on their return home, related what they had seen; and learned men wrote books, containing descriptions of the town, the palace, and the gardens; but they did not forget the nightingale, which was really the greatest wonder. And those who could write poetry composed beautiful verses about the nightingale, who lived in a forest near the deep sea. The books travelled all over the world, and some of them came into the hands of the emperor; and he sat in his golden chair, and, as he read, he nodded his approval every moment, for it pleased him to find such a beautiful description of his city, his palace, and his gardens. But when he came to the words, "the nightingale is the most beautiful of all," he exclaimed, "What is this? I know nothing of any nightingale. Is there such a bird in my empire? and even in my garden? I have never heard of it. Something, it appears, may be learnt from books."

Then he called one of his lords-in-waiting, who was so high-bred, that when any in an inferior rank to himself spoke to him, or asked him a question, he would answer, "Pooh," which means nothing.

"There is a very wonderful bird mentioned here, called a nightingale," said the emperor; "they say it is the best thing in my large kingdom. Why have I not been told of it?"

"I have never heard the name," replied the cavalier; "she has not been presented at court."

"It is my pleasure that she shall appear this evening," said the emperor; "the whole world knows what I possess better than I do myself."

"I have never heard of her," said the cavalier; "yet I will endeavor to find her."

But where was the nightingale to be found? The nobleman went up stairs and down, through halls and passages; yet none of those whom he met had heard of the bird. So he returned to the emperor, and said that it must be a fable, invented by those who had written the book. "Your imperial majesty," said he, "cannot believe everything contained in books; sometimes they are only fiction, or what is called the black art."

"But the book in which I have read this account," said the

emperor, "was sent to me by the great and mighty emperor of Japan, and therefore it cannot contain a falsehood. I will hear the nightingale, she must be here this evening; she has my highest favour; and if she does not come, the whole court shall be trampled upon after supper is ended."

"Tsing-pe!" cried the lord-in-waiting, and again he ran up and down stairs, through all the halls and corridors; and half the court ran with him, for they did not like the idea of being trampled upon. There was a great inquiry about this wonderful nightingale, whom all the world knew, but who was unknown to the court.

At last they met with a poor little girl in the kitchen, who said, "Oh, yes, I know the nightingale quite well; indeed, she can sing. Every evening I have permission to take home to my poor sick mother the scraps from the table; she lives down by the sea-shore, and as I come back I feel tired, and I sit down in the wood to rest, and listen to the nightingale's song. Then the tears come into my eyes, and it is just as if my mother kissed me."

"Little maiden," said the lord-in-waiting, "I will obtain for you constant employment in the kitchen, and you shall have permission to see the emperor dine, if you will lead us to the nightingale; for she is invited for this evening to the palace."

So she went into the wood where the nightingale sang, and half the court followed her. As they went along, a cow began lowing.

"Oh," said a young courtier, "now we have found her; what wonderful power for such a small creature; I have certainly heard it before."

"No, that is only a cow lowing," said the little girl; "we are a long way from the place yet."

Then some frogs began to croak in the marsh.

"Beautiful," said the young courtier again. "Now I hear it, tinkling like little church bells."

"No, those are frogs," said the little maiden; "but I think we shall soon hear her now:" and presently the nightingale began to sing.

"Hark, hark! there she is," said the girl, "and there she sits," she added, pointing to a little grey bird who was perched on a bough.

"Is it possible?" said the lord-in-waiting, "I never imagined it would be a little, plain, simple thing like that. She has certainly changed colour at seeing so many grand people around her."

"Little nightingale," cried the girl, raising her voice, "our most gracious emperor wishes you to sing before him."

"With the greatest pleasure," said the nightingale, and began to sing most delightfully.

"It sounds like tiny glass bells," said the lord-in-waiting, "and see how her little throat works. It is surprising that we have never heard this before; she will be a great success at court."

"Shall I sing once more before the emperor?" asked the nightingale, who thought he was present.

"My excellent little nightingale," said the courtier, "I have the great pleasure of inviting you to a court festival this evening, where you will gain imperial favour by your charming song."

"My song sounds best in the green wood," said the bird; but still she came willingly when she heard the emperor's wish.

The palace was elegantly decorated for the occasion. The walls and floors of porcelain glittered in the light of a thousand lamps. Beautiful flowers, round which little bells were tied, stood in the corridors: what with the running to and fro and the draught, these bells tinkled so loudly that no one could speak to be heard. In the centre of the great hall, a golden perch had been fixed for the nightingale to sit on. The whole court was present, and the little kitchen-maid had received permission to stand by the door. She was not installed as a real court cook. All were in full dress, and every eye was turned to the little grey bird when the emperor nodded to her to begin. The nightingale sang so sweetly that the tears came into the emperor's eyes, and then rolled down his cheeks, as her song became still more touching and went to every one's heart. The emperor was so delighted that he declared the nightingale should have his gold slipper to wear round her neck, but she declined the honour with thanks: she had been sufficiently rewarded already. "I have seen tears in an emperor's eyes," she said, "that is my richest reward. An emperor's tears have wonderful power, and are quite sufficient honour for me;" and then she sang again more enchantingly than ever.

"That singing is a lovely gift;" said the ladies of the court to each other; and then they took water in their mouths to make them utter the gurgling sounds of the nightingale when they spoke to any one, so thay they might fancy themselves nightingales. And the footmen and chambermaids also expressed their satisfaction, which is saying a great deal, for they are very difficult to please. In fact the nightingale's visit was most successful. She was now to remain at court, to have her own cage, with liberty to go out twice a day, and once during the night. Twelve servants were appointed to attend her on these occasions, who each held her by a silken string fastened to her leg. There was certainly not much pleasure in this kind of flying.

The whole city spoke of the wonderful bird, and when two people met, one said "nightin," and the other said "gale," and they understood what was meant, for nothing else was talked of. Eleven peddlers' children were named after her, but not one of them could sing a note.

One day the emperor received a large packet on which was written "The Nightingale."

"Here is no doubt a new book about our celebrated bird," said the emperor. But instead of a book, it was a work of art contained in a casket, an artificial nightingale made to look like a living one, and covered all over with diamonds, rubies, and sapphires. As soon as the artificial bird was wound up, it could sing like the real one, and could move its tail up and down, which sparkled with silver and gold. Round its neck hung a piece of ribbon, on which was written "The Emperor of Japan's nightingale is poor compared with that of the Emperor of China's."

"This is very beautiful," exclaimed all who saw it, and he who had brought the artificial bird received the title of "Imperial nightingale-bringer-in-chief."

"Now they must sing together," said the court, "and what a duet it will be."

But they did not get on well, for the real nightingale sang in its own natural way, but the artificial bird sang only waltzes.

"That is not a fault," said the music-master, "it is quite perfect to my taste," so then it had to sing alone, and was as successful as the real bird; besides, it was so much prettier to look at, for it sparkled like bracelets and breast-pins. Three and thirty times did it sing the same tunes without being tired; the people would gladly have heard it again, but the emperor said the living nightingale ought to sing something. But where was she? No one had noticed her when she flew out at the open window, back to her own green woods.

"What strange conduct," said the emperor, when her flight had been discovered; and all the courtiers blamed her, and said she was a very ungrateful creature.

"But we have the best bird after all," said one, and then they would have the bird sing again, although it was the thirty-fourth time they had listened to the same piece, and even then they had not learnt it, for it was rather difficult. But the music-master praised the bird in the highest degree, and even asserted that it was better than a real nightingale, not only in its dress and the beautiful diamonds, but also in its musical power. "For you must perceive, my chief lord and emperor, that with a real nightingale we can never tell what is going to be sung, but with this bird everything is settled. It can be opened and explained, so that people may understand how the waltzes are formed, and why one note follows upon another."

"This is exactly what we think," they all replied, and then the music-master received permission to exhibit the bird to the people on the following Sunday, and the emperor commanded that they should be present to hear it sing. When they heard it they were like people intoxicated; however it must have been with drinking tea, which is quite a Chinese custom. They all said "Oh!" and held up their forefingers and nodded, but a poor fisherman, who had heard the real nightingale, said, "it sounds prettily enough, and the melodies are all alike; yet there seems something wanting, I cannot exactly tell what."

And after this the real nightingale was banished from the empire, and the artificial bird placed on a silk cushion close to the emperor's bed. The presents of gold and precious stones which had been received with it were round the bird, and it was now advanced to the title of "Little Imperial Toilet Singer," and to the rank of No. 1 on the left hand; for the emperor considered the left side, on which the heart lies, as the most noble, and the heart of an emperor is in the same place as that of other people.

The music-master wrote a work, in twenty-five volumes, about the artificial bird, which was very learned and very long, and full of the most difficult Chinese words; yet all the people said they had read it, and understood it, for fear of being thought stupid and having their bodies trampled upon.

So a year passed, and the emperor, the court, and all the other Chinese knew every little turn in the artificial bird's song; and for that same reason it pleased them better. They could sing with the bird, which they often did. The street-boys sang, "Zi-zi-zi, cluck, cluck, cluck," and the emperor himself could sing it also. It was really most amusing.

One evening, when the artificial bird was singing its best, and the emperor lay in bed listening to it, something inside the bird sounded "whizz."

Then a spring cracked. "Whir-r-r-r" went all the wheels, running round, and then the music stopped. The emperor immediately sprang out of bed, and called for his physician; but what could he do? Then they sent for a watchmaker; and, after a great deal of talking and examination, the bird was put into something like order; but he said that it must be used very carefully, as the barrels were worn, and it would be impossible to put in new ones without injuring the music. Now there was great sorrow, as the bird could only be allowed to play once a year; and even that was dangerous for the works inside it. Then the music-master made a little speech, full of hard words, and declared that the bird was as good as ever; and, of course no one contradicted him.

Five years passed, and then a real grief came upon the land. The Chinese really were fond of their emperor, and he now lay so ill that he was not expected to live. Already a new emperor had been chosen and the people who stood in the street asked the lord-in-waiting how the old emperor was; but he only said, "Pooh!" and shook his head.

Cold and pale lay the emperor in his royal bed; the whole court thought he was dead, and every one ran away to pay homage to his successor. The chamberlains went out to have a talk on the matter, and the ladies'-maids invited company to take coffee. Cloth had been laid down on the halls and passages, so that not a footstep should be heard, and all was silent and still. But the emperor was not yet dead, although he lay white and stiff on his gorgeous bed, with the long velvet curtains and heavy gold tassels. A window stood open, and the moon shone in upon the emperor and the artificial bird. The poor emperor, finding he could scarcely breathe with a strange weight on his chest, opened his eyes, and saw Death sitting there. He had put on the emperor's golden crown, and held in one hand his sword of state, and in the other his beautiful banner. All around the bed and peeping through the long velvet curtains, were a number of strange heads, some very ugly, and others lovely and gentle looking. These were the emperor's good and bad deeds, which stared him in the face now Death sat at his heart.

"Do you remember this?" "Do you recollect that?" they asked one after another, thus bringing to his remembrance circumstances that made the perspiration stand on his brow.

"I know nothing about it," said the emperor. "Music! music!" he cried; "the large Chinese drum! that I may not hear what they say."

But they still went on, and Death nodded like a Chinaman to all they said. "Music! music!" shouted the emperor. "You little precious golden bird, sing, pray sing! I have given you gold and costly presents; I have even hung my golden slipper round your neck. Sing! sing!" But the bird remained silent. There was no one to wind it up, and therefore it could not sing a note.

Death continued to stare at the emperor with his cold, hollow eyes, and the room was fearfully still. Suddenly there came through the open window the sound of sweet music. Outside, on the bough of a tree, sat the living nightingale. She had heard of the emperor's illness, and was therefore come to sing to him of hope and trust. And as she sung, the shadows grew paler and paler; the blood in the emperor's veins flowed more rapidly, and gave life to his weak limbs; and even Death himself listened, and said, "Go on, little nightingale, go on."

"Then will you give me the beautiful golden sword and that rich banner? and will you give me the emperor's crown?" said the bird.

So Death gave up each of these treasures for a song; and the nightingale continued her singing. She sung of the quiet churchyard, where the white roses grow, where the elder-tree wafts its perfume on the breeze, and the fresh, sweet grass is moistened by the mourners' tears. Then Death longed to go and see his garden, and floated out through the window in the form of a cold, white mist.

"Thanks, thanks, you heavenly little bird. I know you well. I banished you from my kingdom once, and yet you have charmed away the evil faces from my bed, and banished Death from my heart, with your sweet song. How can I reward you?"

"You have already rewarded me," said the nightingale. "I shall never forget that I drew tears from your eyes the first time I sang to you. These are the jewels that rejoice a singer's heart. But now sleep, and grow strong and well again. I will sing to you again."

And as she sung, the emperor fell into a sweet sleep; and how mild and refreshing that slumber was! When he awoke, strengthened and restored, the sun shone brightly through the window; but not one of his servants had returned—they all believed he was dead; only the nightingale still sat beside him, and sang.

"You must always remain with me," said the emperor. "You shall sing only when it pleases you; and I will break the artificial bird into a thousand pieces."

"No; do not do that," replied the nightingale; "the bird did very well as long as it could. Keep it here still. I cannot live in the palace, and build my nest; but let me come when I like. I will sit on a bough outside your window, in the evening, and sing to you, so that you may be happy, and have thoughts full of joy. I will sing to you of those who are happy, and those who suffer; of the good and the evil, who are hidden around you. The little singing bird flies far from you and your court to the home of the fisherman and the peasant's cot. I love your heart better than your crown; and yet something holy lingers round that also. I will come, I will sing to you; but you must promise me one thing."

"Anything," said the emperor, who, having dressed himself in his imperial robes, stood with the hand that held the heavy golden sword pressed to his heart.

"I only ask one thing," she replied; "let no one know that you have a little bird who tells you everything. It will be best to conceal it."

So saying, the nightingale flew away.

The servants now came in to look after the dead emperor; when, lo! there he stood, and, to their astonishment, said, "Good morning."

The Ugly Little Duckling

It was lovely summer weather in the country, and the golden corn, the green oats, and the haystacks piled up in the meadows looked beautiful. The stork walking about on his long red legs chattered in the Egyptian language, which he had learnt from his mother. The corn-fields and meadows were surrounded by large forests, in the midst of which were deep pools. It was, indeed, delightful to walk about in the country. In a sunny spot stood a pleasant old farmhouse close by a deep river, and from the house down to the waterside grew great burdock leaves, so high, that under the tallest of them a little child could stand upright. The spot was as wild as the centre of a thick wood. In this snug retreat sat a duck on her nest, watching for her young brood to hatch; she was beginning to get tired of her task, for the little ones were a long time coming out of their shells, and she seldom had any visitors. The other ducks liked much better to swim about in the river than to climb the slippery banks, and sit under a burdock leaf, to have a gossip with her. At length one shell cracked, and then another, and from each egg came a living creature that lifted its head and cried, "Peep, peep."

"Quack, quack," said the mother, and then they all quacked as well as they could, and looked about them on every side at the large green leaves. Their mother allowed them to look as much as they liked, because green is good for the eyes. "How large the world is," said the young ducks, when they found how much more room they now had than while they were inside the egg-shell. "Do you imagine this is the whole world?" asked the mother; "Wait till you have seen the garden; it stretches far beyond that to the parson's field, but I have never ventured to such a distance. Are you all out?" she continued, rising; "No, I declare, the largest egg lies there still. I wonder how long this is to last, I am quite tired of it;" and she seated herself again on the nest.

"Well, how are you getting on?" asked an old duck, who paid her a visit.

"One egg is not hatched yet," said the duck, "it will not break. But just look at all the others, are they not the prettiest little ducklings you ever saw? They are the image of their father, who is so unkind, he never comes to see."

"Let me see the egg that will not break," said the duck; "I have no doubt it is a turkey's egg. I was persuaded to hatch some once, and after all my care and trouble with the young ones, they were afraid of the water. I quacked and clucked, but all to no purpose. I could not get them to venture in. Let me look at the egg. Yes, that is a turkey's egg; take my advice, leave it where it is and teach the other children to swim."

"I think I will sit on it a little while longer," said the duck; "as I have sat so long already, a few days will be nothing."

"Please yourself," said the old duck, and she went away.

At last the large egg broke, and a young one crept forth crying, "Peep, peep."

It was very large and ugly. The duck stared at it and exclaimed, "It is very large and not at all like the others. I wonder if it really is a turkey. We shall soon find it out, however when we go to the water. It must go in, if I have to push it myself."

On the next day the weather was delightful, and the sun shone brightly on the green burdock leaves, so the mother duck took her young brood down to the water, and jumped in with a splash. "Quack, quack," cried she, and one after another the little ducklings jumped in. The water closed over their heads, but they came up again in an instant, and swam about quite prettily with their legs paddling under them as easily as possible, and the ugly duckling was also in the water swimming with them.

"Oh," said the mother, "that is not a turkey; how well he uses his legs, and how upright he holds himself! He is my own child, and he is not so very ugly after all if you look at him properly. Quack, quack! come with me now, I will take you into grand society, and introduce you to the farmyard, but you must keep close to me or you may be trodden upon; and, above all, beware of the cat."

When they reached the farmyard, there was a great disturbance, two families were fighting for an eel's head, which, after all, was carried off by the cat. "See, children, that is the way of the world," said the mother duck, whetting her beak, for she would have liked the eel's head herself. "Come, now, use your legs, and let me see how well you can behave. You must bow your heads prettily to that old duck yonder; she is the highest born of them all, and has Spanish blood, therefore, she is well off. Don't you see she has a red flag tied to her leg, which is something very grand, and a great honour for a duck; it shows that every one is anxious not to lose her, as she can be recognized both by man and beast. Come, now, don't turn your toes, a well-bred duckling spreads his feet wide apart, just like his father and mother, in this way; now bend your neck, and say 'quack.'"

The ducklings did as they were bid, but the other duck stared, and said, "Look, here comes another brood, as if there were not enough of us already! and what a queer looking object one of them is; we don't want him here," and then one flew out and bit him in the neck.

"Let him alone," said the mother; "he is not doing any harm."

"Yes, but he is so big and ugly," said the spiteful duck "and therefore he must be turned out."

"The others are very pretty children," said the old duck, with the rag on her leg, "all but that one; I wish his mother could improve him a little."

"That is impossible, your grace," replied the mother; "he is not pretty; but he has a very good disposition, and swims as well or even better than the others. I think he will grow up pretty, and perhaps be smaller; he has remained too long in the egg, and therefore his figure is not properly formed;" and then she stroked his neck and smoothed the feathers, saying, "It is a drake, and therefore not of so much consequence. I think he will grow up strong, and able to take care of himself."

"The other ducklings are graceful enough," said the old duck. "Now make yourself at home, and if you can find an eel's head, you can bring it to me."

And so they made themselves comfortable; but the poor duckling, who had crept out of his shell last of all, and looked so ugly, was bitten and pushed and made fun of, not only by the ducks, but by all the poultry. "He is too big," they all said, and the turkey cock, who had been born into the world with spurs, and fancied himself really an emperor, puffed himself out like a vessel in full sail, and flew at the duckling, and became quite red in the head with passion, so that the poor little thing did not know where to go, and was quite miserable because he was so ugly and laughed at by the whole farmyard. So it went on from day to day till it got worse and worse. The poor duckling was driven about by every one; even his brothers and sisters were unkind to him, and would say, "Ah, you ugly creature, I wish the cat would get you," and his mother said she wished he had never been born. The ducks pecked him, the chickens beat him, and the girl who fed the poultry kicked him with her feet. So at last he ran away, frightening the little birds in the hedge as he flew over the palings.

"They are afraid of me because I am ugly," he said. So he closed his eyes, and flew still farther, until he came out on a large moor, inhabited by wild ducks. Here he remained the whole night, feeling very tired and sorrowful.

In the morning, when the wild ducks rose in the air, they

stared at their new comrade. "What sort of a duck are you?" they all said, coming round him.

He bowed to them, and was as polite as he could be, but he did not reply to their question. "You are exceedingly ugly," said the wild ducks, "but that will not matter if you do not want to marry one of our family."

Poor thing! he had no thoughts of marriage; all he wanted was permission to lie among the rushes, and drink some of the water on the moor. After he had been on the moor two days, there came two wild geese, or rather goslings, for they had not been out of the egg long, and were very saucy. "Listen, friend," said one of them to the duckling, "you are so ugly, that we like you very well. Will you go with us, and become a bird of passage? Not far from here is another moor, in which there are some pretty wild geese, all unmarried. It is a chance for you to get a wife; you may be lucky, ugly as you are."

"Pop, pop," sounded in the air, and the two wild geese fell dead among the rushes, and the water was tinged with blood. "Pop, pop," echoed far and wide in the distance, and whole flocks of wild geese rose up from the rushes. The sound continued from every direction, for the sportsmen surrounded the moor, and some were even seated on branches of trees, overlooking the rushes. The blue smoke from the guns rose like clouds over the dark trees, and as it floated away across the water, a number of sporting dogs bounded in among the rushes, which bent beneath them wherever they went. How they terrified the poor duckling! He turned away his head to hide it under his wing, and at the same moment a large terrible dog passed quite near him. His jaws were open, his tongue hung from his mouth, and his eyes glared fearfully. He thrust his nose close to the duckling, showing his sharp teeth, and then, "splash, splash," he went into the water without touching him, "Oh," sighed the duckling, "how thankful I am for being so ugly; even a dog will not bite me."

And so he lay quite still, while the shot rattled through the rushes, and gun after gun was fired over him. It was late in the day before all became quiet, but even then the poor young thing did not dare to move. He waited quietly for several hours, and then, after looking carefully around him, hastened away from the moor as fast as he could. He ran over field and meadow till a storm arose, and he could hardly struggle against it. Towards evening, he reached a poor little cottage that seemed ready to fall, and only remained standing because it could not decide on which side to fall first. The storm continued so violent, that the duckling could go no farther; he sat down by the cottage, and then he noticed that the door was not quite closed in consequence of one of the hinges having given way. There was therefore a narrow opening near the bottom large enough for him to slip through, which he did very quietly, and got a shelter for the night. A woman, a tom cat, and a hen lived in this cottage. The tom cat, whom the mistress called, "My little son," was a great favorite; he could raise his back, and purr, and could even throw out sparks from his fur if it were stroked the wrong way. The hen had very short legs, so she was called "Chickie short legs."

She laid good eggs, and her mistress loved her as if she had been her own child. In the morning, the strange visitor was discovered, and the tom cat began to purr, and the hen to cluck.

"What is that noise about?" said the old woman, looking round the room, but her sight was not very good; therefore, when she saw the duckling she thought it must be a fat duck, that had strayed from home. "Oh what a prize!" she exclaimed, "I hope it is not a drake, for then I shall have some duck's eggs. I must wait and see."

So the duckling was allowed to remain on trial for three weeks, but there were no eggs. Now the tom cat was the master of the house, and the hen was mistress, and they always said, "We and the world," for they believed themselves to be half the world, and the better half too. The duckling thought that others might hold a different opinion on the subject, but the hen would not listen to such doubts. "Can you lay eggs?" she asked. "No."

"Then have the goodness to hold your tongue."

"Can you raise your back, or purr, or throw out sparks?" said the tom cat. "No."

"Then you have no right to express an opinion when sensible people are speaking."

So the duckling sat in a corner, feeling very low spirited, till the sunshine and the fresh air came into the room through the open door, and then he began to feel such a great longing for a swim on the water, that he could not help telling the hen.

"What an absurd idea," said the hen. "You have nothing else to do, therefore you have foolish fancies. If you could purr or lay eggs, they would pass away."

"But it is so delightful to swim about on the water," said the duckling, "and so refreshing to feel it close over your head, while you dive down to the bottom."

"Delightful, indeed!" said the hen, "why you must be crazy! Ask the cat, he is the cleverest animal I know, ask him how he would like to swim about on the water, or to dive under it, for I will not speak of my own opinion; ask our mistress, the old woman—there is no one in the world more clever than she is. Do you think she would like to swim, or to let the water close over her head?"

"You don't understand me," said the duckling.

"We don't understand you? Who can understand you, I wonder? Do you consider yourself more clever than the cat, or the old woman? I will say nothing of myself. Don't imagine such nonsense, child, and thank your good fortune that you have been received here. Are you not in a warm room, and in society from which you may learn something? But you are a chatterer, and your company is not very agreeable. Believe me, I speak only for your own good. I may tell you unpleasant truths, but that is a proof of my friendship. I advise you, therefore, to lay eggs, and learn to purr as quickly as possible."

"I believe I must go out into the world again," said the duckling.

"Yes, do," said the hen. So the duckling left the cottage, and soon found water on which it could swim and dive, but was avoided by all other animals, because of its ugly appearance. Autumn came, and the leaves in the forest turned to orange and gold. then, as winter approached, the wind caught them as they fell and whirled them in the cold air. The clouds, heavy with hail and snow-flakes, hung low in the sky, and the raven stood on the ferns crying, "Croak, croak."

It made one shiver with cold to look at him. All this was very sad for the poor little duckling. One evening, just as the sun set amid radiant clouds, there came a large flock of beautiful birds out of the bushes. The duckling had never seen any like them before. They were swans, and they curved their graceful necks, while their soft plumage shone with dazzling whiteness. They uttered a singular cry, as they spread their glorious wings and flew away from those cold regions to warmer countries across the sea. As they mounted higher and higher in the air, the ugly little duckling felt quite a strange sensation as he watched them. He whirled himself in the water like a wheel, stretched out his neck towards them, and uttered a cry so strange that it frightened himself. Could he ever forget those beautiful, happy birds; and when at last they were out of his sight, he dived under the water, and rose again almost beside himself with excitement. He knew not the names of these birds, nor where they had flown, but he felt towards them as he had never felt for any other bird in the world. He was not envious of these beautiful creatures, but wished to be as lovely as they. Poor ugly creature, how gladly he would have lived even with the ducks had they only given him encouragement. The winter grew colder and colder; he was obliged to swim about on the water to keep it from freezing, but every night the space on which he swam became smaller and smaller. At length it froze so hard that the ice in the water crackled as he moved, and the duckling had to paddle with his legs as well as he could, to keep the space from closing up. He became exhausted at last, and lay still and helpless, frozen fast in the ice.

Early in the morning, a peasant, who was passing by, saw what had happened. He broke the ice in pieces with his wooden shoe, and carried the duckling home to his wife. The warmth revived the poor little creature; but when the children wanted to play with him, the duckling thought they would do him some harm; so he started up in terror, fluttered into the milk-pan, and splashed the milk about the room. Then the woman clapped her hands, which frightened him still more. He flew first into the butter-cask, then into the meal-tub, and out again. What a condition he was in! The woman screamed, and struck at him with the tongs; the children laughed and screamed, and tumbled over each other, in their efforts to catch him; but luckily he escaped. The door stood open; the poor creature could just manage to slip out among the bushes, and lie down quite exhausted in the newly fallen snow.

It would be very sad, were I to relate all the misery and privations which the poor little duckling endured during the hard winter; but when it had passed, he found himself lying one morning in a moor, amongst the rushes. He felt the warm sun shining, and heard the lark singing, and saw that all around was beautiful spring. Then the young bird felt that his wings were strong, as he flapped them against his sides, and rose high into the air. They bore him onwards, until he found himself in a large garden, before he well knew how it had happened. The apple-trees were in full blossom, and the fragrant elders bent their long green branches down to the stream which wound round a smooth lawn. Everything looked beautiful, in the freshness of early spring. From a thicket close by came three beautiful white swans, rustling their feathers, and swimming lightly over the smooth water. The duckling remembered the lovely birds, and felt more strangely unhappy than ever.

"I will fly to those royal birds," he exclaimed, "and they will kill me, because I am so ugly, and dare to approach them; but it does not matter: better be killed by them than pecked by the ducks, beaten by the hens, pushed about by the maiden who feeds the poultry, or starved with hunger in the winter."

Then he flew to the water, and swam towards the beautiful swans. The moment they espied the stranger, they rushed to meet him with outstretched wings.

"Kill me," said the poor bird; and he bent his head down to the surface of the water, and awaited death.

But what did he see in the clear stream below? His own image; no longer a dark, grey bird, ugly and disagreeable to look at, but a graceful and beautiful swan. To be born in a duck's nest, in a farmyard, is of no consequence to a bird, if it is hatched from a swan's egg. He now felt glad at having suffered sorrow and trouble, because it enabled him to enjoy so much better all the pleasure and happiness around him; for the great swans swam round the new-comer, and stroked his neck with their beaks, as a welcome.

Into the garden presently came some little children, and threw bread and cake into the water.

"See," cried the youngest, "there is a new one;" and the rest were delighted, and ran to their father and mother, dancing and clapping their hands, and shouting joyously, "There is another swan come; a new one has arrived."

Then they threw more bread and cake into the water, and said, "The new one is the most beautiful of all; he is so young and pretty."

And the old swans bowed their heads before him.

Then he felt quite ashamed, and hid his head under his wing; for he did not know what to do, he was so happy, and yet not at all proud. He had been persecuted and despised for his ugliness, and now he heard them say he was the most beautiful of all the birds. Even the elder-tree bent down its bows into the water before him, and the sun shone warm and bright. Then he rustled his feathers, curved his slender neck, and cried joyfully, from the depths of his heart, “I never dreamed of such happiness as this, while I was an ugly duckling.”

THE LITTLE MERMAID

Far out in the ocean, where the water is as blue as the prettiest cornflower, and as clear as crystal, it is very, very deep; so deep, indeed, that no cable could fathom it: many church steeples, piled one upon another, would not reach from the ground beneath to the surface of the water above. There dwell the Sea King and his subjects. We must not imagine that there is nothing at the bottom of the sea but bare yellow sand. No, indeed; the most singular flowers and plants grow there; the leaves and stems of which are so pliant, that the slightest agitation of the water causes them to stir as if they had life. Fishes, both large and small, glide between the branches, as birds fly among the trees here upon land. In the deepest spot of all, stands the castle of the Sea King. Its walls are built of coral, and the long, gothic windows are of the clearest amber. The roof is formed of shells, that open and close as the water flows over them. Their appearance is very beautiful, for in each lies a glittering pearl, which would be fit for the diadem of a queen.

The Sea King had been a widower for many years, and his aged mother kept house for him. She was a very wise woman, and exceedingly proud of her high birth; on that account she wore twelve oysters on her tail; while others, also of high rank, were only allowed to wear six. She was, however, deserving of very great praise, especially for her care of the little sea-princesses, her grand-daughters. They were six beautiful children; but the youngest was the prettiest of them all; her skin was as clear and delicate as a rose-leaf, and her eyes as blue as the deepest sea; but, like all the others, she had no feet, and her body ended in a fish's tail. All day long they played in the great halls of the castle, or among the living flowers that grew out of the walls. The large amber windows were open, and the fish swam in, just as the swallows fly into our houses when we open the windows, excepting that the fishes swam up to the princesses, ate out of their hands, and allowed themselves to be stroked. Outside the castle there was a beautiful garden, in which grew bright red and dark blue flowers, and blossoms like flames of fire; the fruit glittered like gold, and the leaves and stems waved to and fro continually. The earth itself was the finest sand, but blue as the flame of burning sulphur. Over everything lay a peculiar blue radiance, as if it were surrounded by the air from above, through which the blue sky shone, instead of the dark depths of the sea. In calm weather the sun could be seen, looking like a purple flower, with the light streaming from the calyx.

Each of the young princesses had a little plot of ground in the garden, where she might dig and plant as she pleased. One arranged her flower-bed into the form of a whale; another thought it better to make hers like the figure of a little mermaid; but that of the youngest was round like the sun, and contained flowers as red as his rays at sunset. She was a strange child, quiet and thoughtful; and while her sisters would be delighted with the wonderful things which they obtained from the wrecks of vessels, she cared for nothing but her pretty red flowers, like the sun, excepting a beautiful marble statue. It was the representation of a handsome boy, carved out of pure white stone, which had fallen to the bottom of the sea from a wreck. She planted by the statue a rose-coloured weeping willow. It grew splendidly, and very soon hung its fresh branches over the statue, almost down to the blue sands. The shadow had a violet tint, and waved to and fro like the branches; it seemed as if the crown of the tree and the root were at play, and trying to kiss each other.

Nothing gave her so much pleasure as to hear about the world above the sea. She made her old grandmother tell her all she knew of the ships and of the towns, the people and the animals. To her it seemed most wonderful and beautiful to hear that the flowers of the land should have fragrance, and not those below the sea; that the trees of the forest should be green; and that the fishes among the trees could sing so sweetly, that it was quite a pleasure to hear them. Her grandmother called the little birds fishes, or she would not have understood her; for she had never seen birds.

"When you have reached your fifteenth year," said the grand-mother, "you will have permission to rise up out of the sea, to sit on the rocks in the moonlight, while the great ships are sailing by; and then you will see both forests and towns."

In the following year, one of the sisters would be fifteen: but as each was a year younger than the other, the youngest would have to wait five years before her turn came to rise up from the bottom of the ocean, and see the earth as we do. However, each promised to tell the others what she saw on her first visit, and what she thought the most beautiful; for their grandmother could not tell them enough; there were so many things on which they wanted information. None of them longed so much for her turn to come as the youngest, she who had the longest time to wait, and who was so quiet and thoughtful. Many nights she stood by the open window, looking up through the dark blue water, and watching the fish as they splashed about with their fins and tails. She could see the moon and stars shining faintly; but through the water they looked larger than they do to our eyes. When something like a black cloud passed between her and them, she knew that it was either a whale swimming over her head, or a ship full of human beings, who never imagined that a pretty little mermaid was standing beneath them, holding out her white hands towards the keel of their ship.

As soon as the eldest was fifteen, she was allowed to rise to the surface of the ocean. When she came back, she had hundreds of things to talk about; but the most beautiful, she said, was to lie in the moonlight, on a sandbank, in the quiet sea, near the coast, and to gaze on a large town nearby, where the lights were twinkling like hundreds of stars; to listen to the sounds of the music, the noise of carriages, and the voices of human beings, and then to hear the merry bells peal out from the church steeples; and because she could not go near to all those wonderful things, she longed for them more than ever. Oh, did not the youngest sister listen eagerly to all these descriptions? and afterwards, when she stood at the open window looking up through the dark blue water, she thought of the great city, with all its bustle and noise, and even fancied she could hear the sound of the church bells, down in the depths of the sea.

In another year the second sister received permission to rise to the surface of the water, and to swim about where she pleased. She rose just as the sun was setting, and this, she said, was the most beautiful sight of all. The whole sky looked like gold, while violet and rose-coloured clouds, which she could not describe, floated over her; and, still more rapidly than the clouds, flew a large flock of wild swans towards the setting sun, looking like a long white veil across the sea. She also swam towards the sun; but it sunk into the waves, and the rosy tints faded from the clouds and from the sea.

The third sister's turn followed; she was the boldest of them all, and she swam up a broad river that emptied itself into the sea. On the banks she saw green hills covered with beautiful vines; palaces and castles peeped out from amid the proud trees of the forest; she heard the birds singing, and the rays of the sun were so powerful that she was obliged often to dive down under the water to cool her burning face. In a narrow creek she found a whole troop of little human children, quite naked, and sporting about in the water; she wanted to play with them, but they fled in a great fright; and then a little black animal came to the water; it was a dog, but she did not know that, for she had never before seen one. This animal barked at her so terribly that she became frightened, and rushed back to the open sea. But she said she should never forget the beautiful forest, the green hills, and the pretty little children who could swim in the water, although they had not fish's tails.

The fourth sister was more timid; she remained in the midst of the sea, but she said it was quite as beautiful there as nearer the land. She could see for so many miles around her, and the sky above looked like a bell of glass. She had seen the ships, but at such a great distance that they looked like sea-gulls. The dolphins sported in the waves, and the great whales spouted water from their nostrils till it seemed as if a hundred fountains were playing in every direction.

The fifth sister's birthday occurred in the winter; so when her turn came, she saw what the others had not seen the first time they went up. The sea looked quite green, and large icebergs were floating about, each like a pearl, she said, but larger and loftier than the churches built by men. They were of the most singular shapes, and glittered like diamonds. She had seated herself upon one of the largest, and let the wind play with her long hair, and she remarked that all the ships sailed by rapidly, and steered as far away as they could from the iceberg, as if they were afraid of it. Towards evening, as the sun went down, dark clouds covered the sky, the thunder rolled and the lightning flashed, and the red light glowed on the icebergs as they rocked and tossed on the heaving sea. On all the ships the sails were reefed with fear and trembling, while she sat calmly on the floating iceberg, watching the blue lightning, as it darted its forked flashes into the sea.

When first the sisters had permission to rise to the surface, they were each delighted with the new and beautiful sights they saw; but now, as grown-up girls, they could go when they pleased, and they had become indifferent about it. They wished themselves back again in the water, and after a month had passed they said it was much more beautiful down below, and pleasanter to be at home. Yet often, in the evening hours, the five sisters would twine their arms round each other, and rise to the surface, in a row. They had more beautiful voices than any human being could have; and before the approach of a storm, and when they expected a ship would be lost, they swam before the vessel, and sang sweetly of the delights to be found in the depths of the sea, and begging the sailors not to fear if they sank to the bottom. But the sailors could not understand the song, they took it for the howling of the storm. And these things were never to be beautiful for them; for if the ship sank, the men were drowned, and their dead bodies alone reached the palace of the Sea King.

When the sisters rose, arm-in-arm, through the water in this way, their youngest sister would stand quite alone, looking after them, ready to cry, only that the mermaids have no tears, and therefore they suffer more. "Oh, were I but fifteen years old," said she: "I know that I shall love the world up there, and all the people who live in it."

At last she reached her fifteenth year. "Well, now, you are grown up," said the old dowager, her grandmother; "so you must let me adorn you like your other sisters;" and she placed a wreath of white lilies in her hair, and every flower leaf was half a pearl. Then the old lady ordered eight great oysters to attach themselves to the tail of the princess to show her high rank.

"But they hurt me so," said the little mermaid.

"Pride must suffer pain," replied the old lady. Oh, how gladly she would have shaken off all this grandeur, and laid aside the heavy wreath! The red flowers in her own garden would have suited her much better, but she could not help herself: so she said, "Farewell," and rose as lightly as a bubble to the surface of the water. The sun had just set as she raised her head above the waves; but the clouds were tinted with crimson and gold, and through the glimmering twilight beamed the evening star in all its beauty. The sea was calm, and the air mild and fresh. A large ship, with three masts, lay becalmed on the water, with only one sail set; for not a breeze stiffed, and the sailors sat idle on deck or amongst the rigging. There was music and song on board; and, as darkness came on, a hundred coloured lanterns were lighted, as if the flags of all nations waved in the air. The little mermaid swam close to the cabin windows; and now and then, as the waves lifted her up, she could look in through clear glass window-panes, and see a number of well-dressed people within. Among them was a young prince, the most beautiful of all, with large black eyes; he was sixteen years of age, and his birthday was being kept with much rejoicing. The sailors were dancing on deck, but when the prince came out of the cabin, more than a hundred rockets rose in the air, making it as bright as day. The little mermaid was so startled that she dived under water; and when she again stretched out her head, it appeared as if all the stars of heaven were falling around her, she had never seen such fireworks before. Great suns spurted fire about, splendid fireflies flew into the blue air, and everything was reflected in the clear, calm sea beneath. The ship itself was so brightly illuminated that all the people, and even the smallest rope, could be distinctly and plainly seen. And how handsome the young prince looked, as he pressed the hands of all present and smiled at them, while the music resounded through the clear night air.

It was very late; yet the little mermaid could not take her eyes from the ship, or from the beautiful prince. The coloured lanterns had been extinguished, no more rockets rose in the air, and the cannon had ceased firing; but the sea became restless, and a moaning, grumbling sound could be heard beneath the waves: still the little mermaid remained by the cabin window, rocking up and down on the water, which enabled her to look in. After a while, the sails were quickly unfurled, and the noble ship continued her passage; but soon the waves rose higher, heavy clouds darkened the sky, and lightning appeared in the distance. A dreadful storm was approaching; once more the sails were reefed, and the great ship pursued her flying course over the raging sea. The waves rose mountains high, as if they would have overtopped the mast; but the ship dived like a swan between them, and then rose again on their lofty, foaming crests. To the little mermaid this appeared pleasant sport; not so to the sailors. At length the ship groaned and creaked; the thick planks gave way under the lashing of the sea as it broke over the deck; the mainmast snapped asunder like a reed; the ship lay over on her side; and the water rushed in. The little mermaid now perceived that the crew were in danger; even she herself was obliged to be careful to avoid the beams and planks of the wreck which lay scattered on the water. At one moment it was so pitch dark that she could not see a single object, but a flash of lightning revealed the whole scene; she could see every one who had been on board excepting the prince; when the ship parted, she had seen him sink into the deep waves, and she was glad, for she thought he would now be with her; and then she remembered that human beings could not live in the water, so that when he got down to her father's palace he would be quite dead. But he must not die. So she swam about among the beams and planks which strewed the surface of the sea, forgetting that they could crush her to pieces. Then she dived deeply under the dark waters, rising and falling with the waves, till at length she managed to reach the young prince, who was fast losing the power of swimming in that stormy sea. His limbs were failing him, his beautiful eyes were closed, and he would have died had not the little mermaid come to his assistance. She held his head above the water, and let the waves drift them where they would.

In the morning the storm had ceased; but of the ship not a single fragment could be seen. The sun rose up red and glowing from the water, and its beams brought back the hue of health to the prince's cheeks; but his eyes remained closed. The mermaid kissed his high, smooth forehead, and stroked back his wet hair; he seemed to her like the marble statue in her little garden, and she kissed him again, and wished that he might live.

Presently they came in sight of land; she saw lofty blue mountains, on which the white snow rested as if a flock of swans were lying upon them. Near the coast were beautiful green forests, and close by stood a large building, whether a church or a convent she could not tell. Orange and citron trees grew in the garden, and before the door stood lofty palms. The sea here formed a little bay, in which the water was quite still, but very deep; so she swam with the handsome prince to the beach, which was covered with fine, white sand, and there she laid him in the warm sunshine, taking care to raise his head higher than his body.

Then bells sounded in the large white building, and a number of young girls came into the garden. The little mermaid swam out farther from the shore and placed herself between some high rocks that rose out of the water; then she covered her head and neck with the foam of the sea so that her little face might not be seen, and watched to see what would become of the poor prince.

She did not wait long before she saw a young girl approach the spot where he lay. She seemed frightened at first, but only for a moment; then she fetched a number of people, and the mermaid saw that the prince came to life again, and smiled upon those who stood round him. But to her he sent no smile; he knew not that she had saved him. This made her very unhappy, and when he was led away into the great building, she dived down sorrowfully into the water, and returned to her father's castle.

She had always been silent and thoughtful, and now she was more so than ever. Her sisters asked her what she had seen during her first visit to the surface of the water; but she would tell them nothing.

Many an evening and morning did she rise to the place where she had left the prince. She saw the fruits in the garden ripen till they were gathered, the snow on the tops of the mountains melt away; but she never saw the prince, and therefore she returned home, always more sorrowful than before. It was her only comfort to sit in her own little garden, and fling her arm round the beautiful marble statue which was like the prince; but she gave up tending her flowers, and they grew in wild confusion over the paths, twining their long leaves and stems round the branches of the trees, so that the whole place became dark and gloomy.

At length she could bear it no longer, and told one of her sisters all about it. Then the others heard the secret, and very soon it became known to two mermaids whose intimate friend happened to know who the prince was. She had also seen the festival on board ship, and she told them where the prince came from, and where his palace stood.

"Come, little sister," said the other princesses; then they entwined their arms and rose up in a long row to the surface of the water, close by the spot where they knew the prince's palace stood. It was built of bright yellow shining stone, with long flights of marble steps, one of which reached quite down to the sea. Splendid gilded cupolas rose over the roof, and between the pillars that surrounded the whole building stood life-like statues of marble. Through the clear crystal of the lofty windows could be seen noble rooms, with costly silk curtains and hangings of tapestry; while the walls were covered with beautiful paintings which were a pleasure to look at. In the centre of the largest saloon a fountain threw its sparkling jets high up into the glass cupola of the ceiling, through which the sun shone down upon the water and upon the beautiful plants growing round the basin of the fountain.

Now that she knew where he lived, she spent many an evening and many a night on the water near the palace. She would swim much nearer the shore than any of the others ventured to do; indeed once she went quite up the narrow channel under the marble balcony, which threw a broad shadow on the water. Here she would sit and watch the young prince, who thought himself quite alone in the bright moonlight. She saw him many times of an evening sailing in a pleasant boat, with music playing and flags waving. She peeped out from among the green rushes, and if the wind caught her long silvery-white veil, those who saw it believed it to be a swan, spreading out its wings. On many a night, too, when the fishermen, with their torches, were out at sea, she heard them relate so many good things about the doings of the young prince, that she was glad she had saved his life when he had been tossed about half-dead on the waves. And she remembered that his head had rested on her bosom, and how heartily she had kissed him; but he knew nothing of all this, and could not even dream of her.

She grew more and more fond of human beings, and wished more and more to be able to wander about with those whose world seemed to be so much larger than her own. They could fly over the sea in ships, and mount the high hills which were far above the clouds; and the lands they possessed, their woods and their fields, stretched far away beyond the reach of her sight. There was so much that she wished to know, and her sisters were unable to answer all her questions. Then she applied to her old grandmother, who knew all about the upper world, which she very rightly called the lands above the sea.

"If human beings are not drowned," asked the little mermaid, "can they live forever? do they never die as we do here in the sea?"

"Yes," replied the old lady, "they must also die, and their term of life is even shorter than ours. We sometimes live to three hundred years, but when we cease to exist here we only become the foam on the surface of the water, and we have not even a grave down here of those we love. We have not immortal souls, we shall never live again; but, like the green sea-weed, when once it has been cut off, we can never flourish more. Human beings, on the contrary, have a soul which lives forever, lives after the body has been turned to dust. It rises up through the clear, pure air beyond the glittering stars. As we rise out of the water, and behold all the land of the earth, so do they rise to unknown and glorious regions which we shall never see."

"Why have not we an immortal soul?" asked the little mermaid mournfully; "I would give gladly all the hundreds of years that I have to live, to be a human being only for one day, and to have the hope of knowing the happiness of that glorious world above the stars."

"You must not think of that," said the old woman; "we feel ourselves to be much happier and much better off than human beings."

"So I shall die," said the little mermaid, "and as the foam of the sea I shall be driven about never again to hear the music of the waves, or to see the pretty flowers nor the red sun. Is there anything I can do to win an immortal soul?"

"No," said the old woman, "unless a man were to love you so much that you were more to him than his father or mother; and if all his thoughts and all his love were fixed upon you, and the priest placed his right hand in yours, and he promised to be true to you here and hereafter, then his soul would glide into your body and you would obtain a share in the future happiness of mankind. He would give a soul to you and retain his own as well; but this can never happen. Your fish's tail, which amongst us is considered so beautiful, is thought on earth to be quite ugly; they do not know any better, and they think it necessary to have two stout props, which they call legs, in order to be handsome."

Then the little mermaid sighed, and looked sorrowfully at her fish's tail. "Let us be happy," said the old lady, "and dart and spring about during the three hundred years that we have to live, which is really quite long enough; after that we can rest ourselves all the better. This evening we are going to have a court ball."

It is one of those splendid sights which we can never see on earth. The walls and the ceiling of the large ball-room were of thick, but transparent crystal. May hundreds of colossal shells, some of a deep red, others of a grass green, stood on each side in rows, with blue fire in them, which lighted up the whole saloon, and shone through the walls, so that the sea was also illuminated. Innumerable fishes, great and small, swam past the crystal walls; on some of them the scales glowed with a purple brilliancy, and on others they shone like silver and gold.

Through the halls flowed a broad stream, and in it danced the mermen and the mermaids to the music of their own sweet singing. No one on earth has such a lovely voice as theirs. The little mermaid sang more sweetly than them all. The whole court applauded her with hands and tails; and for a moment her heart felt quite gay, for she knew she had the loveliest voice of any on earth or in the sea. But she soon thought again of the world above her, for she could not forget the charming prince, nor her sorrow that she had not an immortal soul like his; therefore she crept away silently out of her father's palace, and while everything within was gladness and song, she sat in her own little garden sorrowful and alone. Then she heard the bugle sounding through the water, and thought—"He is certainly sailing above, he on whom my wishes depend, and in whose hands I should like to place the happiness of my life. I will venture all for him, and to win an immortal soul, while my sisters are dancing in my father's palace, I will go to the sea witch, of whom I have always been so much afraid, but she can give me counsel and help."

And then the little mermaid went out from her garden, and took the road to the foaming whirlpools, behind which the sorceress lived. She had never been that way before: neither flowers nor grass grew there; nothing but bare, grey, sandy ground stretched out to the whirlpool, where the water, like foaming mill-wheels, whirled round everything that it seized, and cast it into the fathomless deep. Through the midst of these crushing whirlpools the little mermaid was obliged to pass, to reach the dominions of the sea witch; and also for a long distance the only road lay right across a quantity of warm, bubbling mire, called by the witch her turfmoor. Beyond this stood her house, in the centre of a strange forest, in which all the trees and flowers were polypi, half animals and half plants; they looked like serpents with a hundred heads growing out of the ground. The branches were long slimy arms, with fingers like flexible worms, moving limb after limb from the root to the top. All that could be reached in the sea they seized upon, and held fast, so that it never escaped from their clutches. The little mermaid was so alarmed at what she saw, that she stood still, and her heart beat with fear, and she was very nearly turning back; but she thought of the prince, and of the human soul for which she longed, and her courage returned. She fastened her long flowing hair round her head, so that the polypi might not seize hold of it. She laid her hands together across her bosom, and then she darted forward as a fish shoots through the water, between the supple arms and fingers of the ugly polypi, which were stretched out on each side of her. She saw that each held in its grasp something it had seized with its numerous little arms, as if they were iron bands. The white skeletons of human beings who had perished at sea, and had sunk down into the deep waters, skeletons of land animals, oars, rudders, and chests of ships were lying tightly grasped by their clinging arms; even a little mermaid, whom they had caught and strangled; and this seemed the most shocking of all to the little princess.

She now came to a space of marshy ground in the wood, where large, fat water-snakes were rolling in the mire, and showing their ugly, drab-coloured bodies. In the midst of this spot stood a house, built with the bones of shipwrecked human beings. There sat the sea witch, allowing a toad to eat from her mouth, just as people sometimes feed a canary with a piece of sugar. She called the ugly water-snakes her little chickens, and allowed them to crawl all over her bosom.

"I know what you want," said the sea witch; "it is very stupid of you, but you shall have your way, and it will bring you to sorrow, my pretty princess. You want to get rid of your fish's tail, and to have two supports instead of it, like human beings on earth, so that the young prince may fall in love with you, and that you may have an immortal soul."

And then the witch laughed so loud and disgustingly, that the toad and the snakes fell to the ground, and lay there wriggling about. "You are but just in time," said the witch; "for after sunrise tomorrow I should not be able to help you till the end of another year. I will prepare a draught for you, with which you must swim to land tomorrow before sunrise, and sit down on the shore and drink it. Your tail will then disappear, and shrink up into what mankind calls legs, and you will feel great pain, as if a sword were passing through you. But all who see you will say that you are the prettiest little human being they ever saw. You will still have the same floating gracefulness of movement, and no dancer will ever tread so lightly; but at every step you take it will feel as if you were treading upon sharp knives, and that the blood must flow. If you will bear all this, I will help you."

"Yes, I will," said the little princess in a trembling voice, as she thought of the prince and the immortal soul.

"But think again," said the witch; "for when once your shape has become like a human being, you can no more be a mermaid. You will never return through the water to your sisters, or to your father's palace again; and if you do not win the love of the prince, so that he is willing to forget his father and mother for your sake, and to love you with his whole soul, and allow the priest to join your hands that you may be man and wife, then you will never have an immortal soul. The first morning after he marries another your heart will break, and you will become foam on the crest of the waves."

"I will do it," said the little mermaid, and she became pale as death.

"But I must be paid also," said the witch, "and it is not a trifle that I ask. You have the sweetest voice of any who dwell here in the depths of the sea, and you believe that you will be able to charm the prince with it also, but this voice you must give to me; the best thing you possess will I have for the price of my draught. My own blood must be mixed with it, that it may be as sharp as a two-edged sword."

"But if you take away my voice," said the little mermaid, "what is left for me?"

"Your beautiful form, your graceful walk, and your expressive eyes; surely with these you can enchain a man's heart. Well, have you lost your courage? Put out your little tongue that I may cut it off as my payment; then you shall have the powerful draught."

"It shall be," said the little mermaid.

Then the witch placed her cauldron on the fire, to prepare the magic draught.

"Cleanliness is a good thing," said she, scouring the vessel with snakes, which she had tied together in a large knot; then she pricked herself in the breast, and let the black blood drop into it. The steam that rose formed itself into such horrible shapes that no one could look at them without fear. Every moment the witch threw something else into the vessel, and when it began to boil, the sound was like the weeping of a crocodile. When at last the magic draught was ready, it looked like the clearest water. "There it is for you," said the witch. Then she cut off the mermaid's tongue, so that she became dumb, and would never again speak or sing. "If the polypi should seize hold of you as you return through the wood," said the witch, "throw over them a few drops of the potion, and their fingers will be torn into a thousand pieces."

But the little mermaid had no occasion to do this, for the polypi sprang back in terror when they caught sight of the glittering draught, which shone in her hand like a twinkling star.

So she passed quickly through the wood and the marsh, and between the rushing whirlpools. She saw that in her father's palace the torches in the ballroom were extinguished, and all within asleep; but she did not venture to go in to them, for now she was dumb and going to leave them forever, she felt as if her heart would break. She stole into the garden, took a flower from the flower-beds of each of her sisters, kissed her hand a thousand times towards the palace, and then rose up through the dark blue waters. The sun had not risen when she came in sight of the prince's palace, and approached the beautiful marble steps, but the moon shone clear and bright. Then the little mermaid drank the magic draught, and it seemed as if a two-edged sword went through her delicate body: she fell into a swoon, and lay like one dead. When the sun arose and shone over the sea, she recovered, and felt a sharp pain; but just before her stood the handsome young prince. He fixed his coal-black eyes upon her so earnestly that she cast down her own, and then became aware that her fish's tail was gone, and that she had as pretty a pair of white legs and tiny feet as any little maiden could have; but she had no clothes, so she wrapped herself in her long, thick hair. The prince asked her who she was, and where she came from, and she looked at him mildly and sorrowfully with her deep blue eyes; but she could not speak. Every step she took was as the witch had said it would be, she felt as if treading upon the points of needles or sharp knives; but she bore it willingly, and stepped as lightly by the prince's side as a soap-bubble, so that he and all who saw her wondered at her graceful-swaying movements. She was very soon arrayed in costly robes of silk and muslin, and was the most beautiful creature in the palace; but she was dumb, and could neither speak nor sing.

Beautiful female slaves, dressed in silk and gold, stepped forward and sang before the prince and his royal parents: one sang better than all the others, and the prince clapped his hands and smiled at her. This was great sorrow to the little mermaid; she knew how much more sweetly she herself could sing once, and she thought, "Oh if he could only know that! I have given away my voice forever, to be with him."

The slaves next performed some pretty fairy-like dances, to the sound of beautiful music. Then the little mermaid raised her lovely white arms, stood on the tips of her toes, and glided over the floor, and danced as no one yet had been able to dance. At each moment her beauty became more revealed, and her expressive eyes appealed more directly to the heart than the songs of the slaves. Every one was enchanted, especially the prince, who called her his little foundling; and she danced again quite readily, to please him, though each time her foot touched the floor it seemed as if she trod on sharp knives.

The prince said she should remain with him always, and she received permission to sleep at his door, on a velvet cushion. He had a page's dress made for her, that she might accompany him on horseback. They rode together through the sweet-scented woods, where the green boughs touched their shoulders, and the little birds sang among the fresh leaves. She climbed with the prince to the tops of high mountains; and although her tender feet bled so that even her steps were marked, she only laughed, and followed him till they could see the clouds beneath them looking like a flock of birds travelling to distant lands. While at the prince's palace, and when all the household were asleep, she would go and sit on the broad marble steps; for it eased her burning feet to bathe them in the cold sea-water; and then she thought of all those below in the deep.

Once during the night her sisters came up arm-in-arm, singing sorrowfully, as they floated on the water. She beckoned to them, and then they recognized her, and told her how she had grieved them. After that, they came to the same place every night; and once she saw in the distance her old grandmother, who had not been to the surface of the sea for many years, and the old Sea King, her father, with his crown on his head. They stretched out their hands towards her, but they did not venture so near the land as her sisters did.

As the days passed, she loved the prince more fondly, and he loved her as he would love a little child, but it never came into his head to make her his wife; yet, unless he married her, she could not receive an immortal soul; and, on the morning after his marriage with another, she would dissolve into the foam of the sea.

"Do you not love me the best of them all?" the eyes of the little mermaid seemed to say, when he took her in his arms, and kissed her fair forehead.

"Yes, you are dear to me," said the prince; "for you have the best heart, and you are the most devoted to me; you are like a young maiden whom I once saw, but whom I shall never meet again. I was in a ship that was wrecked, and the waves cast me ashore near a holy temple, where several young maidens performed the service. The youngest of them found me on the shore, and saved my life. I saw her but twice, and she is the only one in the world whom I could love; but you are like her, and you have almost driven her image out of my mind. She belongs to the holy temple, and my good fortune has sent you to me instead of her; and we will never part."

"Ah, he knows not that it was I who saved his life," thought the little mermaid. "I carried him over the sea to the wood where the temple stands: I sat beneath the foam, and watched till the human beings came to help him. I saw the pretty maiden that he loves better than he loves me;" and the mermaid sighed deeply, but she could not shed tears. "He says the maiden belongs to the holy temple, therefore she will never return to the world. They will meet no more: while I am by his side, and see him every day. I will take care of him, and love him, and give up my life for his sake."

Very soon it was said that the prince must marry, and that the beautiful daughter of a neighboring king would be his wife, for a fine ship was being fitted out. Although the prince gave out that he merely intended to pay a visit to the king, it was generally supposed that he really went to see his daughter. A great company were to go with him. The little mermaid smiled, and shook her head. She knew the prince's thoughts better than any of the others.

"I must travel," he had said to her; "I must see this beautiful princess; my parents desire it; but they will not oblige me to bring her home as my bride. I cannot love her; she is not like the beautiful maiden in the temple, whom you resemble. If I were forced to choose a bride, I would rather choose you, my dumb foundling, with those expressive eyes."

And then he kissed her rosy mouth, played with her long waving hair, and laid his head on her heart, while she dreamed of human happiness and an immortal soul. "You are not afraid of the sea, my dumb child," said he, as they stood on the deck of the noble ship which was to carry them to the country of the neighboring king. And then he told her of storm and of calm, of strange fishes in the deep beneath them, and of what the divers had seen there; and she smiled at his descriptions, for she knew better than any one what wonders were at the bottom of the sea.

In the moonlight, when all on board were asleep, excepting the man at the helm, who was steering, she sat on the deck, gazing down through the clear water. She thought she could distinguish her father's castle, and upon it her aged grandmother, with the silver crown on her head, looking through the rushing tide at the keel of the vessel. Then her sisters came up on the waves, and gazed at her mournfully, wringing their white hands. She beckoned to them, and smiled, and wanted to tell them how happy and well off she was; but the cabin boy approached, and when her sisters dived down he thought it was only the foam of the sea which he saw.

The next morning the ship sailed into the harbor of a beautiful town belonging to the king whom the prince was going to visit. The church bells were ringing, and from the high towers sounded a flourish of trumpets; and soldiers, with flying colours and glittering bayonets, lined the rocks through which they passed. Every day was a festival; balls and entertainments followed one another.

But the princess had not yet appeared. People said that she was being brought up and educated in a religious house, where she was learning every royal virtue. At last she came. Then the little mermaid, who was very anxious to see whether she was really beautiful, was obliged to acknowledge that she had never seen a more perfect vision of beauty. Her skin was delicately fair, and beneath her long dark eyelashes her laughing blue eyes shone with truth and purity.

"It was you," said the prince, "who saved my life when I lay dead on the beach," and he folded his blushing bride in his arms. "Oh, I am too happy," said he to the little mermaid; "my fondest hopes are all fulfilled. You will rejoice at my happiness; for your devotion to me is great and sincere."

The little mermaid kissed his hand, and felt as if her heart were already broken. His wedding morning would bring death to her, and she would change into the foam of the sea. All the church bells rung, and the heralds rode about the town proclaiming the betrothal. Perfumed oil was burning in costly silver lamps on every altar. The priests waved the censers, while the bride and bridegroom joined their hands and received the blessing of the bishop. The little mermaid, dressed in silk and gold, held up the bride's train; but her ears heard nothing of the festive music, and her eyes saw not the holy ceremony; she thought of the night of death which was coming to her, and of all she had lost in the world.

On the same evening the bride and bridegroom went on board ship; cannons were roaring, flags waving, and in the centre of the ship a costly tent of purple and gold had been erected. It contained elegant couches, for the reception of the bridal pair during the night. The ship, with swelling sails and a favorable wind, glided away smoothly and lightly over the calm sea. When it grew dark a number of coloured lamps were lit, and the sailors danced merrily on the deck. The little mermaid could not help thinking of her first rising out of the sea, when she had seen similar festivities and joys; and she joined in the dance, poised herself in the air as a swallow when he pursues his prey, and all present cheered her with wonder. She had never danced so elegantly before. Her tender feet felt as if cut with sharp knives, but she cared not for it; a sharper pang had pierced through her heart. She knew this was the last evening she should ever see the prince, for whom she had forsaken her kindred and her home; she had given up her beautiful voice, and suffered unheard-of pain daily for him, while he knew nothing of it. This was the last evening that she would breathe the same air with him, or gaze on the starry sky and the deep sea; an eternal night, without a thought or a dream, awaited her: she had no soul and now she could never win one. All was joy and gaiety on board ship till long after midnight; she laughed and danced with the rest, while the thoughts of death were in her heart. The prince kissed his beautiful bride, while she played with his raven hair, till they went arm-in-arm to rest in the splendid tent. Then all became still on board the ship; the helmsman, alone awake, stood at the helm. The little mermaid leaned her white arms on the edge of the vessel, and looked towards the east for the first blush of morning, for that first ray of dawn that would bring her death. She saw her sisters rising out of the flood: they were as pale as herself; but their long beautiful hair waved no more in the wind, and had been cut off.

"We have given our hair to the witch," said they, "to obtain help for you, that you may not die to-night. She has given us a knife: here it is, see it is very sharp. Before the sun rises you must plunge it into the heart of the prince; when the warm blood falls upon your feet they will grow together again, and form into a fish's tail, and you will be once more a mermaid, and return to us to live out your three hundred years before you die and change into the salt sea foam. Haste, then; he or you must die before sunrise. Our old grandmother moans so for you, that her white hair is falling off from sorrow, as ours fell under the witch's scissors. Kill the prince and come back; hasten: do you not see the first red streaks in the sky? In a few minutes the sun will rise, and you must die."

And then they sighed deeply and mournfully, and sank down beneath the waves.

The little mermaid drew back the crimson curtain of the tent, and beheld the fair bride with her head resting on the prince's breast. She bent down and kissed his fair brow, then looked at the sky on which the rosy dawn grew brighter and brighter; then she glanced at the sharp knife, and again fixed her eyes on the prince, who whispered the name of his bride in his dreams. She was in his thoughts, and the knife trembled in the hand of the little mermaid: then she flung it far away from her into the waves; the water turned red where it fell, and the drops that spurted up looked like blood. She cast one more lingering, half-fainting glance at the prince, and then threw herself from the ship into the sea, and thought her body was dissolving into foam. The sun rose above the waves, and his warm rays fell on the cold foam of the little mermaid, who did not feel as if she were dying. She saw the bright sun, and all around her floated hundreds of transparent beautiful beings; she could see through them the white sails of the ship, and the red clouds in the sky; their speech was melodious, but too ethereal to be heard by mortal ears, as they were also unseen by mortal eyes. The little mermaid perceived that she had a body like theirs, and that she continued to rise higher and higher out of the foam. "Where am I?" asked she, and her voice sounded ethereal, as the voice of those who were with her; no earthly music could imitate it.

"Among the daughters of the air," answered one of them. "A

mermaid has not an immortal soul, nor can she obtain one unless she wins the love of a human being. On the power of another hangs her eternal destiny. But the daughters of the air, although they do not possess an immortal soul, can, by their good deeds, procure one for themselves. We fly to warm countries, and cool the sultry air that destroys mankind with the pestilence. We carry the perfume of the flowers to spread health and restoration. After we have striven for three hundred years to all the good in our power, we receive an immortal soul and take part in the happiness of mankind. You, poor little mermaid, have tried with your whole heart to do as we are doing; you have suffered and endured and raised yourself to the spirit-world by your good deeds; and now, by striving for three hundred years in the same way, you may obtain an immortal soul."

The little mermaid lifted her glorified eyes towards the sun, and felt them, for the first time, filling with tears. On the ship, in which she had left the prince, there were life and noise; she saw him and his beautiful bride searching for her; sorrowfully they gazed at the pearly foam, as if they knew she had thrown herself into the waves. Unseen she kissed the forehead of the bride, and fanned the prince, and then mounted with the other children of the air to a rosy cloud that floated through the ether.

"After three hundred years, thus shall we float into the kingdom of heaven," said she. "And we may even get there sooner," whispered one of her companions. "Unseen we can enter the houses of men, where there are children, and for every day on which we find a good child, who is the joy of his parents and deserves their love, our time of probation is shortened. The child does not know, when we fly through the room, that we smile with joy at his good conduct, for we can count one year less of our three hundred years. But when we see a naughty or a wicked child, we shed tears of sorrow, and for every tear a day is added to our time of trial!"

The Flea and the Professor

There was once an aëronaut who suffered a bad accident; the balloon burst, the man tumbled out, and broke into bits. His boy, however, had landed safely with a parachute—that was the boy's luck; he was unhurt and went about with knowledge enough to make him an aëronaut too, but he had no balloon and no means of acquiring one.

But live he must, and so he applied himself to the art of legerdemain and to talking in his stomach; in fact he became a ventriloquist, as they say. He was young, good-looking, and when he got a moustache and had his best clothes on, he could be taken for a nobleman's son. The ladies seemed to think well of him; one young lady even was so taken with his charms and his great dexterity that she went off with him to foreign parts. There he called himself Professor—he could scarcely do less.

His constant thought was how to get himself a balloon and go up into the air with his little wife, but as yet they had no means.

"They'll come yet," said he.

"If only they would," said she.

"We are young folks," said he, "and now I am Professor." She helped him faithfully, sat at the door and sold tickets to the exhibition, and it was a chilly sort of pleasure in winter time. She also helped him in the line of his art. He put his wife in a table-drawer, a large table-drawer; then she crawled into the back part of the drawer, and so was not in the front part—quite an optical illusion to the audience. But one evening when he drew the drawer out, she was also out of sight to him: she was not in the front drawer, not in the back one either, not in the house itself—nowhere to be seen or heard— that was her feat of legerdemain, her entertainment. She never came back again; she was tired of it all, and he grew tired of it, lost his good-humor, could not laugh or make jokes;—and so the people stopped coming, his earnings became scanty, his clothes gave out; and finally he only owned a great flea, which his wife had left him, and so he thought highly of it. And he dressed the flea and taught it to perform, to present arms and to fire a cannon off—but it was a little cannon.

The Professor was proud of the flea, and the flea was proud of himself; he had learned something, and had human blood, and had been besides to the largest cities, had been seen by princes and princesses, had received their high praise, and it was printed in the newspapers and on placards. Plainly it was a very famous flea and could support a Professor and his entire family.

The flea was proud and famous, and yet when he and the Professor traveled they took fourth-class carriages on the railway; they went just as quickly as the first class. They were betrothed to each other; it was a private engagement that would never come out; they never would marry, the flea would remain a bachelor and the Professor a widower. That made it balance.

"Where one has the best luck," said the Professor, "there one ought to go twice." He was a good judge of character, and that is also a science of itself. At last he had traveled over all countries except the wild ones, and so he wanted to go there. They eat Christian men there, to be sure, the Professor knew, but then he was not properly Christian and the flea was not properly a man, so he thought they might venture to travel there and have good success.

They traveled by steamship and by sailing vessel ; the flea performed his tricks, and so they got a free passage on the way and arrived at the wild country. Here reigned a little Princess. She was only eight years old, but she was reigning. She had taken away the power from her father and mother, for she had a will, and she was extraordinarily beautiful—and rude.

Just as soon as the flea had presented arms and fired off the cannon, she was so enraptured with him that she said, "Him or nobody!" She became quite wild with love and was already wild in other ways.

"Sweet, little, sensible child!" said her own father. "If one could only first make a man of him!"

"Leave that to me, old man," said she, and that was not well said by a little Princess when talking with her father, but she was wild. She set the flea on her white hand.

"Now you are a man, reigning with me, but you shall do what I want you to, or else I'll kill you and eat the Professor." The Professor had a great hall to live in. The walls were made of sugar-cane, and he could lick them, but he was not a sweet-tooth. He had a hammock to sleep in. It was as if he were lying in a balloon, such as he had always wished for himself—that was his constant thought.

The flea lived with the Princess, sat upon her delicate hand and upon her white neck. She had taken a hair from her head and made the Professor tie it to the flea's leg, and so she kept him tied to the great red coral drop which she wore in her ear-tip. What a delightful time the Princess had, and the flea too, she thought, but the Professor was not very comfortable. He was a traveler; he liked to drive from town to town, and read about his perseverance and cleverness in teaching a flea to do what men do. But he got out of and into his hammock, lounged about and had good feeding, fresh bird's-eggs, elephant's eyes and roast giraffe. People that eat men do not live entirely on cooked men—no, that is a great delicacy.

"Shoulder of children with sharp sauce," said the Princess's mother, "is the most delicate."

The Professor was tired of it all and would rather go away from the wild land, but he must have his flea with him, for that was his prodigy, and his bread and butter. How was he to get hold of him? That was no easy matter. He strained all his wits, and then he said, "Now I have it."

"Princess's Father! grant me a favor. May I summon your subjects to present themselves before your Royal Highness? That is what is called a Ceremony in the high and mighty countries of the world.

"Can I, too, learn to do that?" asked the Princess's father.

"That is not quite proper," replied the Professor; "but I shall teach your wild Fathership to fire a cannon off. It goes off with a bang. One sits high up aloft, and then off it goes or down he comes."

"Let me crack it off!" said the Princess's father. But in all the land there was no cannon except the one the flea had brought, and that was so very small.

"I will cast a bigger one!" said the Professor. "Only give me the means. I must have fine silk stuff, needle and thread, rope and cord, together with cordial drops for the balloon, they blow one up so easily and give one the heaves; they are what make the report in the cannons inside."

"By all means," said the Princess's father, and gave him what he called for. All the court and the entire population came together to see the great cannon cast. The Professor did not summon them before he had the balloon entirely ready to be filled and go up: The flea sat on the Princess's hand and looked on. The balloon was filled, it bulged out and could scarcely be held down, so violent did it become.

"I must have it up in the air before it can be cooled off," said the Professor, and took his seat in the car which hung below. "But I cannot manage and steer it alone. I must have a skillful companion along to help me. There is no one here that can do that except the flea."

"I am not very willing to let him," said the Princess, but still she reached out and handed the flea to the Professor, who placed him on his hand.

“Let go the cords and ropes,” he shouted. “Now the balloon’s going.” They thought he said “the cannon,” and so the balloon went higher and higher, up above the clouds, far away from the wild land.

The little Princess, all the family and the people sat and waited—they are waiting still; and if you do not believe it, just take a journey to the wild land; every child there talks about the Professor and the flea, and believes that they are coming back when the cannon is cooled off; but they will not come, they are at home with us, they are in their native country, they travel on the railway, first class, not fourth; they have good success, a great balloon. Nobody asks how they got their balloon or where it came from: they are rich folks now, quite respectable folks, indeed—the flea and the Professor!